D0952416

WHEN WE WERE

When We Were Magic

SARAH GAILEY

SIMON PULSE
NEW YORK LONDON TORONTO SYDNEY NEW DELHI

SIMON PULSE
An imprint of Simon & Schuster Children's Publishing Division
1230 Avenue of the Americas, New York, New York 10020
First Simon Pulse hardcover edition March 2020

Jacket designed by Sarah Creech
Interior designed by Mike Rosamilia
The text of this book was set in Chaparral Pro.
Manufactured in the United States of America
2 4 6 8 10 9 7 5 3
Library of Congress Cataloging-in-Publication Data
Names: Gailey, Sarah, author.
Title: When we were magic / by Sarah Gailey.
Description: First Simon Pulse hardcover edition. | New York : Simon Pulse, 2020. |
Summary: When Alexis accidentally kills a classmate on prom night using magic, her best friends Roya, Iris, Paulie, Marcelina, and Maryam join in using their powers to try to set things right. |
Identifiers: LCCN 2019001195 (print) | LCCN 2019002854 (eBook) |
ISBN 9781534432871 (hardcover) | ISBN 9781534432895 (eBook)
Subjects: | CYAC: Magic—Fiction. | Witchcraft—Fiction. | Friendship—Fiction. |
Murder—Fiction. | Lesbians—Fiction. | High schools—Fiction. | Schools—Fiction.
Classification: LCC PZ7.1.G3453 (eBook) | LCC PZ7.1.G3453 Whe 2020 (print) |
DDC [Fic]—dc23
LC record available at https://lccn.loc.gov/2019001195

For everyone who isn't sure yet

1.

I DIDN'T MEAN TO KILL JOSH HARPER.

Really, I didn't. It's just that I was nervous, and condoms are more complicated than I was expecting, and one thing led to another and—well.

Now there's blood everywhere and he's dead.

I wipe my hands on the rumpled sheets until they're clean enough that I can pull my underwear on. I put on my bra, but I can't get the hooks done. My hands won't stop shaking. In the end, I leave it unhooked. I pull my dress on over it, and struggle to grip the zipper on the side. By the time I get the dress zipped up, blood has stopped pumping out of Josh Harper and *naked* feels like a hundred years ago.

I'm not sure where my shoes are. I know that I kicked them off, but I can't remember when or where. I'm turning around in a slow circle, staring at the floor, watching for the flash of my gold heels. I catch a glimpse of myself in the full-length mirror on the back of Josh's door. I'm a blur of bright blue, and I realize that my vision is fuzzy because my eyes are brimming with tears.

"Okay," I whisper to myself. "Okay, okay, just think. Think. Think think think." I wipe at my eyes and try to look at anything that isn't my reflection or the bed. The room is dark save for the light of a desk lamp, which casts a soft yellow glow on the desk and the bed.

Josh is on the bed.

There's so much blood on the bed.

I smooth my skirt. My palm catches on a patch of glitter, which immediately sheds, raining sparkles onto the carpet. I wipe my hand on a non-glittery section of skirt, leaving behind a bright smear of silver. I frown. I hate glitter. Why did I pick a dress with glitter on it? Probably because Roya said it looked good on me. Even as I stare at my skirt, frowning, I know that I'm not thinking straight. *You're in shock*, I think, but I can't stop glaring at that stupid patch of glitter. I want to scream. I can't believe I didn't already scream.

My phone buzzes in my purse and I nearly have a heart attack. My purse is at the foot of the bed. My phone is buzzing and I have to get it and it's on the bed. On the bed where Josh is. On the bed with all the blood.

Shit.

Okay. I can do this. I just won't look.

I reach over and accidentally grab Josh's foot.

It's still warm. And he's still wearing his socks. Ten minutes ago, he was telling me that they weren't his socks. He had borrowed them from his dad. He'd laughed nervously while I'd pushed him backward onto the bed, stopping him from taking them off.

What's your hurry? he'd asked me, and I'd shoved my mouth onto his instead of answering, and then.

I let go of his foot and grab my purse. It's a little tiny sparkly thing that's totally impractical and only fits my student ID and my cell phone. I fumble with the clasp, which is slippery with blood. My phone buzzes inside again, twice in a row.

The group text is going crazy.

It takes me a long time to reply—autocorrect can't even interpret the fumbling input of my shaking hands. **Josh bedroom 911**.

Five minutes later, five girls pour into the bedroom. My best friends. Four one-night-in-a-lifetime dresses plus Paulie's powder-blue tux. They're all in here and nobody is missing them because we all went to prom alone-together in solidarity with Iris after her boyfriend cheated on her. Well, everyone except Roya, and she ditched Tall Matt halfway through the night anyway. The point is that we're all single, but none of us is alone, and that's how we want it. At least until the end of the year. Why am I thinking about this? There's something else I should be thinking about.

Oh. Right.

I look at the girls. They're all gorgeous, all perfectly themselves and shining with party-sweat, and they're all looking at me. They're all looking at me, at me, at me. I can't look back at them. I can't look away. There's nowhere safe for my eyes to land. They're too bright—the colors are too saturated. It's too much. Roya is wearing a deep red gown and I can't look at her. My mouth is dry. My hands are too big. I feel short.

Iris looks at me like I'm a monster. Like I've got an eyeball hanging out. I know what I look like: I look like a girl you'd forget, if she didn't have that just-killed-a-boy aesthetic going on. I look like a girl on a prom night gone horribly, horribly wrong. Wide-set brown eyes that are probably glassy with nauseated fear. Curly brown hair that just passes my shoulders, stiff with hairspray and I-almost-had-sex-mussed. Eyeliner runoff halfway down my cheeks. Blood. Blood everywhere.

I don't need to look in a mirror to know that I'm a mess.

Iris is the one staring at me, and Iris is the first one to speak. "Well," she says. "What the fuck did you *do*?"

Here is what I did.

I tried to have sex with Josh Harper.

I didn't really want to have sex with Josh Harper. But I wanted to have sex with *someone*, and Josh Harper was around, and relatively sober, and I'd felt his boner against the top of my butt when he'd tried to grind on me at prom, so I figured it wouldn't be too tricky to get him to have sex with me. And I was right. Sort of.

* * *

"Oh my god," Marcelina says, covering her black-lipsticked mouth with her hands. "Oh my god, Alexis, oh my god, what happened to his *dick*?"

Here is what happened to Josh's dick.

It exploded.

I was trying to get the condom on him, and I guess I was doing it upside down or something. I don't know, it looked a lot easier in the YouTube video I watched with the banana. But the room was dark and I couldn't really see what I was doing, and it was my first time touching a guy below the waist, and it felt weird, and the condom wouldn't go on. And then Josh asked if it was my first time.

I didn't answer right away. He started to push me away, and he said something about how he didn't want to do anything I wasn't ready for. He was sweet about it. He was kind. But I wanted to have sex with someone, anyone, I needed to just get it over with, and I figured it didn't matter if I was ready or not because Roya was probably going to fuck Tall Matt anyway, so—I lied. I lied and said that it wasn't my first time and that it was fine. I tried to ignore the ache in my chest. I told him I wanted it, even though I didn't.

The lights were off, but I guess Josh heard my voice do that stuffy thing it does when I'm trying not to cry. And he said I didn't sound so sure, and he tried to grab the condom out of my hand, and I got flustered. And we were both struggling with the condom.

And then his dick exploded. And not in the way people joke about, not in the it-happens-to-a-lot-of-guys kind of way.

Every summer Marcelina cuts a hole into a watermelon and jams a handful of cherry bombs into it and then lights them and we run away and watch the carnage.

That's the way Josh's dick exploded.

"Did he try to—" Maryam is getting that face like she's going to kill someone. If Josh wasn't already dead, I'd be worried for him.

"No," I tell her. I tell all of them. "No, he didn't—we were—oh my god." I bury my face in my hands. "I don't know what happened. It was an accident."

Paulie wraps her arm around my shoulder and squeezes. She smells like wine coolers. "Okay, so, okay. So." Her eyes are locked on the bed. She's not blinking. "So, he's dead."

"Oh, for sure," Roya says. "He's one hundred percent dead."

I lean against Paulie. She's shaking hard, still not blinking. Her voice is pitched higher than usual when she asks, "What do we do?"

It takes me a minute to realize that she's talking to *me*.

"I have no idea," I say. They all stare at me. "I don't know. We . . . we have to fix it, but I don't know how. I don't know how to fix it." I'm babbling. I'm a disaster. *Oh god, this is a disaster*.

"C'mon, Alexis, you're the brains of the outfit," Roya says, giggling.

"Shut up, Roya," I snap. I shouldn't be so short with her, but Josh is dead and she's laughing.

Besides, I'm not the "brains of the outfit." That's Iris. And I'm not as cool as Paulie, or as ambitious as Maryam, or as badass as Marcelina, or as funny as Roya. I'm just me, and she's rubbing it in my face.

I should be more upset about Josh being dead than I am about Roya teasing me. But only one of those things feels small enough to fit inside my brain, and it's not the dead boy on the bed in front of me. "You're drunk," I mumble at Roya.

She waves me off. "You would be drunk too, if you hadn't run off to get laid."

As always, Marcelina steps in to save us from ourselves. "Okay, let's just—let's figure out what to do."

"What do *you* think we should do, Marcy?" Roya asks. Marcelina shoots her a look that would down a helicopter, but Roya's too tipsy to apologize for using the forbidden nickname.

"We have to call the cops," Iris says, as if it's the most obvious thing in the world.

Everyone explodes. Or, no, I shouldn't use that word so lightly anymore. Everyone starts yelling. There, that's less . . . evocative.

"No," I say, and I feel dizzy even saying it. "No, no, no—"

"Are you fucking crazy?" Roya shouts. "My mom can't know I'm here!"

"Not all of us are white," Maryam snaps at Iris, crossing her arms.

"How are we going to explain what happened?" Paulie demands. "What, we're just going to tell them about—"

"Guys, quiet," I say, but none of them listen to me. I'm not going to do that thing where I yell super loud to get them all to shut up, that never works. I hold my hand up in the air with my thumb and middle two fingers together, my pinky and index fingers upright—the silent coyote.

The first one to notice is Iris. That's not surprising, since she's always the first one to notice anything. She raises a freckle-covered arm over her head and imitates my gesture. I can tell that she's pissed because her lips press into a pale line—she's a pale ginger, so she changes colors a lot when she's feeling emotions or getting drunk. Right now, she's so many shades of pink and white that I half expect to see steam rising out of her pile of red curls.

The second person to fall silent is Maryam. She always pays close attention to what we're all doing, but she didn't see my silent coyote because she was arguing with Paulie about something. They're really close, which means they fight harder than any of us, except for maybe Roya and me. When Maryam notices my hand in the air, she looks pointedly away from Paulie and raises her chin imperiously at the same time as her own hand goes up. Her hands are covered with gold flash tattoos that match her emerald-green dress, and both are matched by her elaborate eye makeup. Between her aesthetic and the way she's holding herself and her quiet fury at Paulie, she looks like she belongs on a throne.

Marcelina and Paulie follow suit. They couldn't look more different: Paulie is ice where Marcelina is obsidian. Paulie's fitted powder-blue suit is a summer sky next to Marcelina's black velvet gown. Marcelina is tan where Paulie is pale, round and soft where Paulie is tall and willowy. Her thick black hair piles a lot higher than Paulie's thin, straight blond hair can. They don't just look different—Paulie is a cheerleader, and Marcelina is the closest thing our little school has to a real goth, even though she hates it when people call her that. But as opposite as they are, they became friends quicker than anyone I've ever seen. Somehow they wind up doing a lot of things in tandem.

Of course Roya is the last to notice me.

I don't want to look at her anyway. She's in a bloodred gown. That's not an exaggeration: she literally texted us all when she found it, saying that she was going to look like a vampire queen at prom. Her long tangle of black hair is piled on top of her head in a way that looks messy and polished at the same time. She's long-limbed and elegant and glowing and she never pays any attention to what I'm trying to tell her, and as always, Paulie has to slap her arm to make her stop talking and look at me.

Finally, everyone's quiet. There's a moment of peace. The silent coyote prevails again. It's a trick my first-grade teacher used to shut the class up, and it works every single time.

"Okay, so, I guess I have to be in charge right now," I say, my voice shaking. Roya rolls her eyes, and Marcelina throws her a sharp glare. "We can't call the cops," I say. "Roya's mom would kill her, and also, there's absolutely no way to explain why his dick exploded without telling them that we're magic."

I forgot to mention that part. Sorry. I got swept up in the fact that Josh died from a bad case of exploded-wang.

We're all magic.

"So we tell them," Maryam says. She tugs on her sleeve and I can tell she's on the way from frustrated to pissed. "We can't just let Josh be dead without telling anyone. I'm tired of keeping the magic thing a secret, anyway."

Iris suddenly looks very pale under her million freckles. "Maryam," she whispers. "You know we can't do that. My parents—"

"I know," Maryam interrupts, deflating. She covers her face with her hands, and her voice is muffled behind her matte copper fingernails. "Mine too." She doesn't talk much about how her family and her faith community would feel about her magic, but the look she shares with Iris from between her fingers tells me that it probably wouldn't be an easy conversation. Her family doesn't go to a mosque on a regular basis, but they still have a lot of rules, spoken and unspoken. I'd be willing to bet "no magic" is one of them.

Maryam doesn't follow all of their rules. She didn't follow the one that said she shouldn't go to this after-party. But there's a big difference between the kind of trouble she'd face for going to a party and the kind of trouble she'd face for being in proximity to a dead white boy.

"Maryam," I say quietly, and she makes a *hmph* noise from behind her hands. "You don't have to be part of this."

She lowers her hands and looks at me. Her eye makeup is smeared, which I know will infuriate her. "I can't," she whispers. "I'm sorry. It's too dangerous. Even aside from my parents, if the cops found out about this, a girl like me—I can't be involved. I can't."

"It's okay," Marcelina says, smiling at her. "We understand."

"Do we?" Roya asks, eyeing Maryam coolly. "I'm brown too, and I'm staying."

"You're not Muslim," Maryam snaps. "And your mom's a white cop. You'll be fine."

Roya opens her mouth, probably to start up the same argument she and Maryam have every other month—about the ways they're treated differently, about intersections of privilege and marginalization, about modesty and culture. If they have this argument, Roya will accuse Maryam of being protected by her lighter skin color, and Maryam will accuse

Roya of being protected by her mother, and the rest of us will try to stay out of the way as best we can because there are layers to that fight we don't understand from the inside. And because we know better than to get between those two when they're pissed at each other.

But Marcelina throws out her arms like an umpire, and Roya's mouth snaps shut again, and before anything else can happen, Maryam shakes her head. "I don't think I can be here," she says, still looking at me. I nod. She gives me a tight hug before she walks out of the room. When she pulls away, she rests her fingertip on my chin and stares into my eyes. It's something I've seen her mother do to her little sister. "I'm still here for you," she says. "I'm not bailing on you. I just can't do this."

"I know," I whisper, and I feel tears finally spill over. She kisses my forehead and then walks out of the room without looking back at me or at Josh or at anyone. The door closes behind her and my heart sinks. I understand why she can't be part of this, but I wish she would stay.

"Wait," Iris says, "we're letting her *leave*?"

"I trust her," I answer. "We've been through a lot together."

"Right, but what if she freaks out?" Iris's voice is getting higher and faster with every word.

Paulie snaps her fingers in front of Iris's face to get her attention. "No," she says in a voice that brooks no argument. "We trust each other. That's rule one. Right?"

Iris hesitates, then nods. "Right."

Paulie looks to each of us in turn. Her big gray eyes are set in a don't-you-dare glare. "We trust each other. No matter what."

Josh Harper is blond and tall and that's mostly what I know about him. I've gone to school with him for like six years, and I can't remember anything about him other than "blond" and "tall."

A quick survey of his room reveals more about him. Things I didn't notice when I was fumbling his pants off and trying to get him to stop asking if I was sure I was okay.

He liked cars. There are posters of them. Three posters, on the wall above his bed. They're spattered with blood now.

He played lacrosse. When I think about it, I have a hazy memory of him wearing a jersey to school one day, but I don't really follow school sports except for swimming, and our lacrosse team is nothing to pay attention to, so I didn't really put it together. But he definitely played lacrosse—his stick is leaning against the side of his headboard, and a ball rests in the weird net thing on the end of it. They're drenched in blood too.

He liked to read. A low bookshelf is next to his bed, on the other side of the lacrosse stick. It has a water glass on top—I guess he used the shelf as a nightstand. The books are spattered with red. The glass has three inches of blood-pink water in it.

Somewhere downstairs, someone screams. We all jump. Laughter rises from the party like ripples in the wake of the scream, which repeats with a definite note of delight.

"Okay," Marcelina says. The thick layer of black and silver around her eyes makes her look even more intense than usual. "So. What are we going to do?"

"We need a spell," Roya says. Some of the drunken fuzz is gone from her voice. She comes over to stand next to me, and her arm brushes against mine, and my skin jumps like I'm a cat she's petted the wrong direction.

"Yeah," I say, because it's true. There's only one way to fix this, to bring Josh back and make everything the way it was before. "We need a spell that will make this right."

We all look to Iris. She's shaking her head at us, but I can see the gears turning. She closes her eyes and we wait. The glow of her magic shines through her eyelids, illuminating a delicate leaflike tracery of pink veins. We all look away.

Iris's eyes glow when she comes up with spells. It's a whole thing she does. She's the only one of us who can do it—everyone else just kind of Does Magic and whatever happens happens, but Iris can gather our magic together and give it structure if she works on it really hard. But the working-on-it-really-hard makes her eyes glow. She gets so embarrassed about it. We don't tell her that the glow is still totally visible even when her eyes are closed. It's not a big deal to anyone other than her, but we know she would be self-conscious. It's just better if we don't tell her.

We look at each other to keep ourselves from looking at Josh or at Iris. I keep accidentally catching Roya's eyes and then looking away from her. Paulie bumps her shoulder against mine and whispers "You okay?" and I shake my head. I am *absolutely not* okay. I'm overwhelmed and terrified and oddly ashamed. And I'm mad that Roya had a prom date to ditch at all, even though that's not what I should be thinking about right now. It's too hot in the room, too crowded with the five of us plus Josh plus all the blood. Paulie grabs my hand and squeezes it. Her palm is dry and cool and I resist the urge to press it to my forehead.

After a few minutes, the magic glow from Iris's eyes dies away. She looks at me and nods, the motion knocking one red curl into her face. "Okay," she says. "I think I've got it. Let's go."

2.

WE STAND IN A SEMICIRCLE THAT ARCS OUT from Josh's bed. We're staring at our shoes because it's getting harder and harder not to look at Josh. We're all holding hands. Marcelina is next to me. Her hand is soft and warm and it feels like more than I deserve right now. Usually, Iris would be at the end of the line, opposite me—but I think that Paulie, Iris, and Marcelina arranged themselves to stay between Roya and me. It's probably for the best, but it still makes me a little sad.

Here's what you need to know about Roya: She's my best friend. She's on the swim team and she eats more pasta than anyone I've ever met in my life. She talks a lot about macros and carb-loading. She's Afghani. Her mom is the chief of police and her dad is some kind of fancy accountant, but I can never remember what makes him fancier than a regular accountant. Roya's parents adopted her when she was six and then gave birth to her little brother six years later. Being adopted was the first thing we bonded over—there was a thing where everyone was supposed to bring in baby pictures and tell the stories of our families, and we were the only two who didn't know our birth dads' names.

When Roya is really happy and not paying attention, she makes flowers grow. She has this long thick black hair that's always loose in beachy waves, unless she's at a swim meet, in which case it's tucked up under her swim cap and you can see the back of her neck, which is long and slim and covered in these fine hairs that look like they'd be really soft under your fingertips.

Anyway.

Roya's always mad at someone. Right now, the person she's mad at is me.

I thought I wanted this.

"Okay, here's what we're doing," Iris says. Her voice has taken on this businesslike tone that she uses whenever she's being bossy. She's bossy a lot. It's great. Seriously, we all love it—she takes charge like nobody else I know. She's going to run the world someday.

"The spell should clean everything up. And then it'll get rid of the body." She frowns a little. "I think."

"You think?" Marcelina mirrors Iris's frown.

"I'm not sure. It's kind of vague."

"Wait," I say. "That's not what I meant when I said 'make it right.'"

"Oh?" Iris looks at me sharply. Her eyes are flashing, and I know what she's thinking: that I'm the one asking for a huge favor, here, and can I really afford to be picky? Still, I press.

"We have to . . . we have to *fix* it," I say, hating the whine in my voice. "We have to make it right, we have to bring him back. There has to be a way to bring him back."

Iris laughs. Her laugh is only a little cold, not mean, but she's in that mood she gets sometimes, where she knows best and we're all just failing to keep up. "If you think we can bring people back from the dead . . . That's ridiculous, Alexis," she says. "We aren't miracle-workers. It's going to be hard enough just to get rid of him."

It stings when she talks to me that way. And it stings even more because what she's saying is that I've done something that can't be undone. I feel stupid for ever having hoped that things could go back to the way they were before.

I feel so small, and I'm so afraid that they'll leave me all alone with this thing I've done if I ask them for too much help. So I don't argue.

"It's not like we can make it any worse," Roya mutters. Someone knocks on the door, and we all jump. Roya shouts that the room is occupied, suddenly sounding a lot more sober than she did a few seconds before.

"Can we please, please get this over with?" Paulie growls, and everyone nods, and I can't argue with them anymore. I can't ask them for more help than I already have, and I certainly can't ask them to risk getting caught with a dead body with me.

Besides, Iris is really smart. Like . . . *really* smart. If she says this is the only option, I believe her.

"Are you ready?" Iris asks. We all say yes, and then—

Magic.

How can I explain what it's like?

It's like that feeling when you've been cooped up inside all day and then you finally go outside and remember what fresh air tastes like.

It's like when you get up in the middle of the night and your mouth is gross and dry and you take a drink of water and the water is sweet.

It's like watching someone dive into a pool without leaving a ripple.

It's like waking up.

Threads of light swirl up around each of us like spun sugar rising up out of a cotton candy machine. We all do different things with our magic, and we all usually look different when we do it. It's always kind of like light, and kind of like thread, and kind of like neither of those things at all. But when Iris is in control, we all make magic that looks similar. It looks like raw material. Pure. When we work together, Iris's magic is white, and Roya's is pink, and Marcelina's and Paulie's are both blue. I can't see my own. I can see when my hands glow a little, but I can never see the magic coming out of them. Almost none of us can see our own, except for Iris. So, I don't know what mine looks like, but Roya told me once that it's a bright dark purple. I asked how it could be dark when it's bright, and she shrugged and said she didn't make the rules.

She also said it was really pretty. Not that it matters, but she said it, is all. She thinks it's pretty.

A cloud of power roils overhead as we all give ourselves over to Iris. We'll be exhausted after this, but it's worth it to see what she can do. To see the shape of her plan. She reaches up and swirls her hand through the light that's filling the room. She pulls at it and pushes it and wraps her light around ours and clenches her fist tight and then she says "NOW" and we all stop.

Stopping feels like holding your breath—awful and suffocating and a little dizzying after the first minute. But you get used to feeling like that.

Iris lets go of the gathered light she's holding. It settles over Josh's body in a big sheet. We all slump a little as the magic leaves us. The light flares, and as it does, time slows. This doesn't happen with every spell, but this is a big one, and

I guess things are different with magic this size. Or maybe it's just adrenaline making me see every single detail of what happens—I don't know. All I know is, his blood shimmers like oil on water. I can feel it growing hot on my face, on my lips, on the tip of my tongue where I didn't even notice it until now, which seems wrong. You should notice when a boy's blood is on your tongue.

I feel his blood get hot, and I watch it shine on every surface in the room. The pink water lets off a few wisps of steam. The blood that's on my skin hurts. It hurts so much, but I don't let myself cry out and I don't let myself flinch because I know in my heart that I deserve so much more than this taste of pain.

I did this. It's my fault. I deserve worse than what I'm getting.

And then, faster than should be possible, the light of the spell fades, and he's gone. Josh is gone. One second he was there, and everything was covered in blood, and the next—he's not there anymore. All the blood is gone. The strange rush that comes with pain suddenly disappearing washes over me.

It totally worked. I smile, even though I don't really feel happy. It's over. I can pretend that it was all a bad dream.

He's gone.

And then Iris yells and her knees buckle and it's not over after all.

Marcelina grabs Iris before she falls. Her eyes are glowing again, brighter than they usually do—they're blue-white and painful to look at. She's biting her lip hard, making a sound like a held-in scream. Her skin is so pale that her freckles stand out like ink spatters across her cheeks. She clutches at Marcelina's black dress. I hear the fabric rip, and then a louder ripping-fabric sound that can't be Marcelina's dress, it's so loud. It's too loud.

There's a flare of light on the bed. At the exact same moment, Iris faints.

Her dress is pooled around her, a puddle of white satin and gold sequins. Marcelina and Roya drop to the floor beside her without hesitating. They both know CPR—Roya from being on the swim team, Marcelina from when she used to be a Girl Scout—and they're checking her pulse and looking inside her mouth and saying things quietly to each other that I don't really understand.

"She's okay, I think," Roya says.

"She . . . doesn't look okay," Paulie replies.

Roya ignores Paulie. She puts her hands on Iris's temples. A soft pink glow shines out from under her palms. Her jaw clenches—she should be drained of magic right now. She must be drawing on some deep reserve. Iris's eyes flutter open, and she looks at Roya with a dreamy kind of smile.

I look away.

That's when I notice Josh.

"Um, guys?" I say it too quietly at first and nobody notices me. "Guys," I say again. "We've got a problem."

They all look up at me, and I point at the bed.

"No way," Paulie says.

Marcelina looks up at the bed. "Way," she responds quietly.

"What is it?" Iris says from the floor. Her words are a little slurred. She tries to sit up, and Roya puts a hand on her chest, gently pushing her back to the floor.

"Josh is back," I say.

"Well. Sort of," Paulie adds.

Sort of.

I took biology in my freshman year of high school. It's where I met Paulie. At first, I thought she was just another pretty, preppy blond cheerleader-type. I was kind of a shallow, judgy freshman, and I thought high school was going to be all about cliques and groups. So, when I sat down on my first day of class and the girl next to me was a shiny-haired Taylor Swift lookalike in a cheer uniform, I rolled my eyes. I braced myself for a whole year of stupid questions and conversations about diets and boy drama and . . . well. I was kind of a dick to Paulie for the first month of school.

But then we got paired together for a dissection. It was a cow eye—we were supposed to cut it open and find the lens, and draw diagrams of the sclera and the retina and the optic nerve. The teacher came around to our lab tables with a big bucket and dropped an eyeball onto each of our dissection trays.

"Whoa," Paulie said when the eyeball splatted onto our tray. "Cool."

I remember being surprised at her reaction. "Cool?" I repeated. "It's pretty gross."

"*Yeah*," she said, and she looked up at me with this kind of wild, excited smile. "It's *totally* gross. And it's also *cool*."

We dissected our cow eye and then we talked about other cool, gross things. I realized how wrong I'd been about Paulie. We became friends in that immediate way that happens when you find someone amazing and don't want to let go of them for anything, and it only took a month for us to realize that we were both keeping the same secret. I'd always thought I was weird for being magic. I'd known I wasn't the only one, because of Roya and Maryam, but I thought we were freaks. I tried to love our magic then, but I couldn't help feeling like something was wrong with us. Paulie thought she was weird too, but she thought it was cool. "Like a cow eye?" I'd asked the first time she told me so.

"Exactly like a cow eye," she'd said.

"Okay, so, it didn't work," Marcelina says. She's staring at the bed and fidgeting with a curl that's come loose from her prom updo.

"It *kind of* worked," Paulie says.

"What happened?" Iris asks.

Here is what happened:

Josh came back. But not all of him. And not all in one piece.

His head is there. His spine is there, although it takes me a minute to realize that's what the little pile of round bones is. A big purple cushion-looking thing is there, which I will later figure out is his liver. His hands are piled one on top of the other, and his feet are at either end of the bed. They are not attached to his arms and legs, which are stacked like firewood at the foot of the bed.

His heart is there. It's sinking into the bed, like it's heavy, heavier than any of the other parts of him that are there. It's translucent and shiny and it looks . . . cold.

All of the parts are clean and really pale. There's no oozing blood. The sheets look cleaner than they did when I came into the room the first time, and they'd looked clean enough then that I'd been willing to lose my virginity on them.

It's helpful. It makes everything look kind of fake, like drawings in a textbook. Although there is a smell. A sweet, cooked-meat kind of smell.

It's not a nice smell.

When Iris sees what's on the bed, she covers her mouth with her hand. Her voice shakes. "I'm really sorry," she says.

"It's okay," Roya says. She's kneeling behind Iris, helping her sit up.

"No," Iris says. "It's not okay, it's not—we have to try again. Let's try again."

Roya looks up at the rest of us with alarm on her face. "We can't, guys." Her hands are resting on Iris's shoulders, and

I notice that her palms are still glowing pink. I give her an is-she-okay look, and she responds with a minute shake of her head.

"We have to try again," Iris repeats, and her voice is getting high and shaky the way it does before she has a panic attack. Her breathing is fast and shallow. I sit down on the floor in front of her and grab her hand in both of mine, then let it go, because I don't know what will happen if I hold someone's hand. Because I don't know how much I might hurt someone. I can't believe I did magic with them without thinking of it—of what might be inside me, waiting to come out. Of how I might have hurt all of them.

I can't believe I did that.

What's wrong with me?

I push back a wave of shame and fear because now isn't the time. Iris needs me. She needs someone to help anchor her, to keep her from spinning out. I sit on my hands, trying to stay solid for her.

"It's okay," I say. Her eyes are shot with the dark red of burst blood vessels. "It's okay. We can deal with this." Paulie and Marcelina settle on either side of me, and they make soothing noises too.

"We can totally deal with this," Marcelina says.

"Piece of cake," Paulie adds.

"Piece of Josh," Roya says, and we all laugh desperately. Iris cracks a smile.

"Too soon," she whispers. She's still breathing a little fast, but it seems like we've successfully derailed her anxiety spiral before she went into a full-on panic attack. "We could try again, though," she says.

Sometimes Iris says things that she doesn't mean just so one of us will reply with the thing she knows to be true. Like, she'll say, "What if nobody likes me?" so that someone outside of her brain can respond, "Lots of people like you." It's a coping mechanism we've all developed together. It's not manipulative, and it's not fake. It's just that sometimes she needs to hear someone else confirm reality.

"We can't try again," Roya says softly, and Iris closes her eyes and listens. "That spell not working was really bad for you. I don't know what it did exactly, but . . ." She pulls her hands away, extinguishing the pink light, and Iris gasps with pain. "Yeah," Roya says, returning her hands. Iris sighs as the pink light returns. "I don't think you should do magic for a few days. Actually, I don't think you should do *anything* for a few days."

"Okay," Iris says. She looks up at Marcelina, then makes a dismayed sound. "Oh, Marcelina, oh no. I ripped your dress."

"I could probably try to fix it," Roya says halfheartedly. "Later, when I've got a little more to give." The muscle under her eye is twitching the longer she keeps her hands on Iris, though, and I can't imagine that she'll have anything left by the end of the night.

Marcelina waves the apology away. "It's fine," she says, but her chin wobbles a little in that trying-not-to-cry way. We all know it's not fine—she worked evening shifts at the Crispy Chicken for four months to save up for that dress. She cried when she finally bought it—she said it was the nicest thing she'd ever owned. It's black, like all of Marcelina's clothes, but it has little silver stars stitched into it. There's a huge rip in the bodice now. It's definitely ruined. "We've got more important things to worry about," she says.

It's true. It's not right, but it's true.

We help Iris stand up. Her legs are trembling. Her freckles are stark—something she'd love if she was doing it on purpose. Her freckles are her favorite part of herself, her best-beloved feature. She's told me that they're the thing that make her feel most beautiful. But right now, she just looks sick. She keeps muttering, "I don't know what happened." Roya keeps a hand on Iris's shoulder, pouring that pink glow into her. We stand there, our arms around each other, staring at the body parts on the bed.

"I have an idea," Paulie says. She unthreads her arm from around my waist and goes to Josh's closet.

"Wait," I say, "what are you doing?"

"Trust me," she calls back, rummaging. Downstairs at the party someone's turned the music up, and the bass vibrates through the floor. Paulie emerges from the closet clutching a pile of bags.

"Duffels," she says, dropping them on the floor next to the bed.

"Duffels?" Marcelina repeats blankly.

"Knew he'd have a buttload of 'em," Paulie says. "Lacrosse dudes love duffel bags."

I nod as if that's a truth universally acknowledged. "Sure," I say. "But what are we . . . ?" Paulie folds her arms and waits for the penny to drop. And then it does. "No. No way."

"Yeah," Paulie says, looking uneasily at the bed. "We gotta get him out of here."

Roya is the first one to make a move. She gives Iris a squeeze, then steps toward the bed. Iris makes a small noise in the back of her throat and looks a little gray, but she stays standing under her own strength. Roya grabs a duffel and moves to the bed. In one brisk motion, she grabs an arm and a leg and stuffs them into the bag. She zips it up and takes two fast steps backward. Her lips are pressed together and her nostrils are white. She nods, staring straight ahead without seeming to see anything.

"Right," Marcelina says. "Sure." She picks up a duffel and scoops the hands and feet into it. She looks at the floor and bobs the bag up and down, like she's testing its weight.

Paulie takes the arm and leg that Roya didn't grab. She doesn't say anything, and after she's zipped up her duffel, she sits down on the floor, cradling it in her lap.

"Okay," Iris whispers over and over again. "Okay, okay, okay, okay." She grabs a drawstring backpack and yanks the top open, then rests it on the bed and starts to load the vertebrae into it one at a time. It takes a while. Her hands are shaking. "Thirty-one, thirty-two, thirty-three," she mutters. She shakes the bag a little to settle the bones in the bottom of it, then peers inside at the amount of room that's left. After a moment of deliberation, she picks up the liver and jams it into the bag. She cinches the backpack shut and swings it onto her back, wincing at the rattle of the bones inside.

Marcelina looks up, something dawning across her face. "Oh shit, actually. Iris?"

"Yeah?"

"Can I trade you?" She holds out her duffel, with the hands and feet inside. Iris stares at her and she shrugs. "I need the spine for something."

Iris shakes her head. "I don't want to know." She holds out her bag of bones and Marcelina takes it.

"Thanks." Marcelina passes over her bag of extremities and beams at Iris, who can't help smiling back. Nobody can help smiling back when Marcelina turns up the wattage like that. Her cheeks go all round and dimply and everything feels brighter. It's not magic, but it's close.

Once the exchange is done, they both turn and look at me. I look around the room. They're all watching me. Waiting.

"My turn, right?" I say. My voice seems too loud. Downstairs, the party is chanting something, and the chants dissolve into a general all-purpose party-yell.

"Your turn," Roya says. I look up at her, and she gives me an encouraging little smile. I feel some of the tension slip off my shoulders. *Maybe she's not mad at me after all.*

"My turn," I repeat. I grab the last bag—a beat-up backpack with Josh's name scrawled on it in Sharpie. It was probably his schoolbag last year. I look inside: a highlighter with no cap on it rolls around in the bottom, next to a crumpled Skittles wrapper and a few curly edges from torn-out notebook pages. I turn the bag over and let the trash fall to the floor. It doesn't feel right to leave it in there.

I step up to the bed feeling like a spotlight is on me. Gingerly, I pick up his head. The eyes are closed, and he would look like he was sleeping if it wasn't for the blue tint of his lips and the deathly pallor of his skin. His head is lighter than I would have anticipated. I wonder if his brain is still inside.

I hold the head in both of my hands. His hair is soft under my palm. There had been some sort of gel in it before, when we were making out, but now it's just clean. I bite my lip and put his head into the backpack as gently as I can manage. Then, before I have time to hesitate, I grab his heart.

I gasp without meaning to. "It's wrong."

"What do you mean?" Iris asks.

I shake my head. "Feel." I hold the heart out to her, and she pokes it with a tentative fingertip.

"Oh, fuck," she whispers. "It's . . . it's so *cold*?"

No one else wants to touch the heart, and I can't blame them. It feels awful. It's like glass, hard and smooth and cold and much too heavy. Warmth seeps out of my hand and into the heart by the second. I stare at it. It's almost translucent, but not quite, and I feel sure that if I just moved into better light, I could see all the way to the center of it. I can feel something in me moving toward it—something stirring deep inside me, being pulled toward the thing at the core of the heart, the thing I can't quite see—

Roya grabs the heart out of my hands and drops it into my backpack. She zips it up without looking at where the heart has landed.

"Maybe don't hold that thing in your hands for too long, huh?" she says, dipping her head low to look into my eyes.

"Yeah," I say, shaking myself. "Thanks. Let's get the hell out of here."

"Wait," Roya says. "How are we doing this?"

"We each get rid of our pieces," Iris replies in her bossy-voice.

"I want to be with you guys," I add quickly. "When you do it."

"What?" Paulie asks. "Why?"

"I just . . . I did this," I say. "And you guys don't have to help me. But I *know*"—I hold up my hand to stem the tide of of-course-we're-helping objections—"I know you're going to help me. So I want to at least be there with you when you get rid of your . . . your parts. Okay?"

Marcelina nods. "Yeah. That makes sense."

"Thanks," I say. There's an awkward moment where none of us knows what to say to each other. Roya breaks through it by opening the door to the bedroom. She walks out without another word. Iris smiles at me over her shoulder, then follows Roya out. Paulie goes after her.

I look at Marcelina. "Um, this is awkward, but . . ."

"What?" she asks.

"I told my parents I was sleeping over at your house tonight," I say.

She narrows her eyes at me. Her smile is always luminous, but when she's mad, she looks like a lioness. "Because you were going to stay here?"

I shrug, trying not to look away. "I wasn't sure where I was going to stay. Anyway, um. I can't stay here tonight. Obviously."

"Obviously," she says. She hefts her duffel and purses her lips for a moment before shrugging, and I know I've been forgiven for using her in my lie. "Of course you can stay at my place tonight, Alex. Now let's get the fuck out of here. This place is giving me the creeps."

I pick up my bag full of Josh Harper and turn off the desk lamp before we go. I shut the door behind me. I don't look back.

3.

MARCELINA IS COMPLICATED.

She's this tiny, plump Filipina girl with the most perfectly round face you've ever seen. She's small and soft and likes to tell people that she's only four feet tall, just to see if they'll call her bluff. She does the whole cute-goth thing really well: lots of black lipstick and eyeliner but also occasionally some silver glitter. Her hair is long and black and she piles it up tall most of the time. She wears high heels that she buys cheap, and then she paints them or glues studs and feathers to them until they look like something you'd have to get on a waitlist to buy.

She doesn't really seem like the type of girl who would live on a farm, but if you decide you're going to tell Marcelina what kind of person she's supposed to be? Well . . . good luck with that, is all I can say.

Marcelina likes to say that her family is land-rich. They're in a rambling one-story house with a lot of DIY additions tacked onto the sides. It sits on twenty acres of undeveloped land that butts up against the woods, and they kind of think of the woods as their property too. Marcelina especially, since her best magic is tree magic.

We all have something like that. We can all do a lot of the same little things, like knocking over trash cans from across the room or drying each other's hair or warming up our hands when it gets cold out. Some of us can do stuff that the others can't, like how Marcelina can talk to trees and Paulie can make water into shapes. And each of us has something we're best at—something we practice all the time, something that feels more *right* than any other magic we do. For Marcelina, it's plants. Trees especially, but really, all plants. She understands them on a level that I can't even comprehend, and a lot of the time it seems like they understand her back. I know how it sounds, but it's true.

We walk along the edge of the woods with our shoes in our hands, the grass soft and cold and already a little dewy between our toes. My dress is still shedding glitter, so my feet are shining everywhere that they're not muddy. I wonder if, come morning, there will be a sparkling trail to mark where I walked. The idea gives me a brief spasm of desperate hope, like I could follow the trail back to the beginning of the night, before I decided to sleep with Josh.

Before something broken and awful rose up inside me and killed him.

Marcelina pauses and rests her free hand against the trunk of a twisting black oak. She looks like a storybook witch in her torn starry dress, with moonlight on her face and a gnarled old tree casting curlicue shadows across her cheeks. I tell her as much and she gives me one of her amazing Marcelina-smiles. It's a high compliment to her aesthetic.

"So what's up?" I ask, nodding to the tree.

Marcelina hands me her shoes so she can lay both palms on the bark. She leans her cheek against it too, and the leaves of the tree rustle as if there's wind. Which there isn't. "I'm just checking in on her," she says. "It's been a hard year. Remember that lightning storm we had in March?"

I don't remember, but I nod anyway, because I want to hear how the tree is doing.

"Well, she didn't get hit, but one of the trees she's friends with did. It's really hard on both of them. She's been giving up a lot of minerals to help her friend recover."

I blink at her. "What?"

She waves a hand at me. "It's a whole thing with the root systems and fungal exchanges. I'll tell you about it sometime." She presses her forehead against the tree's trunk and whispers something. Then we're walking along the tree line again, toward the dark house. Josh's backpack bumps against my back, and I suppress a shudder at the thought of his face mashed against the canvas.

"I'm really sorry, Marcelina." My voice is shaking and I try to take a deep breath, try to imagine that my lungs are big billowing sails and I'm filling them with wind. It's something Iris taught me—a trick she uses to manage her anxiety. It works well enough that I'm able to look at Marcelina, who's swinging the string backpack like a handbag. "I'm sorry that I got you into this."

Her face is still angled up at the trees, and the white light of the moon catches on a smear of glitter that I think is probably secondhand, shed from my dress onto hers. The rip in her gown gapes open, and the moonlight illuminates a stripe of bare skin. I wonder if Roya will ever be able to fix the dress. I wonder if I'll ever be able to make up its loss.

"It's not a big deal," she says quietly, but her hand rises to that tear in the bodice of the dress she worked so hard for. And even if the dress was intact . . . Josh is dead and his head is in a *backpack*.

"Um, I think it's a pretty big deal," I say. She just shakes her head.

"It's nothing you wouldn't do for any of us," she says, and we're quiet until we get to the house. She lifts up the manual garage door with one hand, shuts it after us as we slip inside. It's completely dark in the garage, and musty. It smells like cigarettes.

"Did your dad start smoking again?" I whisper as we feel our way across the garage.

"Him, or maybe Uncle Trev," she says. Uncle Trev is her mom's friend from college—he's been staying with them for the past two months while his wife decides whether she's going to divorce him or not. To hear him tell it, the only thing that went wrong in their marriage is that he lost his job. He never says anything bad about his wife, though, which makes me trust him a little more. Pop told me a long time ago to never trust guys who have a lot to say about how awful their exes are.

"Oh." I don't know what else there is to say. Sometimes I don't know what to say, and it never feels like it's okay to not know. Roya would know what to say. It would probably go a little too far, but still. She wouldn't be quiet in this moment.

We get into the house and whisper-greet the two giant shaggy farm dogs that are sleeping in the mudroom. For anyone else, they'd do big deep fearsome woofs, but I hold out my hands and they stand there, wagging, until I pat their heads and tell them they're good dogs.

They shove wet noses against my palms and huff hot air against my wrists. They lean against my legs, trying to tell me about the grass and the cat and the one amazing smell they found and rolled in. I smile in the dark and tell them to go back to sleep, that I'll hear all about it in the morning.

I tell them without words. I tell them the same way that Marcelina tells the tree she's going to help it however she can. It's my thing, the thing that only I can really do as far as I know. Fritz and Handsome love me, because they can tell me all the dog-things that no other human seems to understand, and because I listen to them. I listen as much as I can, at least.

We put on the house slippers that are lined up by size in a long row next to the inside-door. Then we sneak down the hall past Marcelina's parents' room, past the guest bedroom where Uncle Trev sleeps.

We pass the kitchen. The whole house smells like Clorox wipes, except for the kitchen, which always smells like whatever Marcelina's mom has been cooking. Her mom is an amazing cook. She's left a huge disposable pan of something on the countertop, covered with foil. As we pass, I can smell something that smells like salt and vinegar and the color red, and my mouth waters until I remember how it felt when Josh's blood was burned off my tongue. Marcelina lets out an exasperated sigh in front of me, and I know she's rolling her eyes at her mom leaving out a whole pan of food for just her and whoever she happened to bring home. I don't grab her and pull her into the kitchen to eat like I usually would, because I'm sure that I'll throw up if I try to eat right now, but still. It smells fantastic in that kitchen. Almost good enough to make me hungry.

Marcelina's bedroom is exactly what you'd expect it to be—lots of black, lots of posters featuring bands where the guys wear more makeup than the girls and everyone's hair is super long. But it's also got a million plants in it, and a sunlamp, and a terrarium with a fat lizard inside.

Marcelina walks around the room touching the plants, greeting each one by name. "Hey, Bert," I say to the lizard, and he blinks a sleepy eye at me.

She opens a drawer and tosses me a pair of sweatpants and a T-shirt that says "Haunt me Siouxsie Sioux" on the front in a cute font. "Go take a shower," she says.

"Do I smell?" I ask, trying to discreetly sniff-check my armpits.

"No, but you're fucking *covered* in glitter from that stupid dress," she answers. "And I need a few minutes alone."

I nod. Marcelina's not exactly an introvert, but sometimes she hits a wall and needs to just be alone with her plants. She's had a hard night—it makes sense that she'd want to be alone right now.

I don't want to be alone. I don't ever want to be alone again. But I figure I don't exactly have the right to make anything else about me tonight.

I sneak back down the hall to the bathroom and climb into the tub to take my dress off, hoping to contain the inevitable glitter explosion that will come when I step out of it. It's not a bad strategy, although I'm not totally sure what to do with the dress once I've got it off. I lean out of the tub and reach for the trash can, then pull out the plastic bag that's lining it and stuff my dress inside. Thankfully, the bag is empty—no ear swabs or wadded-up pads or used tissues to stick to my dress. But once I've got the dress in the bag, I know that it wouldn't matter anyway. It may not have any blood on it anymore, but I'm still going to throw it away as soon as I can.

I'm never wearing that dress again.

When I turn the water on, it's freezing. I stand under it, shivering and covering my chest with my arms, and wait for it to warm up. The cold is punishing, but I don't move.

I don't move because Josh is dead.

Once the water gets warm, I drop my arms and shove my face into the spray. It's hot enough that it doesn't remind me of the way his blood felt when it hit my skin, but the comparison still comes to mind and I gag. I brace myself against the wall and let the water get hotter, hotter, scalding. The horror I've been pushing away all night rises around me like threads of magic, if they were made of barbed wire. I shiver once, and then again, and then I can't stop shaking.

Josh is dead. Josh is dead because of me. Because I killed him. Somehow, I killed him.

I don't know how it happened. I know I said that already, but I mean I really don't know how it happened. I didn't just not-do-it-on-purpose—I didn't know it was possible. To explode someone. To kill someone, just like that, just because of a slip of magic. It's like if I tripped and fell and accidentally levitated. Except that I have accidentally levitated before, and that's how magic has always felt—floaty and personal and friendly. Harmless. I've never seen Iris get hurt this way before. *I've* never hurt anyone this way before.

I've also never tried to use anyone the way I tried to use Josh. I push the thought aside before I can really get my teeth into it, though. It's not what I want to be thinking about right now.

What happened tonight was something dark and different. That's what matters. It's new, and it terrifies me. And my friends are going to help me get out of this; they won't let me do it all on my own, and that terrifies me even more.

The water is really hot now. Steam is rising up around me, and my skin is turning pink. There's a mirror suction-cupped to the tile inside the shower—Marcelina's dad uses it to shave, I think—and I wish it would fog over, because I don't want to see myself right now. I lather soap between my hands and spread it across the surface of the mirror.

I grab Marcelina's mom's fancy apricot scrub and start scouring my body. Iris's spell took all of Josh's blood off me, but I can still feel the burn of every drop. I can feel it all, lingering there like flecks of glitter. I scrub until it hurts. I wish I had just had sex with him. I wish I had never tried to have sex with him. I wish I had done whatever I needed to do to keep from *killing* him.

Josh is dead because of a horrible kind of magic that is apparently inside me. I scrub as if I can get to that magic and wash it out. My skin is a bright, livid red, and I make myself stop before I draw blood.

Before I draw *more* blood. There's been so much blood tonight. Oh god, it was in my *mouth*.

I stand under the water until the heat makes me dizzy. After I turn it off, I lean my head against the tile and finally, finally, I let myself cry.

When I get back to Marcelina's room, she's sitting cross-legged on the floor. She's wearing black sweats and a black tank top. Her hair is in a messy topknot, and she's taken all her makeup off.

She looks a little naked without makeup. People always

talk about how wearing makeup isn't natural, how "real" women look better, but that's bullshit. Marcelina is perfectly lovely with or without makeup, but the "real" Marcelina likes wearing a ton of eyeliner and dark lipstick and sometimes does really incredible things with eyeshadow that I don't fully understand. She and Maryam spend hours experimenting on each other's faces, turning each other into mermaids and vampires and starlets. She's good at makeup and she loves it and if that's not "real," I don't want real.

Anyway.

She's sitting on the floor, and there are two piles in front of her on a piece of spread-out newspaper. It looks like the classified ads—the paper, not the piles. I lean my head to one side and scrunch a towel through my hair as I watch her work.

She's holding a vertebra in one hand. There are maybe ten or twelve of them in a pile in front of her left knee. In front of her right knee, on the newspaper, is a pile of white powder.

I don't ask what she's doing, because she's doing magic, and watching Marcelina do magic is just amazing. I mean, everyone looks amazing when they do magic, because it's *magic*, but Marcelina is especially cool to watch at it. She lifts the bone to her lips and starts whispering to it, a steady stream of suggestions and secrets. I can't hear everything she's saying, but I catch the words "together" and "dark" and "settle." The vertebra starts to glow blue from within, like a flickering fire is burning in the bone. Marcelina breathes over it, a breath that's heavy with magic and meaning, and then she's not holding a bone anymore—she's holding a handful of white powder. She adds it to the pile and picks up another vertebra.

This is her magic: the magic of quiet moments. Where Iris's magic is showy and enormous and awe-inspiring, Marcelina's magic is soft and subtle and works its way into everything. Where Paulie's magic is experimental, Marcelina's magic is certain. Watching her work is like watching a time-lapse video of a river's course changing.

"Do you want help?" I ask softly, not wanting to disturb her. She shakes her head and looks up at me. Her face has gone soft and peaceful, and her lips are tinged with a faint glow, like the magic she's whispering has left her with a Popsicle stain.

"Okay," I say, and I sit beside her to watch her work. She raises the bone to eye level and starts whispering to it, and I don't say another word until after she's done.

There are a million stars. It's one of the nice things about living so far outside the city—we get stars here. I look up at them as often as I can, because when I go to college in the fall, there probably won't be that many stars.

I try not to think about it too much. I'm going to miss the stars. I'm going to miss a lot of things. But Maryam and Roya and I are all going to State together, so at least I won't be alone in the dark of the city.

Marcelina is walking in front of me, a teardrop-shaped silhouette against the tree line. The trees rustle a little as she passes them. They don't bend toward her, but they notice her. I'm carrying a shovel. Handsome—the shaggier of the two farm dogs—lopes along beside me, his nose skimming the ground as he tries to take in every new smell in the grass. He whined when we snuck out, but once I told him that he could come with us, he shut up.

Yeah, I know. I'm a sucker.

Marcelina stops in front of the black oak she touched before. At least, I'm pretty sure it's the same one—I don't recognize individual trees the way she does, but there's a big knot in the trunk that looks familiar. Marcelina confirms my guess when she puts her hand on the trunk and says, "I told you I'd come back."

She's holding the sheet of newspaper from her bedroom in one hand. It's wrapped around the bone dust and twisted at either end, like a huge hard candy. She sets it down next to the tree, then looks back at me and holds her hand out.

"Let me," I say, and she hesitates for only a moment before nodding.

"Okay," she replies, "but you have to dig where I tell you to, or you'll hit her roots."

I pat Handsome on the butt and tell him to go have fun. He's off before I finish telling him to come back within an hour, vanished into the trees to chase some sound or smell or dog-adventure that I'm sure he'll spend the whole morning telling me about.

"You told him to come back, right?" Marcelina asks, peering into the trees.

"Yeah, but he'll come back anyway," I answer. "He doesn't want to sleep outside anymore. His hips are bothering him."

Marcelina frowns into the trees but doesn't ask any other questions. She knows that Handsome is getting older, and that I'll tell her if he has any serious problems. He's doing okay for now. His hips hurt, and his vision isn't so good, but he's old and he's pretty much all right.

"Here," she says, pointing at the ground between her feet. "Dig straight down, three feet. Don't go to either side, though. There's a root there and a gopher tunnel on this side."

"Got it," I say, and she backs away a few feet so I can dig.

It feels good. The night air is warm, and the soil is soft, and there's something satisfying about the sense that I'm doing work. That I'm fixing something.

When the hole is dug, Marcelina kneels in the soil and pushes the newspaper down into it. With both of her hands in the earth, she tears the paper open. She scoops a few handfuls of soil back into the hole, then kneads the bone dust into it. She hesitates. But not for long. Marcelina never hesitates for long. She pushes her fingers down into the loose mixture, and threads of blue shoot through the soil like an electric current. They disappear into the walls of the hole I dug almost as quickly as they appear.

"What are you doing?" I whisper, but either it's too quiet for Marcelina to hear or she's ignoring me. The question is answered within the next heartbeat as tiny tendrils creep out of the soil and brush against her fingertips. Marcelina breathes on them, and they shiver.

She glances up at me with a moon-bright Marcelina-smile and says, “Roots.”

The tendrils dive down into the bone-and-soil combination as Marcelina nudges the rest of the dirt back into the hole. I tamp it down gently with the back of the shovel—there’s a tiny mound left, but Marcelina puts a hand on my arm before I compress it all the way. “Leave some room,” she says. “She’ll need to breathe.”

We sit in the grass and wait for Handsome to come back from the woods. It’s probably one in the morning, and the dew is starting to gather. The seat of my pants gets damp, but I don’t stand up.

“So that’s what you needed it for?” I ask.

“Yeah,” she says, running her fingers through the grass.

“Why?”

“Minerals,” she says. “She’s been depleted because she’s been sending minerals to her friend. The bone dust should help a little.”

“Oh,” I say, because I don’t know what else to say. Then: “Should we put the liver in there too?”

“No,” she says. “It would screw up the balance of the soil. We’ll deal with it later. Besides, I kind of think we should do the different parts separately, don’t you? So each one gets our attention? I wouldn’t want to get rid of anything without thinking about it.”

I swallow hard. I know exactly what she means. I don't want any part of Josh to disappear without me knowing. I don't want to look away from any part of this, no matter how hard it is for me to see what I've done. What we're doing. "Sure," I whisper, digging my fingers into my thighs. "Totally. I'll talk to the other girls about it too, yeah?"

Marcelina nods, then goes quiet. She's really good at comfortable silences—it never feels awkward to just be together, not talking about anything, looking up at the moon. After a while, Handsome comes loping out of the forest and sits next to me. I pick pine needles out of his fur and he pants happily, occasionally twisting around to aim a lick at my arm.

"What were you doing with Josh?" Marcelina asks after a few minutes. "I mean, I don't care who you sleep with, it's just . . . I didn't even think you knew Josh."

I glance over at her, but she's not looking at me. She's staring down at the clover next to her, gently brushing her palm across the tops of the leaves. I can't tell what they're saying to her, or what she's saying to them. Or maybe it's neither—maybe they're just sitting there in a companionable silence, like she and I were until a second ago.

"I don't know," I reply. "I guess I just wanted tonight to be special."

The lie is as obvious as Handsome's dog-smell. Marcelina is quiet, waiting for me to tell the truth. Giving me a chance. I keep picking pine needles out of Handsome's fur. After a long time—long enough that I start to feel guilt creeping up the back of my neck—Marcelina stands up and brushes grass off her butt.

"It's gonna be okay," she says. "I know it doesn't feel like it's gonna be okay, but it is."

"But what if it's not?" I ask, burying my face in Handsome's fur. He smells like pine and dog and wind. I feel Marcelina's footsteps behind me, soft and patient in the grass.

"Then you won't be alone with it," she says. "We'll all be not-okay with you."

I stand up and Handsome stands with me, his tail already wagging. He looks back toward the house.

"Come on," Marcelina says. "The rest of it will still be there in the morning. We'll do the liver another day."

We walk back to the house together, me and Marcelina and Handsome, and for the time it takes us to get there, I believe her. Maybe things will be okay.

4.

WHEN I WAKE UP ON THE FLOOR OF MARCELINA'S bedroom, I don't remember right away. I lie in the early-morning grayness under a pile of lap blankets stolen from the living room. My mouth is dry and my shoulders ache a little, but I don't have that sense of oh-shit-where-am-I that happens sometimes when I wake up someplace that isn't my own bed. I'm not hungover, because honestly, I was too nervous to drink at the party. I just feel sleepy. That's all. Just sleepy.

I reach up a hand to rub my face, and a flicker of something crosses my brain. *You should be feeling bad about something.*

Then I remember.

Josh. Blood everywhere—on my cheeks and burning and coppery in my mouth and sprayed across posters of cars. Maryam leaving. Roya's incredulous glare. My fault. My fault. My fault.

Before I can think about it, my hand shoots out. My fingertips find canvas, a zipper, a solid lump. My stomach turns.

It was all real.

There is no part of me that thinks, *Maybe this is all a terrible dream.* It hurts to realize that *Josh exploding is just a nightmare* was a safe psychological harbor I passed by without docking.

"Marcelina?" I whisper. She doesn't answer. I poke my head up and can see the small hill that is her and her million tangled blankets. She's motionless in the bed, sleeping so soundly that I'd be worried she was dead if I hadn't seen her sleep a hundred times before. Still, I wait to see the slow rise of her breathing before I trust that she's really just asleep. I get up as quietly as I can, gathering my own nest of blankets in one arm and slinging the backpack across my shoulder with the other. I close her bedroom door behind me, holding the latch back with my thumb until the last possible second.

I dump the blankets into the basket next to her parents' couch. I sneak into her kitchen and grab a roll of duct tape from the junk drawer. I rip off a five-inch strip and slap it over the place on Josh's backpack where his name is scrawled in Sharpie. For good measure, I put another piece on top of that one. It's bad enough that I'm coming home from prom with no dress and a strange bag; I can't have a boy's name on the bag. A dead boy's name. *No*, I remind myself, *a* missing *boy's name*. As far as everyone else knows, Josh is missing. Nothing more.

I ease the bag open just a little and reach in, my fingertips finding the smooth, glassy surface of the heart. It feels a little warmer than it did last night—still hard, still wrong, but just a tiny bit warm. I press gently with my fingers, trying to figure out if it's softened, if it's really warmer or if I'm just imagining things. *Why would it be different?*

"How was prom?" The voice comes from right behind me. I jump a mile and whip around to glare at him—Uncle Trev is there, and he holds two hands up, lifting his shoulders in a whoa-don't-kill-me stance. "Sorry," he says, aiming an awkward grin at me. "Didn't mean to scare you."

"Well, you did," I say, breathless, my heart pounding. I adjust the backpack onto both of my shoulders. *Oh god, I'm talking to Trev and there's a head in my bag.* "Prom was fine. What are you doing awake?"

"I've got a workout this morning," he says. "Just 'fine'?" he asks, leaning a shoulder against the wall and crossing his arms. His biceps swell a little with the motion. Trev took up weightlifting after he lost his job, and I'm never sure if he's showing off his muscles on purpose or if that's just what happens when you train for three hours a day. He looks like what I imagine Josh would look like if he grew up, stayed sober, got divorced, and did a lot of CrossFit. Tall, blond, trying a little too hard but not in an irritating way. "Did something happen?" he asks.

I've always liked Uncle Trev, but right now I really hate how interested and engaged he is all the time. "Um, nothing big," I say. "Just some drama." That's normally a foolproof way to get adults to mind their own business—explanations of drama are usually drawn-out, expansive diagrams of high school social politics. The only people who hate high school social politics more than actual high schoolers are adults who are pretending to be interested.

“Did you and Roya have a fight?” he asks, tipping his head to one side.

“What? No. What? We didn’t—why would you think that?” I’m talking too fast and my ears feel hot. Trev laughs.

“Okay, well, if you ever want to talk about it, you know where to find me,” he says.

“Thanks, Trev,” I say awkwardly. He shrugs and walks out of the kitchen.

The first time I told my dads about Uncle Trev, they exchanged a long look and then had a talk with me about Red Flags and What to Watch Out For and Adult Men and Grooming Behavior. And I’ve watched out for all the red flags—but honestly, Trev is just a nice guy. I talk to Marcelina about it all the time: how much it sucks to have to be suspicious of a grown man just because he’s kind and thoughtful and listens. But then again, Marcelina and I also talk a lot about grown men we were right to be suspicious of. The kinds of grown men who pretend to be interested in our lives and then start texting us late at night. The kinds of grown men who ask for hugs. The kinds of grown men who say they want to be our friends, who try to tell us secrets because they think we don’t know what it means when a grown man tries to tell a teenage girl a secret. Uncle Trev isn’t like them, and I know that, but it’s awful to be constantly watching just in case he turns out to be that kind of guy.

It's exhausting.

Anyway.

I go through the mudroom to get out, because Handsome and Fritz would never forgive me if I left without saying goodbye. I sit down and let them bombard me with dog-dreams and news and sheer unbridled affection. They both try to shove their noses into my backpack. Even though they listen when I tell them to leave it alone, I get up and go pretty fast. It doesn't feel right, sitting there with Josh's head and his all-wrong heart and letting the dogs tell me how great I am.

Nothing feels right.

I walk home. It's only about a mile, and the fresh air is nice. It's early enough that not many people are awake. I pass the places where Marcelina and I used to ride our bikes around when we were kids, before we knew that magic was more than just a game we played. Houses that we'd decided were haunted, or where we said a murderer probably lived. Sidewalks that we dusted with chalk rainbows before rainstorms, so that when the weather started to turn, we could watch the colors run.

I wonder when the days stopped feeling endless. It was definitely long before I had a backpack full of body parts to dispose of.

My house is just like all the other houses on the block. It's squat and square and has a big window in the front and a little yard next to the driveway. It's light blue, and the one on the left of it is white and the one on the right of it is brown, and that color pattern repeats over and over for about eight blocks in every direction.

The only thing that makes my house stand out is my dads' garden. It's one of the many Couples Hobbies they've taken up together over the years in an attempt to stay "connected." It's not that their relationship is bad or anything—it's just that they're both trial lawyers, which means that they're both always busy. I guess when you're that busy, it doesn't matter if you're madly in love with the person you want to spend the rest of your life with—it's still easy to drift apart. So my dads have golfed and tennis'd and biked and run marathons, and now they're gardening. The front lawn is a patchwork of garden beds that are exploding with flowers—mostly orange and pink ones right now, although they put some blue hydrangeas in for me.

I feel weirdly guilty whenever I see the hydrangeas, even though I know that they planted them to make me happy and it's not a big deal. I don't like feeling like I disrupted their color scheme. But then, if I ever told them I felt bad about it, they'd make a big deal about how it's *not* a big deal. So I don't say anything, and I tell myself that it's not something I should feel guilty about.

I walk inside as quietly as I can, thinking I'll be able to sneak into my bedroom without getting noticed or talked to, but as soon as I step inside, I'm thwarted by my little brother. Nico's wearing his soccer uniform and he's got his cleats on, even though he's not supposed to wear them in the house and Pop will definitely kill him if he sees.

Nico looks nothing like me, which makes sense since we were adopted from entirely different families. Where my hair is brown and curly, his is black and straight and stands up in every direction even when he doesn't put too much gel in it. We both have brown eyes, but mine are dark and his are light in a way that I'm sure girls his age think is dreamy. He's two years younger than me, and he goes to a STEM magnet school that's annoyingly close to my school. He's getting taller every half hour or so, which means that his elbows are pointy and his neck is weirdly long and he's developing horrible posture because he doesn't know how to be tall yet. He'd be really good-looking if it wasn't for the slouch. And if he wasn't my little brother. And if he wasn't *constantly* underfoot, like he is now.

"What are you doing up?" I ask. He looks down at his soccer cleats and then raises his eyebrows at me like I'm ten cents short of a dime, which . . . fair.

"Dad said you weren't coming to my game today because you'd probably be hungover from prom," Nico says.

"He did not say that," I snap back at him. I want to yell at him to stop slouching, just to annoy him. I don't have that many months left to be an annoying older sister who yells at my kid brother.

He rolls his eyes and heads toward the kitchen, his cleats pulling at the carpet.

"Whatever," he yells over his shoulder. "Dad, Pop, the prodigal daughter has returned!"

I love my little brother, but he's at an age where he thinks he's clever. Normally I would say that I want to kill him, but . . . that's a little close to home right now. I don't know if I'll ever be able to say that again, to be honest. I turn down the hallway that leads to my bedroom, hoping against hope that I'll be able to get there without interruption, but apparently, it's not a good morning for hoping.

"How was prom?" Dad pokes his head out of the bathroom. He looks a lot like Nico, which he swears wasn't intentional, but which makes people think that Nico is his son from a previous marriage or something. He has the sticking-up-everywhere black hair and the lighter-than-mine brown eyes and the altitude. But his black hair is starting to become salted with white, and his brown eyes have a web of laugh lines around them, and he's what people call "olive" where Nico is just vampiric.

He's my dad, and he's got toothpaste foam on his chin, and he's kind of the best. And I would give anything to not have to talk to him right now, because I'm tired and I have body parts in a bag and what if I get mad at my dad and hurt him somehow? I wasn't even mad at Josh when I killed him, but it still happened.

You weren't mad at him, something in me whispers. *You were* lying *to him.*

"Prom was fine," I say, and that lie doesn't kill my dad, so I push away the thought that it might matter.

"Just fine?" he asks, and I want to scream.

"It was great," I answer, forcing a smile. "I'm just tired."

"Okay, well, we didn't even know that you'd be back this morning, so you're free." He sticks his toothbrush back into his mouth and makes a series of unintelligible noises. I decide to interpret them as "By all means, go lie in the dark in your room and try to figure out how you're going to dispose of that nice boy's head."

"Love you," I say, and he waves at me, and his salt-and-pepper head disappears back into the bathroom. I walk into my bedroom, shut the door, and allow myself an all-out dramatic sigh, complete with a slouching lean against the door.

I think I've earned some melodrama.

I pull out my phone before I've finished crossing the room to flop onto the bed. I have a million notifications, and I dismiss all of them except for the text messages. I don't have the energy for social media yet.

I have a bunch of texts from Maryam.

She's doing that thing where she's anxious, but she doesn't want to put what she's anxious about in writing, so she's overexplaining and being vague at the same time. She wants to know if everything's okay, and if everyone's on the same page, and if there's anything she should know about, and if we can have a phone call, or maybe a phone call's a bad idea, and maybe we shouldn't even be texting, and can I delete her texts just in case?

I hesitate, then delete all of the messages she's sent in the last twelve hours. There are nineteen of them. I send a thumbs-up emoji, and nothing else, because I don't know what I could possibly say that wouldn't make her worry even more. She replies immediately with a message that says simply *I love you no matter what*.

She loves me no matter what. Even if I'm a murderer. Even if I'm a monster—because, let's face it, the kind of person who does what I did? That's a monster. It wasn't on purpose, but that doesn't really feel like it matters.

Something is wrong inside me, something I don't understand and can't control, and Maryam wants me to know that she loves me anyway.

The group text thread is pretty quiet. I'm not the only one who doesn't know what to say. I can't blame them—I don't know what to say either. I draft and delete nine messages before chickening out and sending a string of heart emojis.

The only texts I haven't read yet are the ones from Roya.

My mouth is too dry for me to read the texts from Roya. When did my mouth get so dry? It wasn't like this until I saw her name on the screen.

I hate seeing her name on the screen. I wish I saw it more.

I slip out of my room, hoping no one will ambush me in the hall to ask if prom was *just fine*. I can hear Dad and Pop and Nico making leaving-noises in the front entryway. I stand at the sink, drinking water and trying to get my heart rate to settle down a little. I open the texts from Roya.

Hey did you get home ok?

Marcelina says you're staying at her place, lmk if you need anything

Man, this duffel bag I'm thinking of buying is an ~arm and a leg~

I let out a long, slow breath that would be a laugh if I wasn't so dizzy. Of course Roya's got jokes. She's always got jokes.

"Well, go find them," Dad says from the entryway, and I catch a note of exasperation in his voice. It's always like this, trying to get Nico out the door—a thousand loose ends, everything last-minute and forgotten. Dad's pretty type-A, and he tries hard not to expect Nico to be as organized as he is, but it definitely drives him up the wall.

"I think they're in Alex's room," I hear Nico call back behind him, and then his cleats are tearing up the carpet in the front hallway, and—

"Shit," I mutter, dropping my glass into the sink hard enough that I have to check to see if it's cracked. It isn't. "Shit, shit, shit." I run for the hall. My bedroom door is ajar, and when I walk in, Nico is rummaging around my desk. No no no. The head is in here. The heart is in here. *He* can't be in here.

"What are you doing?" I shout. I'm a caricature of a pissed-off big sister. "Get out of my room!"

"I need my headphones," he says. "I can't find them. Didn't you borrow them yesterday when you were doing your hair or whatever?"

"No," I snap. "You probably washed them *again*. Take shit out of your pockets next time."

"Don't swear at me or I'll tell Dad and he'll make you do Conflict Resolution," Nico says. I scowl because he's right—Dad would totally sit me down to go over the rules of engagement. No swearing, no yelling, no specious allegations, no hearsay. *We are not a yelling household*, and other totally normal things to say during an argument.

Nico looks something less than smug but more than satisfied. He runs a hand through his hair, which he does whenever he knows he's winning. I hope the gel leaves his hand gross and sticky. "I know you borrowed them. I just need to find them before I go, or else I won't have anything to listen to during warm-ups." He turns around and his eyes land on the backpack.

He reaches for it.

"No," I say, but he's not paying attention.

He's holding the backpack and ignoring the hell out of me.

"Nico," I shout, "give me the damn bag!"

"I just need my headphones. God, don't be such a bitch."

I snatch the bag out of his hand just as he's reaching for the zipper. "Don't call women bitches," I snap. "I don't have your headphones."

"I wouldn't call you a bitch if you weren't being a bitch," he snaps back, and we would probably devolve into a shouting match, but Pop calls from the garage.

"Are you coming to the game, Lex?"

Nico and I stare at each other hard. He smiles. I shake my head. His smile broadens, and he calls over his shoulder.

"Yeah, Pop, she's coming! She's just getting her shoes on now."

I growl at Nico and push him out the door so I can change into clothes I didn't sleep in. I shove the backpack under my bed as far as it'll go. When I pull my arm out from under the bed, my fingertips brush across something that feels unfamiliar. I grab it and pull it out.

Nico's tangled headphones dangle from my hand.

"Ah, shit," I mutter.

Nico gloats for the entire drive to his game. I should have just tossed his headphones into his room and let him warm up with no music, but I'm not that cruel of a sister. Pop is on a call with his assistant for the first half hour of the forty-minute drive, but the second he hangs up, his eyes find mine in the rearview mirror.

"So!" He does the bright, excited voice that means "I'm sorry for taking a work call on the weekend, it won't happen again, except actually it definitely will and I'll make up for it by sending you to a nice college someday." "Prom, huh? Was it the best night of your life?"

I swallow an incredulous laugh, and his eyebrows go up. "Uh, no," I say. "I sure hope not. It would be a bummer to peak this early."

He smiles, rolls his eyes. "Did you have a good time, though?"

"Yeah, it was fine."

"Just fine?" he asks, and I realize that I've died and gone to a special section of hell where people won't accept "fine" as an answer.

"It was fun," I revise. "The music was great. I felt like a princess the whole time."

Pop doesn't laugh. His eyebrows come together, which isn't hard, since they almost meet in the middle anyway.

They're the only hair on his entire head, but they kind of work overtime. When he frowns, they form one long, worried line. "Did something happen?"

"No," I say, sharper than I intend. "Nothing *happened*, Pop, it was just—it's a dance. Everyone thinks it's more than that, but it's not. It's just a dance. And it was *fine*."

"I think she had a fight with Roya," Dad whispers. "Roya went with Tall Matt." Pop keeps glancing at me in the rear-view mirror. When Dad says "Tall Matt," Pop's eyes get wide and his eyebrows rocket around like they're motorized.

"Why does everyone think that?" I retort. "I didn't have a fight with anyone, I had a good time, I don't even care about who Roya went to prom with, it was—"

"'Fine,' we know," Nico interrupts. He's texting someone, probably about how he was right and I had his headphones all along. "If you didn't have a fight with Roya, you must be on your period or something."

"Nico," Dad says in a warning tone. "Don't do that."

"What?" Nico says, not looking up from his phone. "All I said was—"

"Nope, don't even try," Dad interrupts, examining his stubbly chin in the pull-down mirror. He's being the stern one this morning, since Pop is all guilt-ridden from his long work call. "You're deliberately pushing her buttons. I know you don't talk to *Meredith* that way."

Nico's ears turn red and he doesn't say another word until we get to the soccer field. Meredith is his girlfriend—his first real one—and Pop's right. Meredith would never let Nico talk to her the way he talks to me. I mean, Nico shouldn't talk to me the same way he talks to his girlfriend. That would be weird. But I could learn a thing or two from her about silencing glares.

It's hot outside in that threatening way late-spring mornings have, where you can tell that it's going to be unbearable in the sun by noon. Gina Tarlucci waves at me from the bleachers. Her little brother is on the soccer team too, and she's another senior, so it's kind of strange that we've never hung out. We've always had classes together, although this year we only share study hall. I like her fine—but I've always had my friends, and she's always had hers, most of whom are in the photography club and way too intense for me. She's one of those girls who's super serious about becoming a photographer. She carries around an old camera and rolls her eyes when people take selfies on their phones. She verges on being annoying about it, but she's also really good. Or at least, she always takes a lot of pictures that get into the yearbook. She's tall and broad and wears super-shiny lip gloss and bright, patterned dresses that I think she makes herself.

I should probably talk to her, but I can't deal with the slightly awkward why-aren't-we-better-friends conversation right now. I can't make small talk after the night I had. I wave back at her, then head for the shade behind the bleachers, where hopefully I won't have to talk to her.

I could stay out on the field and just pretend that I have to stick by my family, but if I did that, I'd have to talk to all of Nico's friends' parents. It's not that I don't like them—they're nice people. But I can guarantee that they'll all have the same five questions. *How's school? Where are you going to college? What do you want to major in? What's your five-year plan? How was prom?*

The answers are *fine, State, I don't know, (screaming internally)*, and *fine*, respectively. I can deal with answering the first two questions, which nobody actually cares about unless they went to State, in which case they'll start giving me all kinds of advice about professors I might have and classes I might take. The last three questions hurt in ways it's hard to articulate. Before last night, the last question was always *Are you excited for prom?*, which also hurt in ways it's hard to articulate. It's like every adult I talk to has some weird combination of expectations. They want me to be living in the now and enjoying "the best years of my life," sure—but at the same time, I'm supposed to know what income I'll need to afford the thirty-year fixed-rate mortgage I'll be signing up for in ten years.

It's just a lot, is all. So yeah, sometimes I hide, or pretend to be totally absorbed in my phone, or whatever. Because sometimes I don't want to have to know where I'll be in ten years and how I'll get there. Sometimes I don't want to be experiencing the Fullness of Teendom.

Sometimes I just want to be able to exist as I am without having to worry about anything bigger than how I'll dispose of Josh Harper's head and heart.

I check the group text and, apparently, a million things have happened since the last time I looked at it. Roya is hungover, and Iris is in trouble with her parents as always, and one of Maryam's prom makeup tutorials got picked up by some big clickbait website. Everyone is trying not to talk about what happened; they're all acting like everything's fine, like our normal problems matter. It's an enormous relief. While I'm composing my response, three dots appear at the bottom of the screen, the indicator that someone is typing.

I wait. I want to see what someone else says before I hit *send*. I wouldn't want my response to interrupt someone else's thought. I wonder sometimes if everyone else thinks this way too—if they're also always trying to make sure that they're not taking up too much space.

I don't have to wait long. It's only a few seconds before Maryam's message comes through.

We have to talk about last night

The air feels humid and close and suffocating.

Sure thing but not in text, comes Roya's reply. She and Marcelina negotiate a time and place for all of us to meet: Marcelina's house at dawn. Paulie protests, because of course she does, but agrees to the plan after a single message from Maryam:

Please. It's an emergency.

I haven't sent a reply yet. I can't find a reply that fits, so after a minute, I send a thumbs-up emoji. It looks wrong, so I follow it with the word **Thanks**, then **Sorry**, then **Thanks** again. Nothing feels right, and I start to think that maybe nothing ever will.

I lean against the bleachers so that I can feel the vibrations of footsteps against my back. I can hear Pop yelling "Go Nico!"

as loud as he can, even though he doesn't understand the game.

Then I hear Dad's voice, much closer than Pop's.

"Yeah, sorry, I just had to get away from the field," he's saying. "It's loud as heck out here. What were you asking?"

He walks around the corner of the bleachers, his shoulders sagging with relief as he steps into the shade. His face is already shining with sweat from standing in the sun—it's beading in his five-o'clock shadow and making his hair foof up into curls. He must have pulled a late night last night to have skipped shaving this morning. He'll have a sunburn later, and Pop will nag him for not wearing sunscreen—you can count on it. He squints around in the shadows while his eyes adjust, and then he spots me and does a combination oh-hi-you're-here and sorry-I'm-on-the-phone pantomime. I smile and wave him off. It's the same exchange we go through every time he tries to sneak away to take a work call during family time, only to run into me in one of my hiding places.

I'm not paying him any attention—I've spent my whole life learning how to tune out his meandering conversations with clients and colleagues—but some part of my brain must be listening, because I snap to attention when I hear the name "Josh."

". . . wasn't at a friend's house?" Dad is saying, and a sick kind of heat rises in my chest. "Well, I don't know. He definitely wasn't with us." He pauses, and I'm not even trying to pretend that I'm not listening. I know that if I tried to act disinterested, I'd fail, so I let him see that he's caught my attention, that I'm worried. I hope that he only sees "worried," and not "pissing myself with fear." He holds up a finger, frowning—the other person on the line is still talking.

"Hang on," he says after a long time. "I have Alexis right here. I'll ask her." He covers the mouthpiece and looks up at me. "Hey, bug, did you see Josh Harper last night?"

Let me take a moment to explain why I say what I say next. I've grown up with two lawyer dads. Trial lawyer dads. They both work defense cases, which means they could find a loophole in a mountainside and turn it into a tunnel big enough for a steam engine to pass through. They're also both *great* at spotting lies. They trust me a lot, and they let me get away with a lot, but they expect the truth from me, and most of the time, I give it to them.

On my very best, sneakiest day, when Pop and Dad are both way overwhelmed and barely have time for me, I can maybe get away with "I'm staying over at Marcelina's house tonight" when really I mean "I'm going to lose my virginity to whatever boy is nearby tonight."

Today? With Dad looking straight at me, worry draped across his brow like a flower crown? Not a chance.

So I say yes.

"I saw him at prom," I say. "And . . . at the after-party." I let myself look a little guilty about the after-party, and Dad's eyebrows go up in a decent imitation of Pop's surprised-face. He gives me a *we'll talk about that later* look, then uncovers the phone.

"Yeah, she saw him," he says. "He was at a party. Whose house?" He looks at me.

"His house," I whisper. Dad's eyebrows go down into a furrow.

"Your house," he says, and the person on the other end talks a lot. I wave my hands and shake my head. "Hold on," he says into the phone. "Maybe I misunderst—hold on, okay?"

"Sorry," I say, "it was at his dad's house, not, uh. Not his mom's house."

"I see," Dad says. "And I take it his father was out of town?"

I bite my lip and nod. Dad's lips tighten into a thin line, and I know that there will be a Long Conversation about this in my future.

He relays the information into the phone, then says, "I'm sure he's fine," and "Let me know if there's anything we can do to help." Then he hangs up.

"What's up?" I ask. "Is everything okay?" There's fear in my voice, and I hope to god that Dad thinks it's just fear of the consequences of having gone to the party.

"I'm sure everything's fine," he says, crossing his arms. "That was Mrs. Harper. Apparently, Josh didn't come home last night, and he isn't answering his phone."

"Oh," I say, looking at the ground. I wonder if Iris's spell got rid of his phone, or if it's in his bloodless bedroom at his dad's house, ringing and ringing and ringing.

"Hey," he says, walking toward me and putting his phone into the pocket of his cargo shorts, which Pop calls his "soccer dad" shorts. "I'm not thrilled about this party, but you know I trust you, right?" He ducks his head to look into my face. My eyes are stinging with guilty tears.

"Yeah," I whisper. "I know."

"Then all I need to know is, were you safe there? Were you with your friends, and did you all keep an eye on each other and get home safely and responsibly?"

The tears spill over, and I hiccup once. "Yeah," I say. "Yeah, we were all together. And we were safe."

Dad puts an arm around me and pulls me into a hug. I lean my face into his shirt. He smells like deodorant and bar soap, and I cry for everything that I can't tell him.

"Hey, bug, hey, it's okay," he says, rubbing my back like he did when I was a little kid. "I'm sure Josh is fine. He probably just overslept and forgot to charge his phone or something. He'll turn up."

I don't answer, because I can't. The tears won't stop coming. I cry until I'm tired and drained. I cry until I feel as empty as the duffel bags that Josh abandoned at the bottom of his closet. I cry until I hear Pop shouting for one of Nico's goals, and then I pull away from Dad, and wipe my face, and give him a weak smile.

"It'll be okay, bug," he says, trying to look comforting but really just looking worried.

"I know," I say. But I don't know.

I don't know at all.

5.

THE NEXT MORNING, I WAKE UP WHILE THE STARS are still out. I sneak out of the house without turning any lights on, leaving a note on my door that says I caught a ride to school with Paulie. I walk to Marcelina's woods and listen to the way the world sounds different before dawn. I wonder why I don't wake up this early more often—it's kind of beautiful, the way everything is still and silent. The way the world feels half-finished in the almost-light.

My backpack is heavy. I've still got Marcelina's shovel, plus all my school stuff.

Plus the head and the heart.

I checked on them before I left the house. Nothing about the head has changed. Something about Iris's spell preserved the flesh, held it in a state of suspended animation. The heart, though—I wasn't imagining things the other day. It's just the slightest bit warm. As if someone was holding it right before me and their skin left a trace of heat on its glassy surface. I turn the beginning of an idea over in my head as I walk, but it's loose, ill-formed, and I lose track of it too quickly.

When I get to Marcelina's house, I'm the last one there. Everyone else is standing around, silently watching their shoes soak up the morning dew. They stand at the edge of the woods, barefaced and sleepy-eyed. Marcelina's got her palm pressed to the trunk of a tree, and when I look down at her feet, they're on either side of a mound of fresh-turned earth. This is where we buried the spine, then—this is the tree that Josh's bones helped.

"How's she doing?" I whisper to her, lifting my chin toward the tree.

She smiles and nods. "Better."

"This is everyone," Roya says, her voice a little too loud. Paulie catches my eye and her lips tighten.

"Thank you all for coming." Maryam is stiff, oddly formal. Her hands are tucked into the big front pocket of her hoodie. "I'm really sorry, but I just—I needed to talk to you all about what happened, and what you're going to do about it."

"I thought you didn't want to be part of this," Iris hisses. Her eyes are mean.

"I don't want to be part of it," Maryam snaps back. "But I love you all, so I want to talk to you about it because I'm worried, okay?"

"We've got it under control." Roya's too loud again, and Marcelina glances back toward the house. No lights come on, but Roya notices and closes her mouth pointedly.

I clear my throat. "What do you want to talk about, Maryam? I think that if we tell you what we're going to do with the body, that kind of makes you part of it, right? So we probably shouldn't do that."

Maryam flinches at the word "body." She folds her arms across her chest, then thinks better of it and unfolds them, shoving her fists back into her pocket. "I'm sorry," she whispers. "But I think this is wrong, you getting rid of the body. It's not just that I can't be a part of it. *None* of you should be a part of it. This kind of thing, it stays with a person's soul."

Iris starts to say something, but Marcelina gets there first. "I think you're right," she says. "I haven't been able to stop thinking about it. But . . . but what else are we supposed to do? How are we supposed to explain it?"

"We don't even have the whole body," Roya says. "It's all in pieces now, and the pieces are—"

"They're weird," Iris interrupts. "They're preserved and weird and if we brought them to the cops, there wouldn't be any way to explain why they're like this. We don't have a choice. We have to get rid of the pieces." She sounds certain, like she always does.

"Did you even *try* to bring him back?" Maryam asks. She asks it softly, gently. She already knows the answer. Iris folds her arms and looks away.

"Iris?" Paulie whispers. She's being painfully gentle. "Did you try to come up with a way to bring him back? Or did it feel too impossible?"

Iris doesn't look back at any of us. She's staring into the tree line as if she's watching the woods for something. Everyone is so still that I can hear Paulie breathing next to me, slow and even, the way she breathes when she's trying to stay calm.

"I didn't . . . It didn't occur to me to bring him back until Alexis asked about it," Iris says at last. "I mean, it would have been impossible, right? I didn't try to come up with a way to do it because it just felt so outrageous to even consider it."

"Even just getting rid of him seemed too hard," Roya says. "Hell, it *was* too hard. We didn't even pull that off. How are we supposed to try to bring him back?"

Paulie wraps her arms around herself. "What if something even worse happens?"

"I get it," Maryam murmurs. "But we have to at least make an effort. I think we have to try to do the right thing, before we can find excuses for having done the wrong thing."

What she's said settles over us. It's heavy with truth.

Roya swears, then lets out a noise that's between a sigh and a growl. "You said 'we.' Does that mean you're with us?"

Maryam nods. "I still can't help you get rid of a body, but if there's something I can do to help you bring him back, I will."

We all look to Iris. She's still staring at the woods. It's light out enough now that I can make out her face pretty clearly. She's chewing hard on her lip, fighting an internal battle. I think I can guess the conflict.

"Iris?" I venture. "I don't think you did anything wrong. You were trying to help. But maybe—maybe this can help too?"

She shakes her head, then shrugs and says, "Fine. Do you all have your parts? Let's get them together. Maybe we can make it work."

Everyone except for Marcelina drops a duffel bag or a backpack to the ground. Marcelina has to go back to the house to get hers. She asks me if I'll come with her, and I hand my backpack to Roya, relieved. I know that she won't hesitate to pull out the heart and the head while I'm gone.

I won't have to do it.

It's not that I'm grossed out. It's not that I can't face what I did. It's just that I don't want anyone to see. I don't want them to see me cradling Josh's head in my hands, my fingers in his hair. I don't want them to see me with my thumbs over his eyelids or my palm on his cheek. I don't want them to see his face and remember that he was a person, and that he might deserve more than having his head in a backpack.

I keep Fritz and Handsome quiet while Marcelina sneaks into the house. When she comes back out, she's carrying a dark bundle—the liver, wrapped in a T-shirt I don't recognize. We walk back to the rest of the girls in silence, our feet swishing through the grass. Just before we reach the group, Marcelina pauses.

"Are you doing okay?" she whispers.

"Yeah," I reply, because it's the only answer that feels allowed. I'm the reason everyone is in this mess—what right do I have to be anything less than okay? Marcelina nods, and I think she understands that *yeah* is all I've got right now.

We get back to the group as the sun crests the horizon. It had felt like morning already, with the sky growing light and the air getting warmer, but now the first tendrils of light are touching the tops of the trees, and it feels like dawn. Iris is flipping through her big journal of How Magic Works. It's thick and worn, full of extra pages that she's stapled in, bursting with her notes and charts and theories. She hasn't cracked the Why or How of our magic yet, but she hasn't given up either. I don't think Iris knows how to give up.

I join the circle as Marcelina crouches, gently placing Josh's liver near the middle of the odd arrangement of his limbs. Every part of Josh that we have is placed in an approximation of a boy-shape: arms, legs, hands, feet, head, heart, liver.

"Oh," Maryam says, looking at his heart. "That's not right, is it?"

I shake my head. *Not right* is an understatement.

"Where's the spine?" Iris asks.

"I already got rid of it," Marcelina replies. "It was buried there." She points to the little hill of soil just behind Josh's head.

"Shit," Roya hisses. She laces her fingers behind her head and breathes in long and deep, her chest steadily rising.

"Yeah, shit," Paulie says. "Should we dig it up?"

Marcelina shakes her head. "It's powder. I ground it into powder."

Roya releases the deep breath in one shocked gust. "You—what? Powder? What the *fuck*, Marcelina?"

"It's fine," Iris interrupts. "We'll just have to hope it's enough."

We stand in a loose circle—Paulie is on my right, near Josh's feet, and Marcelina is on my left. Roya is across from me, next to Maryam. Iris stands just above the head. She closes her notebook with a decisive slap, slips it into her bag, and tucks her hair behind her ears. She takes Marcelina's and Maryam's hands and holds them in a white-knuckled grip.

"Do you think it'll work?" Paulie mutters.

I reach out and squeeze her hand. "Yeah," I whisper back. "I really do." It's the second time I've lied today, and the sun hasn't even finished coming up.

The spell starts out like it did the last time: all of us spinning loose magic up for Iris to work with, her fists in the air gathering spools of raw power. The air feels tight on my skin. The magic doesn't make a sound, but it *feels* like it's crackling. It builds and it builds and it builds and it *builds* and then—

It breaks.

Iris falls sideways into Marcelina, her arms falling limp by her sides. The spools of magic around her fists fall too, landing on the pieces of Josh in huge bright sheets. We all scramble, kicking up loam and running into each other. Paulie shouts, and then her hand is on my arm, pulling me away from the body. My feet slip out from under me, but Paulie keeps yanking on me and I don't get a chance to fall, and by the time I've got my balance, we're fifty feet away.

Roya grabs my hand tight, looking across me at Paulie's

wide eyes. Iris is pale, leaning heavily on Marcelina. Maryam is covering her face with both hands, staring at the smoke that rises from the place where she was standing just a few moments before.

"What are those?" Roya asks in a hoarse whisper. Her fingers twitch in mine. They're thin and cool and soft, and I do not trace the shape of her first knuckle with the pad of my thumb. How could I even think of that, at a time like this one?

She points to the ground where we had been standing. Our circle has been replaced by six little hills. From where we are, they look like piles of earth. I squeeze Roya's hand gently, then let it go and take a cautious step toward the body. There's smoke there, but no fire. The air feels thick, humid. Close.

"Alexis, don't—"

"Don't what?" I look over my shoulder, but Maryam just shakes her head. I give her what I hope is a reassuring smile.

"Don't touch them," she says.

I'm not sure what she means. Not until I get a little closer. My breath catches in my throat at what I see.

Six hawks. Gorgeous, full-feathered ones. Harris hawks, I think, although I've never seen one this close before and my eyes catch on so many little details that I can't be sure. They're huge, with hooked yellow beaks and tawny wings and white-tipped tails, and they're beautiful, and they're dead.

Six hawks, right where we were standing.

"They fell out of the sky," Paulie whispers, and I turn to find her standing next to me. She sinks her teeth into her bloodless lower lip briefly before clearing her throat. "One almost—it almost hit you, when it fell."

"His feet," Marcelina says. "They're gone." Her eyes are on the lingering smoke that curls up from the place where Josh's feet had been.

"Fuck," Iris croaks. "I'm sorry. I couldn't—"

"It's okay," Maryam says, laying her fingers gently across Iris's forehead. "You did your best."

I step between two hawks, trying not to look at them. It feels like my feet are sinking into the earth a little too deep—the soil isn't steady beneath me. I stare at the heart.

It throbs once. I watch it, unable to make myself so much as blink. The other girls notice and look over to see what I see, and they see it too: after a few seconds, it throbs again.

It's beating.

The soil in Marcelina's woods is still soft from the heavy rain we got all spring. I find a spot that's far enough from the tree line to feel private. As I dig, I wonder if the trees will report back to Marcelina the next time she checks in. *There was a girl in the woods.*

It didn't work. Iris tried her best, but it didn't work.

Josh is still dead.

I'm the only one who stayed. Everyone else is gone, doing the things that come between dawn and the first class of the day. We were all freaked out about how things went down—

about the heart and about the hawks, and about how badly our attempt to set things right hurt Iris. Roya started asking if the heart was coming back to life, if that meant we could bring every piece back to life but couldn't put them back together, and Maryam had to calm her down before she hyperventilated. And Iris . . . Iris was in bad shape, pale and unsteady on her feet.

Even after everyone had calmed down, I wasn't ready to go home, and I didn't want to talk to anyone about what had just happened. About our failure, and about what would come next. I told them to go ahead without me.

So instead, I'm burying the head.

I dig as the sun comes up. The shovel crunches through the top layer of dirt and into soft soil, well churned by industrious worms. All I hear as the sky lightens overhead is my own steady breathing and the rhythm of the shovel shifting mound after mound of earth. School starts in a couple of hours—the first day of the last month of classes—and I need enough time to bury the head, go to school, shower, change, and buy a crappy day-old bagel from the cafeteria. The ground is much softer than I anticipated. The digging is easy, and before I know it, I've got a pretty deep hole.

I jump down into it and keep going. I dig until the top of the hole is over my head, until I'm surrounded on all four sides by close walls of loose, crumbling earth. Josh is still dead. The hole is only just wide enough for me to stick my elbows out and turn around in a circle. I can't see anything but hole anymore, and my breath catches in my throat. Josh is still dead. I make an unintentional ragged sound as my lungs clench with the certainty that I've dug too deep, that I'm trapped, that someone will find me here in a hole with a head in a backpack next to it.

Josh is still dead. And the only thing we can do is try to hide the evidence.

I take deep breaths. I imagine that I'm coaching Iris through a panic attack. I imagine that I'm floating in a tropical sea, staring up at the moon. None of it works, though, because every time I open my eyes, I'm still in a grave. *I have to get out of here.*

I toss up the shovel and try to jump. When I bend my knees, I find that there's barely room for even that—my butt bumps against one side of the hole and my knees bump against the other. I push off and get maybe a foot of height, and when I grab at the edge of the hole, I succeed only in pulling dirt down into my face. I spit mud and try again, keeping my arms over my head this time. I get a little higher and grab at fistfuls of grass near the sides of the hole. Painfully, bracing my feet on opposite sides of the too-small grave, I pull myself up. Soft soil rains down into my shirt and shoes and hair. I have my eyes scrunched shut to keep the dirt out of them, and I don't open them again until I'm sprawled, panting, on the ground beside the hole I've made.

The tree I've chosen to bury Josh's head under is, I think, the lightning-struck tree that Marcelina was worrying about.

It's a huge, gnarled black oak with a squat trunk. Branches shoot up out of it like grasping fingers, and there's a black scar that travels the entire length of the tree, from the tallest branch to the roots. It's still alive, but it's struggling—there are an awful lot of brown leaves, and I can't see any tender new growth on the tips of the branches.

I pull the head out of my backpack, trying not to touch his eyes or his lips. I drop it into the hole and start shoveling soil back over it. It takes longer than I thought it would—I figured I'd be able to just kind of push a whole pile of dirt into the hole, but it doesn't quite work that way. I try to shove the pile, and it topples. I have to shovel the dirt in the same way I got it out—one scoop at a time. I'm thankful for the work, for the way my palms burn and my back starts to ache, because Josh is dead and there's nothing I can do to fix it. I'd let myself hope, and that was a mistake, because there's nothing I can do but try not to get caught.

I wanted to do the right thing. I tried to do the right thing.

By the time I finish, I'm sweating hard, and the sun is already bright in the sky. I wipe my face off on the inside of my shirt, although both are so dirty that I'm sure I'm just smearing mud between the two.

I can't make this right, but at least I can make it useful. Before I drop in the last few fistfuls of soil, I crouch next to the little mound. I push my fingers into the loose dirt—the grave dirt—and close my eyes.

I don't have Marcelina's focus when it comes to plants. Her

ability to draw the other tree's roots to the new nutrient-source is something I'd never even hope to achieve. But I can do something, in my own way, to help. I push magic out into the earth. All of my muscles relax as I let it flow through me and into the tiny tunnels and warrens and scent-trails of all the small eyeless underground creatures that live in the shelter of this tree. *Come here,* I tell them without words. The ground pulses faintly, all the dead leaves rustling wherever my magic flows. *There is meat. There is a carcass here. Do your work.*

A thousand sightless consciousnesses turn to me, touched by the message that I've sent to them. Normally, they'd be drawn by the smells of decay, but not this time. This time, they'll be the first to the meal.

I snip off my magic like threads on a loom, leaving trails that can be followed. There's a shudder beneath my feet, and I pull my fingers out of the dirt fast. An underground stampede is happening—an army of burrowing beetles and worms and mites are coming to see why I called them. I use the shovel to spread the last of the dirt in an even layer over the mound, and then I leave. I want to be gone before they try to thank me for the gift of Josh's head.

I walk away without looking back, because there's nothing else for me to do.

Against my back, through the thin canvas of my backpack, I can feel the way Josh's glass heart starts to beat just a little harder.

6.

THE WALK TO SCHOOL IS STRANGE. I KEEP expecting people to pull over and ask me why I'm covered in filth, but there are almost no cars on the road. I suppose it's still too early for them—the sun is up, but only because it's practically summer. An empty bus passes, and the driver lifts his hand to me without looking at me. I lift my hand back anyway. The back of it is covered in grime, and half of my sparkly prom-manicure has chipped off. My fingernails look like treasure maps.

If Roya was here, she could will the dirt away from me. It's something we figured out when we were kids, back when we were first realizing that the things we could do weren't just in our imaginations—that I really could talk to her cat, that she really could kiss a bruise and make it disappear. We were alone at her house, playing. Roya's parents were at a doctor's appointment—they would come home with glowing smiles and a blurry black-and-white photo of Roya's little brother. But all we knew then was that we had the run of the house, and we took full advantage of it. We poured tall glasses of grape soda and smeared our faces with Roya's mother's forbidden lipstick and pulled all of her father's shirts out of the closet for some grand dress-up scheme.

You can imagine what those shirts looked like by the time we'd finished with them. Each and every one, indelibly stained in ways that we somehow failed to notice while we were playing. I remember staring at one mark on the shirt I'd just taken off, then looking at all the others with increasing horror as the stains and lipstick-smears seemed to multiply. It was like that thing where you notice one ant, and then another, and then you realize that they're *everywhere*.

Roya squeezed her eyes shut and pushed her hands at the pile of ruined shirts, and the next thing either of us knew, they were back on their hangers, clean and pressed as if nothing had ever happened. Roya's pupils were dilated for the rest of the day, and she was way too quiet, but her parents never knew what had happened.

I always think of her magic as fixing-things magic. Roya can heal people, like she did when Iris was hurt on prom night, and she can clean things, like with her dad's shirts. She has a lot of other magic—we all do—but she's the only one of us who can do those particular things. She hates it. She says it's regressive. But then, she can also start a car just by laying her hands on the engine block, and she set my arm with an audible crunch back when I broke it in fifth grade, so . . . I think she's just looking for something to be mad about.

Which isn't all that surprising. It is Roya, after all.

If she was here, she'd will me clean. But she's not here.

I come onto campus the back way and head for the gym lockers, which are in a low-ceilinged, temporary-looking building between the pool and the auditorium. There's no proper door on either of the locker rooms, which has always seemed weird to me—just a curving wall at the entrance that hides the inside of the rooms from passersby, like at a rest-stop bathroom. The entire school is like that: built sometime in the late eighties to fulfill a design aesthetic that seems halfway between airplane hangar and National Park outbuilding. There are lots of low timbers and metal crossbeams, and everything needed to be power-washed about ten years ago. There's new paint every year, covering up old graffiti and trying to make the place look fresh, but the stucco and cinder-block never really stops being outdated.

I walk into the locker room, feeling furtive and victorious, and head for the showers. I drop my backpack on a bench without breaking stride. I strip off my shirt as I go, raining dirt that no one will notice onto the pebbly, never-mopped floor. *Clean,* I think, reaching back to unhook my bra. *So close to being clean—*

"I don't know."

I freeze with my fingers on the clasp of my bra. The echoes of a voice, distorted by the way the sound bounces around the locker room. No one is supposed to be here this early. Shit. I can't tell where the voice is coming from, so I race toward the showers, hoping to duck behind a curtain before anyone sees me. Before anyone can ask what I'm doing here and why I look like a swamp creature.

"Just ask her," another voice answers just as I reach the showers. Too late, I realize that I've come closer to the voices, rather than farther from them. I duck behind a shower curtain and whip it closed just as the sound of shower shoes slapping wetly on the floor reaches me.

"She won't tell me," the first voice answers, and I realize who it is I'm hearing.

Roya.

The footsteps stop just outside of my shower stall, and a locker swings open. The voice that answers Roya is unmistakable, now that it's close enough not to echo off the metal lockers. It's Iris. "Well, maybe if you didn't—"

Oh, thank god, I think, and I open the shower curtain again. Iris and Roya are right there, and they freeze at the sight of me. "You guys scared the shit out of me," I say.

They don't answer. They're staring at me. Iris is clutching the top of her towel, and Roya has frozen halfway through drying her mass of hair.

"What the hell," Iris breathes, and I realize what I must look like—hair in a half-fallen-out topknot, dirt caked into my every pore, shirtless, my bra hanging halfway off. I'm not sure if I look better or worse than I did on prom night. At least I'm not covered in blood this time.

"Um," I say.

"Holy shit, Alexis," Roya says, and then she starts cackling at me, a desperate kind of "oh thank god I can still find things funny" laugh. "It's only been like . . . an hour and a half. What *happened* to you?" Roya gasps.

"Lots," I snap. "Lots of stuff happened to me." I pull the shower curtain closed and strip, throwing my filthy clothes out past the vinyl. Every item I toss elicits a new round of laughter from Roya—I can hear Iris joining in, less enthusiastically, but she's laughing all the same. "It's been a long morning," I say, turning on the water and tipping my head back to shake the dirt out of my hair.

I do not think of the fact that I am in here, naked, and Roya is out there, wearing only a towel. I *do not think about it*, okay? Not at all. Not even a little.

"Do you need soap?" Roya asks. Before I can answer, her hand thrusts through a gap in the shower curtain, holding a bottle of the mint body wash she loves. Her wrist brushes my stomach as she waves the bottle back and forth. I can't breathe.

"Yes, thanks," I say, grabbing the bottle in a wet hand. Our fingers tangle for a moment before she lets go of the bottle.

I shove my face into the spray. She's my best friend. I don't think about it.

"What are you guys doing here so early?" I call. "I thought you'd go back to bed."

"Practice," Iris answers, and that's all she needs to say. They must have come straight here from Marcelina's house. There's a big meet coming up, but "practice" would have been the answer even if there hadn't been a single meet on the calendar. With his two best swimmers about to leave, the swim coach has been driving the team hard all year. If I breathe deep enough, I can smell the chlorine still clinging to Roya's hair and skin.

And Iris. It's also clinging to Iris. Not just Roya. Not just Roya's skin.

I lather, rinse, and inspect. Still dirty, although the first round got most of the loose dirt off.

"Hey, do you want me to do your hair?" Roya calls. I start soaping up again, trying to get some of the more stubborn dirt off my hands and arms.

"Why?" I ask as I rinse.

"So you don't have to wash it," she says. "I should be able to get the dirt out without getting it wet."

"Too late," I reply, turning off the water and wringing out my hair, and I hear her mutter an *I told you so* to Iris. "Um, speaking of which," I add, but before I can finish, Roya's arm thrusts back into the shower, this time clutching an only-slightly-damp towel. "Thanks," I say sheepishly. After I take the towel, her arm hesitates for a moment.

I stare at the soft inside of her wrist. It's a lighter shade than the deep brown-gold of the rest of her, but still dark enough that my fingertips look ghostly against the backdrop of her skin. A bangle, gold with dark green stones, hangs just above the jut of bone at the base of her hand. It's the bangle I gave her for her birthday last year.

Her fingers flex. I don't know what she's waiting for. Slowly, *slowly*, I reach out and brush my fingers across her palm.

A soap bubble drifts by. I snatch my hand back, my cheeks and throat and chest all burning. What was I thinking? *The soap*. Of course she's waiting for the soap. I grab it and fumble it into her hand, then towel myself off roughly. My breath comes fast and shallow, and I want to smack my head into the wall until the embarrassment fades.

Maybe she didn't notice. Maybe she thought it was the towel or my hair or something, anything but my fingertips.

"See you at lunch?" Iris calls, and I can hear them zipping up backpacks. "There's some stuff I wanna run by you."

"Yeah, sure, perfect!" I call, my voice too bright and brassy.

"Bye," Roya says, and I know it's just in my head, but there's a softness to her voice. A waiting-ness. I know it's all in my imagination, but it feels like she's saying something more than just "bye." It feels like years of longing are contained in those three letters.

I shove my face into the towel and hold back a scream of frustration. Years of longing in three letters? God, I'm pathetic. She was just saying "bye." Normal people say "bye" to each other *all the time*.

I don't come out of the shower until long after their footfalls fade from my hearing. I throw my filthy clothes into the trash on my way out the door, because I can't bear the thought of carrying grave-dirt-covered clothes with me all day. I buy my day-old bagel from the cafeteria, and I make it to my first class just before the bell rings. All morning long, my fingertips sweetly ache where they brushed Roya's palm. It feels just like it does when I'm pushing magic out of myself and into the world, and I can't stop checking to see if they're glowing.

I'm still staring at them when my math teacher announces that Josh is missing.

7.

I HAVE CALCULUS FIRST PERIOD. MY TEACHER, Mr. Wyatt, is kind of a mess. His divorce was finalized at the beginning of the school year, and he's been trying to date since winter break. School gossip has been unrelenting, with reports circulating of his unsuccessful dates with all of the single female teachers (and, uncharitably, a couple of the married ones). Sometime around January he bought a motorcycle and stopped buttoning the top few buttons of his shirts. I'm sure he's a great guy and all that, but his midlife crisis is a little overwhelming to witness. We all try to be gentle with him, which adds an extra layer of hard-to-watch to his announcement about Josh.

"Anyone who has any information about Josh's whereabouts should head to the front office right away. You won't get in trouble if you know where he is." He's trying to look calm and comforting, but also stern and authoritative, which results in a facial expression I can only describe as "clenched." "His family is worried about him, guys," he says in a scolding tone that implies we all know where Josh is but think it's fun to keep the information to ourselves. "Think about what they're going through. Do the right thing."

I glance around the room. Some people are casting worried looks at each other, mouthing, "Did you hear from him?" One girl is texting under her desk without watching the screen, her thumbs moving fast while she stares at Mr. Wyatt with a fixed, I'm-definitely-listening look on her face. A few people look totally locked down—they're not responding well to Mr. Wyatt's tone, his assumption that we know something but aren't telling.

Maryam sits two rows in front of me. I can't see her face, and the back of her head tells me absolutely nothing about whether she's mad or scared or sad or what. All I know is that she's sitting very still. She doesn't raise her hand and say, "I know who killed him!" She doesn't look back at me. There's nothing she could possibly do in this moment to make me feel better, but still—a bright knot of worry tightens in my belly at the sight of her stillness. What if this morning she was giving us all some kind of last chance? What if she's decided that telling someone what happened is the Right Thing to Do?

Mr. Wyatt finally finishes staring at all of us like we're hiding his car keys, and transitions to handing out the day's worksheet. We're doing worksheets for the entire last month of school, because he knows that every senior he teaches has one foot out the door. He gives us completely unnecessary instructions, which basically boil down to "Answer all the questions on the page instead of screwing around for the next hour," then sits down at his desk to fiddle with his profile on this month's dating site. There are no pretenses here. The second his butt hits the chair, the classroom erupts into whispers.

Nikki Palay, who sits in front of me, gets up and we swap seats. It's a long-standing arrangement that lets me talk to Maryam while Nikki talks to her best friend, who sits in the back row.

"Hey," I say as I slide into Nikki's still-warm chair. Maryam turns around to look at me. She's styled herself in the last couple of hours. Her eyeshadow is silver and blue today, with sharp black cat-eye liner framing her lids on either side. The second I see her makeup, I breathe a sigh of relief—I realize that part of me was afraid she'd turn around and still be barefaced, grieving. Haunted by what I did.

Or worse: afraid of what I am.

"Hey," she says, layering her hands over mine. She gives my fingers a squeeze. "How are you?"

Her smile makes my chest ache. "I'm okay," I say weakly, and we both laugh. "I mean, I'm awful, but I'm okay now. I was worried about you."

She shakes her head at me. "Don't worry about me," she says. "I'm fine. It's fine."

"Are you really fine?"

"No," she says, smiling a little. "But I know you guys tried your best," she says, then glances away. "And I know we'll figure something out. Together."

"You don't have to be—"

She cuts me off. "So, my video went viral this weekend."

Her eyes are wide and serious. I blink a couple of times. What the hell does her video have to do with anything?

She nods once, then repeats herself, more slowly this time. "So. My video. Went viral."

Oh.

She's asking me for a break. She's asking me to talk about this other thing, this significant thing that isn't as significant as *I murdered a boy with magic I don't understand* but that matters to her, that matters to our friendship. She's asking me for time.

I can give her that.

"Tell me every single thing" I say, and just like that we slide into a conversation about her viral makeup tutorial. It has something like a million views now. She's getting a shockingly low volume of hate mail, considering the usual tone of people on the internet. Marcelina is monitoring the comments section to report anything nasty in there. Maryam talks about the responses she's getting with a brightness that almost reads as true. It's the kind of conversation we'd be having if prom had gone any other way—a conversation about her ambition.

She talks about makeup, and she talks about making the video, and for half an hour, everything is fine.

Here's what you need to know about Maryam. She does these video tutorials even though, strictly speaking, she doesn't need to know any of the skills in the videos. Her strongest magic is color, and she could do her makeup without ever picking up a brush. She can do things to pigment that I could never even imagine attempting, and she's got an understanding of the structure of the human face that blows me away. She can will a color change or a pattern onto her lids without blinking.

But she doesn't usually do it that way—instead, she's spent hours perfecting techniques and making videos to teach strangers on the internet how to achieve the things that she can do without thinking. She's been working on it since middle school, when she first realized that she could change her lip color without lifting a finger.

I'll never forget when she showed Roya and me what she could do, behind the school administration building during lunch one day. We were in sixth grade, and she was just starting to cross the line with Roya and me—the line between friends and *best* friends. She told Roya her secret first, and then, when Roya vouched for me, she told me what she could do. We asked if we could see. She asked us if we could really keep secrets, like for real, and we all pinky-swore, and then she lifted her fingers and twitched them and turned Roya's hair pink.

I'll never forget the uncertainty in her eyes in the moment before Roya and I started falling over each other to reveal our own secrets. I'll never forget the feeling that we'd unlocked something together, the three of us—some secret to friendship and teenagedom and grown-upness. Maryam has worked tirelessly since that day to perfect her control of her powers—and to make sure that she doesn't *need* them to pursue her passion. She's one of the only people I know who's always had a plan for what she's going to do with her life. She's the kind of person who you can tell is going to be a big deal someday.

After we part ways at the end of class, I notice that my manicure is restored. I didn't even feel her do it. There's a tiny black heart on each sparkling nail—a little thing to make me smile all morning, so long as I don't think about Josh's heart when I look at my hands. That's Maryam for you. She's an amazing friend, and I realize: part of me was worried that I'd lose her over Josh. I don't know how I ever could have doubted her, even in the scared part of me that doesn't want to be left alone. She would never bail over a guy.

Even a dead one.

I don't see any of the girls again until lunch. We text between classes, but it's still a relief to find them all crowded around our usual table. I think some part of me was expecting them to be gone. To have left me behind to deal with what I've done and whatever it is that I'm becoming.

But of course they would never do that. Of course they're still here, and they've still saved me a seat.

I watch them from the burrito line. Roya is devouring a pile of cold pasta salad, holding her hair back into a ponytail with one hand and shoveling carbohydrates into her mouth with the other. By the time I get to the table with my foil-wrapped burrito, she'll have finished her pasta, and I'll have to defend the first half of my lunch from her appetite. Paulie has a thick sandwich, half of which she's already passed to Marcelina. Iris is squeezing a ketchup packet out all over the top of a pile of soggy cafeteria french fries—her defense mechanism against Roya, who won't eat them if they're already contaminated. Maryam is ignoring her boxed salad in favor of adjusting Iris's eyeliner to be curlier at the inside corners. Her brow is furrowed and she's saying something in that quiet I'm-right-next-to-your-eyeball way she talks when she's doing makeup, and Iris is pursing her lips.

I can quote the conversation by heart: Maryam is trying to get Iris to let her experiment with contouring, and Iris is responding that she won't cover her freckles. And Maryam is saying that there are ways to accentuate the freckles while still highlighting the bone structure, and Iris is saying that she wants her freckles to show exactly as they are because she worked so damn hard to love them and now they're her favorite thing about herself, and Maryam is saying that she knows, and then they're starting all over again.

Except that Maryam looks a little more animated than usual, and Iris is a little more gentle. Usually, Maryam leaves a lot of space for Iris to be opinionated and stubborn—no small sacrifice, given how opinionated and stubborn Maryam is on her own. But right now it looks like she's pushing harder than usual, and I know Iris well enough to know what it looks like when she bites her tongue.

If I had to guess, I'd say that Iris is giving quarter because she feels guilty for our failure this morning. And Maryam is pushing her, trying to make her feel like everything's okay. Like everything's normal. Just like this morning in class, when she tried to make me feel like everything was normal.

Maybe I'm overthinking things. But then again, maybe I'm not. Maybe I should stop worrying about overthinking things and just trust that I know my friends better than anyone should know anyone.

Paulie spots me and waves, and I wave back, pissing off the burrito-lady, who has to ask me twice if I want bean-and-cheese or chicken. "Chicken, thanks," I say, even though we both know that there won't be any chicken in there. The school burritos are beans, rice, and tortilla—filling enough that I can sacrifice the last few bites to Roya, cheap enough that I can use the remainder of my lunch money to buy a bag of chips to split with Marcelina. I almost always want to take a carb-crash nap during fifth period, but it's study hall anyway, so nobody notices if my eyes droop a little.

I start to make my way toward the table. Iris catches my eye, and I remember that she wanted to talk to me about something—she wanted to "run something by me." I'm trying to figure out how I'm going to pry Maryam off her when something happens.

It's that thing where all the attention in a room shifts, and without anyone saying anything, you know that you need to look. Maybe it's the way conversations shift to whispers; maybe it's the way heads turn to point in the same direction. Maybe it's one of those shared-consciousness things, where everyone is sharing a wavelength, and it twitches toward danger. Meerkats poking their heads up out of holes, looking at a shadow on the horizon.

That's the thing that happens. Without knowing why or how, something in the room makes me look up at the door to the cafeteria.

There's a cop.

Her eyes sweep across the cafeteria. She's wearing a full uniform. Dark blue, designed to make sure everyone around her remembers the authority she has over us. We're small enough that we don't have a dedicated police officer who works here all day, like some of the bigger schools do. But still, it's not rare to see cops here. Kids get caught with drugs or they start fights or get the wrong person on staff mad, and the police show up.

It always feels wrong to see them on campus, though.

Even if the fear I feel right now is amplified and more personal than usual, I've always been afraid of cops. Maybe it's because I've seen how some of my friends get treated differently by police than I do. Or maybe it's Dad's and Pop's stories of things that have happened to them and their friends at protests and marches and parades and all the little moments in between those things. Or maybe it's because police officers bring loaded guns into schools where we have regular drills about how to hide from people who bring loaded guns into schools. I don't know—they just scare the shit out of me, okay? And they scare the shit out of just about everyone I know.

I don't know how to reconcile how I feel about the police with how I trust Roya's mom. I've known her since I was too young to remember ever not having known her. She's put Band-Aids on my knees and made me grilled cheese sandwiches. It's hard to think of her as the same kind of person who makes Pop's hands tighten on his steering wheel when she drives behind him. But then again, I don't often see Roya's mom in uniform. She wears suits most of the time. I don't think I've ever seen her with a gun in her hand.

Maybe I wouldn't trust her so much if I saw her with a gun in her hand.

The cop in the doorway doesn't have a gun in her hand, but she's resting her hands on her belt, which hangs heavy with threats—baton, taser, cuffs, pistol. She's got short gray hair and a long, hawkish nose. She looks like she's seen it all before, twice, and wasn't impressed. Assistant Principal Toomey stands behind her, and they're both looking around as if all eyes aren't on them.

I'm holding my breath, trying hard to look normal. The cop's flat stare passes over my face without pausing. It lands on the table where we usually have lunch, and she points, and they start walking toward the place where everyone but me is sitting.

I slide onto a bench and watch what's happening across the cafeteria. The girl I'm next to—an underclassman I've never met—gives me a look, but doesn't tell me to leave. Toomey and the sharp-nosed cop walk up to the table and say something. Paulie answers, and Iris nods. Maryam's eyes are locked on the officer's gun, and I see Marcelina grab her hand under the table to give it a squeeze.

Roya stands up, shaking her head and looking pissed. She gestures to Iris's fries, and the assistant principal shrugs. The cop rests a hand on the butt of her baton and gives Roya a sizing-up look, and my stomach clenches.

"Ah, fuck!"

I turn to look at the girl next to me, the one who frowned when I sat at the end of her bench. She's swearing, and she's got one hand cupped underneath her nose, which is streaming blood. No, not streaming—gushing.

"Are you okay?" I ask, grabbing a pile of napkins from the freshman at the opposite end of the table. As I do, I notice that my palm is glowing. *Oh god, what did I do?*

"I'm fine," she says, grabbing a fistful of napkins from me and mopping up her chin and upper lip. "I think—I think it's over, actually? That was so weird, I never . . ."

I don't catch the rest of what she's saying, because I catch movement out of the corner of my eye. When I look over, Iris is standing up and putting her hand on Roya's arm. Maryam is staring at the table, her face fixed, her gaze distant. Roya sinks back into her chair, her arms folded, and glares at the cop. Iris says something to Marcelina. Then she walks out of the cafeteria in front of the assistant principal, her posture defiant, high red ponytail swinging. She doesn't turn back, doesn't pause before leaving. She looks like a warrior.

The cop stays behind, saying something to Roya, who rolls her eyes. They exchange a few more words before the officer leaves. I finally let myself inhale. My breath comes as ragged as if I'd been drowning.

I don't come to the table until she's gone. Maybe I'm a coward, but I don't think I could have kept my shit together in front of those handcuffs. In front of that gun.

"What was that about?" I ask as I hand my chips to Marcelina. Paulie gives me a Significant Look.

"They want to know about Josh," she says.

"Why would they think Iris knows anything about Josh?" I ask, ripping foil off my burrito. My fingers tremble a little, but then Roya leans over and takes a huge bite right out of my hands, spilling rice all over me. I glare at her, and she winks, her cheeks bulging. "You're gross," I snap, my voice harsher than I want it to be.

"You wuff it," she replies, her voice muffled by burrito. I roll my eyes, but I can't help smiling, because . . . it's Roya.

"The cop said that they found texts from Iris on Josh's phone," Maryam says, pulling Iris's abandoned fries across the table with a shaky hand. "From the night of the party."

"That doesn't mean anything," I say.

"Well, that's not what the cop said," Marcelina interjects.

We all turn to look at her—Marcelina isn't usually one to correct people, not unless it really matters. "Sorry," she says, looking everywhere but at us. "It's just that, well. Um."

"It's fine," Maryam says, although she sounds irritated. "Go ahead."

"Okay, well, what she said was that they found Josh Harper's cell phone, and that there was evidence indicating that Iris had been in contact with him in the time adjacent to his disappearance, and that they wanted to discuss the situation further without disrupting her class schedule." She's talking fast, and her voice rises with every new clause. "And then Roya said that they were disrupting her lunch, and that seemed more important than Iris missing Econ, and then—"

She trails off, red splotches rising on her chest.

"You okay?" Paulie asks softly.

"I don't know," Marcelina says. "Sorry." Maryam's face softens, and she watches Marcelina carefully. Roya lays the back of her hand against Marcelina's forehead, maternal. Marcelina flinches away. "I'm fine," she says. It's a transparent lie, but we don't push it. Marcelina will tell us when she's ready. She always does.

"So what do you guys think Iris is going to tell them?" Paulie asks, expertly redirecting our attention. Marcelina gives her a grateful smile.

"Not a damn thing," Roya says, reaching to the bottom of the french fry pile to extract an unsoiled wedge. "There's nothing to tell."

Paulie rolls her eyes. “Okay, but they’re going to ask if she knows where Josh is, and—”

“And she doesn’t,” Roya interrupts. “None of us do. We all know where *some* of Josh is,” she adds in an undertone, “but none of us are ever going to know where *all* of Josh is.”

“Except me,” I murmur.

“Except you,” Marcelina says through a mouthful of fries.

“Speaking of,” Roya says, reaching for my burrito, “are you doing anything tonight?”

“What? Tonight? Why?” I see Marcelina and Maryam exchange eye rolls. They start talking to each other about some makeup trick they want to try, and Paulie joins in on the conversation, even though she almost never wears anything beyond lip balm. And just like that, Roya and I are alone in the middle of the cafeteria. She watches me with raised eyebrows. “I mean, yeah, why?”

“I want to go to the reservoir,” Roya says around a large bite of my lunch. A piece of rice is caught in the divot of her top lip, and she flicks out the tip of her tongue to get it. I steal a sip of Paulie’s water, but it doesn’t make my mouth feel any less dry.

“Sure,” I say. “To, uh . . . take care of a thing?”

“Yeah,” Roya says. “To take care of a thing. You walked today, right? I can drive us there after sixth period.”

“Okay,” I say, and then Paulie is asking me a question about makeup that I don’t know the answer to, and the moment’s over. Under the table, Roya’s foot brushes against mine, and Paulie has to repeat herself three times before I answer.

"Oh, fuck," Roya mutters. I glance over, and she's looking behind me.

Her mom is standing in the doorway, and she doesn't look happy. She's wearing slacks and a fitted black blazer—the outfit she calls her "head-bitch-in-charge uniform." Her badge hangs from her belt and her hair is up in a tight, shiny brown bun, and there's no two ways to look at it: she's here in a professional capacity, and she does not have time for games. She points at Roya, then hikes a thumb over her shoulder. Roya stands up, slinging her backpack over one shoulder. She jams her hands into her pockets and stalks out of the cafeteria without saying goodbye to any of us.

As she disappears through the doorway, my phone rings. I look down. It's Roya's name and face on the screen. I answer, expecting it to have been a butt-dial, but a muffled version of Roya's mom's voice comes through. I put my phone on speaker and rest it in the middle of the table. We all lean forward to listen.

"Were you at that party?" Chief Cassas is asking. There's rustling. I'm pretty sure Roya's got her phone in the front pocket of her hoodie.

"Yes." That's Roya's voice, loud and clear. She called me from inside her pocket on purpose, I'm sure of it now. Two things dawn on me at once: First, the fact that Roya knows that we would all lie to her mom to protect her, and she wants us to have our stories straight. Second—the fact that she can call me without looking at the screen.

I bite my lip and try not to smile. She has me on speed-dial.

It's probably nothing. She probably has all of us on speed-dial.

Or maybe not. Maybe it's just me.

"I can't believe this," her mom is saying. "You told me you were going to be at Alexis's house. Are you lying to me now? Is this what we're doing?" Roya says something I don't catch, and there's another rustle. "I don't care if you wanted to go, you know the rules, and—"

"It was worth it," Roya says. "I'm never going to have another prom night, Mom. I wanted to be with my friends. I would do it again."

There's a long silence, and I turn the volume on my phone all the way up, thinking that maybe Roya's covered the mouthpiece of the phone by accident. It turns out to just be a pause in the conversation. Her mom's answer comes through at top volume, and we don't miss a single word.

"Do you know what happened to Josh Harper?"

We all wait, holding our collective breath. Marcelina snaps the hair tie around her wrist in a quick, steady rhythm.

"No," Roya answers simply, and we can hear her mom's sigh.

"Okay," Chief Cassas says. "Okay. We'll talk about the rest of it tonight, then."

"Fine," Roya says. "Am I grounded, though? I was going to go to the reservoir with Alexis this afternoon and . . ." Her voice has gone vague, uncomfortable. There's a sudden cacophony of rustling, like she's shoved both hands into her pocket and is fumbling with the phone. We don't hear the rest of her question or her mom's answer, and then the line goes dead, and the bell rings.

None of us move. All around us, people stand up, clearing their tables and dropping trash into the row of huge gray garbage cans in the middle of the cafeteria.

"Okay," I say. "Well. See you guys later?"

"Yeah," Paulie says. She's the first to go. She plants a kiss on top of my head, then walks away without saying goodbye.

"Don't worry," Marcelina says, running both hands through her hair before starting to put it up in a messy bun. "Roya and Iris are solid. They'll be fine."

I stay at the table as they all leave, knowing that I'll be late for study hall but not caring. I stare at the ten black hearts on the backs of my nails and imagine all of my friends, one by one, lying about whether or not they know what happened to Josh.

If Marcelina's wrong, and they're not fine, it will be because of those lies. It will be because they lied to protect me. If they're not fine, it'll be all my fault. But I'm too scared to do the right thing and turn myself in, or at least tell them they don't have to lie.

My friends love me more than I deserve. That's never been a question. The question is, how long will it take them to realize that?

8.

WHEN I GET TO THE PARKING LOT AT THE END of the day, Roya isn't there yet, so I walk up and down the rows of parking spaces looking for her car. My phone is buzzing in my pocket, but I don't pull it out, because I know what the notifications will be.

Did you hear about Josh?

Do you know what happened?

Did they call you in for questioning?

I heard he ran away from home.

I heard he got kidnapped.

I heard he died.

It's all anyone can talk about. Josh is missing, and the cops are asking students about it, and nobody seems to know what happened. That gray-haired cop let Iris go after a few questions about the party, but that wasn't the last time I saw the cop—she's been pulling kids out of classes all day. Everyone is trying to figure out who was at the party, who saw Josh leave, who he was with. Everyone is trying to figure out if they should be sad or scared, or if they should admit that they didn't really know him that well, or if it even matters that they didn't know him. Because if one of your classmates vanishes, even if you never talked to him before, it still hits you. We all know that we can disappear, even if we don't really feel it in our bones yet. We've spent our whole lives being reminded that we can disappear, from don't-talk-to-strangers to don't-drive-drunk. But it's hitting a lot of people now for the first time that *other* people can disappear. That people *they care about* can disappear.

That they might be the ones left behind with their grief and uncertainty and no idea where to start looking for the person they lost.

I find Roya's car and lean against the hood. Roya drives a mint-green Subaru that she named Nathan after the guy who owned it before it was impounded and sold at police auction. It's a good car for driving around in late at night with the windows down, listening to the wind and the crickets.

Last summer, right after she got the car, we all crammed our stuff in there and went on a camping trip a few hours away. I forgot my sleeping bag, so I slept in the backseat with the moonroof open. I woke up covered in dew, only to find Roya curled up in the passenger seat. She opened her eyes and looked right at me and smiled. When I asked what she was doing in the car, she said she hadn't wanted me to be alone all night. She reached out a finger and tapped my nose, and my entire body felt warm, and then the dew was gone and she winked at me and left to wake up everyone else. I sat there in the backseat feeling the afterglow of the warmth she gave me. I watched her cross the campground, banging a spoon against a pot, and I felt like no one in the entire world had ever felt as happy as I did right then.

It's a good car.

I nearly jump out of my skin when the car alarm starts going off. I leap away from the hood, looking around frantically as the horn honks an irregular STOP-THIEF rhythm. There's a beep, and the honking stops, and I turn to see Roya doubled over with laughter. She's got her hands braced on her thighs, and her hair falls in a thick black curtain around her face. When she throws her head back, the sun glints off her smile.

"That," she gasps, "was hilarious. You looked like you were gonna pass out."

"Yeah, it was great for everyone involved, asshole," I say, trying to look pissed but failing to hold back a smile. She slings an arm around my shoulder and gives me a squeeze, then folds herself into the car. She immediately rolls down the windows and cranks the air-conditioning, then gets back out of the car.

"It's like . . . a billion degrees in there," she says, slipping off her blouse and tugging at the tank top she's wearing underneath so it'll lie straight. Since the new dress code was instituted, this is standard procedure for most of us—the second we're beyond the reach of administration, we change into clothes that will keep us from dying of heat exhaustion.

I've already got my shirt and jacket stuffed into the top of my backpack.

I don't watch her tug at her tank top. Best friends don't stare at each other as they adjust their clothes. I wouldn't ever think to notice something like the way the scooped neck of her shirt moves across her skin as she pulls on the straps. I don't notice anything like that at all.

"Hey, let's get going. You're contributing to global warming," I say in that way that's half teasing, half previous-generations-have-left-us-a-planet-in-crisis. Roya shrugs, then reaches an arm into the car to see if it's livable in there yet. She climbs in a moment later, and I get into the passenger seat, and neither of us buckles our seat belts because the metal is still too hot to touch. The air-conditioning isn't cold yet—it's like standing in front of a giant's mouth and letting him breathe on you. We leave the windows down as she starts to drive. The wind whips Roya's hair back and lifts it into wild, twisting tentacles. She leans her head toward the window and lets the breeze hit her full in the face. She's glowing—not magic-glowing, just. Happy-glowing.

"What?" she says.

"What?"

"You're looking at me."

"Nah," I say, and she grins. I rest an arm on the window-sill and then snatch it back, rubbing the spot where the metal burned my skin. "So how did things go with your mom?"

"Eh, shitty," she says. "Could be worse. She's pissed about the party, but not as bad as I would have thought, to be honest."

"For real? I thought she'd freak out." Roya's mom is a decent-enough person, but she's high-strung and incredibly strict. She raised Roya to be fierce and independent, and I know she's really proud of how Roya turned out, but they go head-to-head a lot. Some nights the group text lights up with Roya's fury at her mom's rules; other nights she needs a place to stay so they can both cool off.

It's not that her mom is mean or abusive or anything like that. She's never raised a hand or even her voice to either of her kids. She tries her best not to bring her work home, but the way Roya explains it, her mom sees the worst of people. She wants to protect her family however she can.

But sometimes that protectiveness makes her hold on to Roya and her little brother with too tight a grip. Roya bucks against it, hard and often. Her brother usually just ducks his head and gets quiet, which makes Roya even angrier.

"Yeah, it's kind of weird," she says. "I thought she'd freak out too. I already knew that I was gonna tell her I was at the party," she adds, darting a glance at me out of the corner of her eye. "I mean . . . she was going to find out sooner or later. But I put it off until today because I figured, you know."

"You figured she'd be so pissed that you'd have to camp out at my house for the rest of the week?"

"Pretty much," she says. "But I told her why I lied about it, and I told her that I didn't regret anything, and she kind of cooled off right away."

"Wow." We turn off the main road and onto a two-lane,

oak-shaded stretch of asphalt that winds around the hill up to the reservoir. The leaves turn the bright summer heat into dappled shade. I reach forward and turn off the struggling air conditioner, and the car fills with the green-smell of the trees that line the road.

"Yeah," she says. "I think she understood. She wasn't happy, but . . . she seemed to get it."

We're quiet for the rest of the drive to the reservoir. Roya pushes her sunglasses up on top of her head. She accelerates into each curve, one hand gripping the shifting knob even though the car's an automatic. There's no one else on the road—we're alone out here, just us and the trees, and it's another one of those perfect moments. I try to hang on to it, try to tell myself I'll never forget *this*. I know that eventually it'll blend into whatever picture of summer-in-high-school I'll have when I'm old, but for now, it's high-res. Roya's hair tangling in the wind. The tree branches arching overhead. Her fingers drumming on the steering wheel. The birds that wait on the road until what feels like the last possible second before flying out of the way of the car. Her smile when she glances over and catches me staring.

It's a perfect moment, and it almost doesn't feel like I killed a boy, and I want to bottle it. But then we pull into the parking lot for the reservoir, and it's over, and the tide of guilt starts rising again. *My fault, my fault, my fault*.

The reservoir used to be a gravel quarry. It's weird to think of a whole quarry just for gravel. I kind of always figured gravel was just . . . *around*. But I guess it wasn't just *around* fifty years ago, so some company came and used dynamite to core the hillside like an apple. And then they let it fill up with water and told kids to swim in it. Instead of calling it what it is, which is a hole in the hill, we call it a reservoir. We call it that even though nobody is ever going to use the water in it for anything other than swimming and telling scary stories about bodies being dumped in there by the mafia.

Because the reservoir isn't really a reservoir, there's no infrastructure to it at all. There's no guardrails anywhere, no parking lot, no changing stalls. There are some trees that you can go into if you have to pee or dry off or make out with someone, and there are a few flattish outcroppings of rock that are good for sunbathing. Other than that, it's just the hole—deep and dark, without a shallow end to speak of. There's a long rope ladder that hangs down into the water, so you can climb out once the cold seeps into your bones. The water is always cold, and it's a relief from the heat, but it's unbearable after the first ten minutes or so. The rope gets replaced every year, and every year it's made of the same frayed, knotted plastic material. Everyone who grew up near the reservoir knows the awful feeling of it digging into their bare hands and feet as they shiver their way up to where their towels wait in the sun.

The flat rocks are crowded with towels. Every so often, someone gets up from their towel to jump in the water. A long trail of wet footprints leads from the top of the ladder to the broad, blinding patch of sun. Roya and I slip our shoes off and walk past the patchwork of beach towels. We settle in a splotch of shade at the edge of the outcropping, dangling our feet in the air over the water and watching people jump. A scrawny kid stands at the edge looking down. His friends are yelling from the water. He's got his arms wrapped around his ribs, and he keeps walking up to the edge and then flinching away.

Roya cups her hands around her mouth. "You gotta run at it!" she shouts. The kid looks over at her—he can't be older than thirteen. "Close your eyes and run!" Roya says, then waves her hands at him, egging him on. His eyes flick down to her legs, dangling over the edge of the rock. She's wearing shorts, and the dusky brown of her skin glows against the dark rock. "Do it!" Roya shouts, and a few people lift their heads from their towels to stare.

The kid nods, jogs backward, and screws up his face. Then he runs, his arms pumping, and like a cartoon character, he runs straight off the edge of the rock. He seems to hover in the air for a second, and then he's yelling, and then there's a splash and all his friends cheer. Roya cheers too, clapping her hands and peering down into the water below us.

"Way to go, kiddo!" she cries, and she's grinning at him, and the poor kid is looking up at her like she hung the moon.

"You know he's in love with you now, right?" I say, and she laughs one of her big laughs, the kind that makes other people smile even though they didn't hear what was funny in the first place. Below us, the kid is getting splashed by his friends.

"He won't be scared to jump next time, though," Roya says,

kicking her feet. "That's the key to doing stuff you're scared of. You gotta run at it."

I glance over at her, and she's staring down into the water with a little secret smile on her lips. Her hair hangs down over her shoulder in a waterfall of tousled waves. I lean back onto my elbows and close my eyes, listening to the splashing and yelling that echoes up from the water. I can't pick out any individual voices—they all blend together in a wash of summer-noise. I swing my legs through the air and wonder if, a hundred years from now, some other girl will be swinging her legs in this same spot, feeling all the same things that I'm feeling. I think probably not, but maybe something close. Maybe she'll feel everything I do, minus the murder-anxiety.

"Hey." Roya's voice is about an inch from my ear, and I jump, and she lets out another big laugh. "You startle so easy, Alexis. If I was meaner, I'd think it was funny." Her hair is brushing my shoulder and her face is right next to mine, so close that almost all I can see is her eyes, but then I look down and I realize that I was wrong because I can see her mouth, too. She boops my nose with hers and then leans back onto her elbows, mirroring my pose. "I'm gonna miss this," she says.

"Hnngmh?" I'm going for nonchalant-interrogative, but it comes out slightly strangled, because of the way her hair slid over my shoulder.

"Hanging out like this," she says. "In the fall. It'll be hard, being apart from everyone."

"We'll still hang out, though, right?" I say. Do I sound clingy? I hope I don't sound clingy. I hope I don't sound desperately afraid that she and Maryam will abandon me the moment we all set foot on campus at State. "I mean, like . . . at school and stuff?" I add in a pathetic attempt to remain nonchalant.

"Of course we will, dummy," she says, shoving my arm with one hand. "Like all the time, are you kidding? Me and you and Maryam are gonna be all sewn together into one giant three-headed sweater. You two aren't allowed to stray more than a hundred feet from me at any given moment."

"Okay, okay, I get it—"

"It's just that I'll miss *this*," she says. She gestures at the reservoir. "I mean . . . I want to leave and everything. I want to get out of here and never look back and all that. But . . . I don't know." She runs a hand through her tangled hair, pausing to tug thoughtfully at the end of one twisted-up tendril. "I've never lived anywhere else, you know?"

"Yeah," I say. And I do know. I've been talking all year about how I can't wait to leave. About how great it'll be to go somewhere *else*, where everyone in town hasn't known me since I was knee-high to a tree frog. And I mean it. I really do. But I also can't help but feel a little spark of fear, like . . . what if I leave, and it turns out that this town is the best place there is? What if I go out there and I'm too small for the rest of the world? What if I can never come back, and everything out there is too much, and there's no place for me after all?

"I'll miss it too," I add, because that's the only way I know how to say it.

"But at least we'll be together," Roya says, and she bumps her shoulder against mine. "Me and you and Maryam."

"Yeah, us and Maryam," I say, because I don't want to say *yeah, but me and you*.

"Anyway," she says, and she gets up and brushes her hands on her shorts. Then she unbuttons them.

"What are you—" I start, but then I realize that she's wearing a swimsuit under her shorts. "Were you wearing that all day?"

"No, weirdo," she says, sliding the shorts down her legs and stepping out of them, one foot at a time. One of her feet lands right next to my hand, and almost against my will, my fingers rise to wrap around the gentle curve of her ankle. She leans down and rests a hand on my shoulder for balance as she picks up her shorts. "I put it on after school. It's why I took forever getting out to the parking lot." She pulls her shirt off over her head, exposing a long stretch of heavily muscled abdomen. Her lats are swollen—her coach has been drilling her on her hundred-meter fly. I'm almost grateful for the reprieve when she throws the shirt at my head. "Hang on to that for me," she says, and by the time I get her shirt off my face, she's started walking away.

I look around just in time to see her slinging an old backpack over her shoulders. It's one I haven't seen in years—a tiny old string backpack covered in flowers. She used it all through middle school, until one day Kevin Ng spilled

Dr Pepper all over it. It's still stained brown in a lot of places. I don't know how I missed her bringing it with us.

"I didn't know you still had that," I say, and she looks over her shoulder with a shrug.

"My mom found it in the garage the other day," she says. It hangs oddly, and I realize what must be inside it a moment before she turns and walks back toward me. She crouches in front of me.

"I'm gonna put it in the reservoir," she murmurs.

"But—"

"It'll sink," she adds. "I put a cinderblock inside. By the time the fabric rots away, the arm will have rotted too."

I look around, but no one is close enough to hear us. "Is the leg in there too?"

"Nah," she says, "it wouldn't fit. Besides, Marcelina said something about doing the pieces separately and I think she's right."

"She told me that too," I whisper, nodding. "I get it. But what about—people will notice you dropping a bag into the water, won't they?"

She gives me a smile and a wink. "I'm not gonna drop it in," she says. "I'm gonna leave it in."

And then she stands up and runs off the edge of the rock. I hear her high whoop, followed by a huge splash. I peer over the edge of the rock, into the water. When Roya surfaces, her hair is draped over her face.

"You look like a sea monster!" I yell down to her, and she

parts the hair over her mouth so I can see her beaming.

"Jump in!" she yells back.

I shake my head even though I know she won't see me. I could yell down a million excuses—I'm not wearing a suit, I have to watch our stuff, the water is cold, I don't have a towel. But none of them would matter. Roya would yell at me to jump in, and I would listen, and our stuff would get stolen and I'd catch a cold and I wouldn't regret a second of it.

Instead, I watch her. She swims over to the kid who she told to jump in, and she gives him a high five. I look around at everyone else in the water, watching for anyone who might have seen the backpack, anyone who might have noticed her dropping it. There are a lot of eyes on Roya—but not a soul is looking for the backpack she ditched. They're watching her, watching the way she cuts through the water like a shark, watching the way her hair fans out behind her. Watching her legs, her arms, her back, her smile.

I look down at my own legs and frown. They're fine, as far as legs go. I'm not insecure about them or anything. But every now and then I wonder if I'm supposed to be insecure about them. My thighs spread out when I sit down, and I don't really know if that's normal or not. There are some girls at my school who brag about the gaps between their thighs. I don't have a gap, but then, I don't really want one either. A long stripe of dark hair runs up the side of one of my calves, where I missed a whole section of my leg when I was shaving. I don't have the huge defined quads that Roya and Iris do. Just like in everything else, I'm ordinary. Just plain old Alexis. Nothing to see here.

As I inspect myself, I notice a dark spot on my knee. At first, I think it's a shadow, but I look up and there's nothing between me and the sun. When I look back down, my breath catches because it's spreading. It's *deepening*. It goes from brownish to blue-black, with a green corona around the outside of it. I watch the bruise grow with increasing horror—and then I realize that my hands are tingling.

"Gah!" I clench my fists and try to *stop*, even though I don't know what it is that I'm *doing*. It works, although I'm not sure if it's my startled reaction or my attempt at control that does the trick. What the hell just happened?

What did I just *do?*

I peer over the edge of the reservoir and spot Roya. She lifts a hand to me, then heads toward the ladder from there and starts climbing. I can't see her goose bumps from where I am, but her shoulders are hunched and she's shivering a little. I aim a small thread of magic at her. It's tiny enough that anyone looking could mistake it for a sunbeam, or a butterfly maybe, or a leaf on the wind. It reaches her and she looks up at me. She's only halfway up the ladder, but because of my magic, she's warm and dry. I give her a thumbs-up.

"Thanks for that," she says when she's up the ladder and back to me.

"Least I can do," I answer, and she shrugs. "Hey, can you look at something for me?"

She lifts an eyebrow. "What's up?" I point at my knee,

which is mottled with purple and green bruising that wraps almost all the way around my leg. “Oh shit,” Roya breathes. She crouches to look closer. “What did you do?”

“I’m, uh. I’m not sure,” I say. It’s hard to come up with words when I can feel her breath on the soft skin at the inside of my leg. “It kind of just happened?”

She lets out a low whistle, then rubs her hands together fast to heat them. “This thing’s so ugly it’s almost pretty,” she says. She presses her palms to my leg, and immediately, a deep, bright heat spreads through the joint. My breath catches in my throat as her fingertips graze the hem of my shorts.

“Does it hurt?” she asks.

“Not too much.”

“Are you sure?”

“Yes.” I swallow hard.

“How’s that?”

When she lifts her hands away, the bruise is gone.

“Thank you. You’re amazing,” I say, grinning up at her.

“Aw, shucks,” she says in a goofy voice, bracing her hands on her thighs to push herself upright.

“No, seriously. Thank you. For everything.” I say. “It’s . . . it means a lot to me that you’re helping with this.” I gesture at the water so she knows that I don’t just mean her help with my crazy, sudden bruise.

“That’s what friends do for each other,” she says. Something inside my stomach drops. Right. Friends.

“You’re a good friend,” I say, looking out over the water.

Roya doesn't answer. We're quiet for a while, and then, without either of us having to say we're ready to go, we grab our stuff. Roya slides her shorts back on, jams her shirt into her bag. She eases into the driver's seat, and it's cooled down enough outside that she doesn't turn the air-conditioning on. She doesn't even start the car right away. She twists in her seat to look at me.

"You okay?" she asks.

I don't answer immediately. I don't want to lie to her. "I don't know," I finally say. She grabs my hand and gives it a squeeze.

"I don't just mean since prom. I mean . . . are you okay?"

"I don't know what you mean," I say, even though I do.

"It's just not like you," she says. "To go with somebody to their room at a party. You've never done that before, not even people you were in relationships with. You don't have to tell me about it, but . . ."

I can't look at her. I can't. "I'm okay," I say, and I squeeze her hand back so she knows I'm sorry for lying.

"Okay," she says. "If you want to talk about it—"

"I'm okay," I repeat, a little harder this time. A little louder.

". . . Okay. Sure." Roya turns the car on, and when I look up at her, her face is closed off. A muscle in her jaw is clenching and unclenching, a sure sign that she's hurt and angry. Her eyes are shining, so I know she's furious. Roya pretty much only cries when she's mad.

She's right to be mad at me. I'm mad at me too, and I don't

have nearly as much right to be mad as she does. Even if she doesn't know why.

We're both quiet on the drive to my house. When she drops me off, she gives me a big, tight hug. It's the kind of hug that means she'll forgive me once she's done being mad. I inhale the mint-and-reservoir-water smell of her and hold my breath until she's gone. Then I exhale. I breathe a little cloud of Roya out into my front yard. It's not the same as having the real thing here, but it'll have to do until tomorrow. When I get to see her again. I breathe in and try to taste the hint of mint left on the air. Until tomorrow.

I go inside to check on the heart. It's no warmer than it was when I left for school—it's no softer, no closer to normal. But it's still a little bit warm, and it throbs in my hands once every few seconds, a slow spasm that ripples irrepressibly across the glassy surface.

The idea that's been slowly taking shape inside my head solidifies. Roya just got rid of a piece of Josh's body, but the heart isn't any different. Something was different this time.

Something didn't work.

9.

ON TUESDAY MORNING, DAD INSISTS ON DROPPING Nico and me off at school.

"But it's so *early*," Nico whines. He's not wrong—it's way too early, and I'm exhausted anyway. Which is weird, because every night, I've been sleeping deeply—but it feels like I've barely rested at all. It's not bad dreams, either. I've been scared of nightmares since Josh died, but I haven't had any.

In fact, I realize, I haven't had any dreams at all.

That can't be right, I think—but I can't remember the last time I dreamed, not since prom, and something behind my navel twists with dread. *That can't be right,* I think again.

"Yeah, well, that's too bad," Dad says to Nico, checking the expiration date on a yogurt he dug out of the back of the fridge. He scratches the long stubble on his face, which is apparently the beginning of an attempt at a beard. None of us have acknowledged it yet. "I gotta drop you guys off in time for my eight-o'clock conference call."

"Why can't we just walk, though?" Nico asks. He and Dad

are staring at each other with identical stubborn expressions, and they look uncannily alike. "I'm gonna get to school like an hour before class starts—"

"And I'm gonna get to school fifteen minutes before that," I say, nudging him. "We can deal for one day, Nic." He looks at me. I shake off my worry about the dreams and try to make my face significant.

Dad's acting like he's dropping us off for no reason, but I saw him and Pop talking this morning before Pop headed out to a client meeting. Pop's eyebrows were a low furrow across the bridge of his nose. They were looking at each other the same way that they looked at each other last night, when Josh's face was on the news. "Just go with it," I mutter to Nico.

He scowls at me, but there's a question in his eyes. I glance over at Dad and back, giving a quick shake of my head. Nico sighs elaborately and slouches off to his bedroom to put too much gel in his already-sticking-up hair.

"I know it's not convenient," Dad says behind me. I turn around to see him putting mayonnaise on a slice of wheat bread. "But I just . . . would rather drive you kids today."

"That's fine," I say. "It'll be nice to have some time with everyone before class starts."

"Yeah?" Dad slices thick chunks of leftover ham and layers them on the bread. His voice is way too casual. "Who are you going to be seeing?"

"Uh, probably . . . the whole gang?" I venture. "Although

Maryam probably won't show up until a few minutes before the bell—why?"

"No reason. Just want to know what's going on in your life."

There's not a chance I'm going to tell him that. "You're being weird," I say, but I lean across the kitchen counter to kiss his stubbly cheek. "You're a weirdo."

"Yeah, well. That's what dads are for," he says. "Go get your backpack. We're leaving in five."

I go to grab my backpack from my room. My phone buzzes in my pocket—I have about thirty new notifications, all messages. Iris is stressing about something, as usual. I skim the group chat for context, but it doesn't really make sense. Marcelina is talking about how she can't forget something, but I can't tell what she's referring to. I figure I'll ask her at school, or else someone else will understand what she means and I'll ask them.

I pause before I walk out of my bedroom. I briefly consider grabbing the other backpack—the one that's under the farthest corner of my bed—but I don't know how I'd explain two backpacks to Dad. *When the time is right*, I tell myself. I don't stick around long enough to let myself wonder when that might be.

When I get back to the kitchen, there are two brown bags sitting on the counter. One of them says "Nico!" in blue Sharpie; the other one has "Alexis!" scrawled across it.

"What's this?" I call out, even though it's totally obvious

what "this" is. At the same time, Nico barrels out of his bedroom, headphones draped around his neck, backpack swinging from one shoulder.

"What's what?" he asks, and then he stops short next to me.

I sniff the air. "Why do you smell like Pop?"

He flushes. "Meredith didn't like the way my cologne smelled, so I'm trying his. Are those . . . lunches?"

I peer into the bag with my name on it. There's a ham sandwich, a banana, and a granola bar. Nico shows me his—he has the dubious yogurt instead of the granola bar.

"Why is Dad packing us lunches? He's never packed us lunches before."

"Just take it," I whisper. "You'll hurt his feelings if you don't."

Nico shoves the bag into his backpack. He looks indignant. "I know," he mutters. "I'm not a total idiot."

"Hey," I start to say—but he's already gone, walking out to the garage to wait for Dad in the car. I sigh and drop my own bag lunch into my backpack. I catch Dad doing his tie in the hall mirror. I give him a hug, a long one.

"What's this for?" he asks.

"Just . . . thanks for the lunch," I say. He rests his scratchy chin on top of my head and gives me an extra squeeze, and I know that my life is better than I'll ever deserve. Because of my friends. Because of my brother. Because of my dads.

I wish there was some way for me to be good enough for them.

* * *

When I get to school, almost no one is there. I walk to my locker to drop off my sad bag lunch, and I don't see a single person on my way. The school feels so liminal when it's empty—there are scuff marks on the linoleum but no sneakers leaving new ones. Rows of empty desks in every dark classroom I pass. Half the lights in the halls are still turned off. There's gum *everywhere*. I get distracted by how haunted and strange the school is, and I almost walk right by the flowers without noticing them.

The senior lockers are all in the same hallway, so it stands to reason that Josh's locker would be near mine. I've probably passed him standing by his locker a dozen times without noticing him. I've probably bumped into him on his way to class.

It shouldn't surprise me, is what I'm saying.

And yet it does. The third locker from the end of the hallway. It must be his, because it's been turned into a kind of altar. Someone put his yearbook photo on it. Drugstore carnations are heaped against the base of the locker, and notes stick out through the ventilation slits in the door. Someone duct-taped a teddy bear to the metal. I stare at it. It's a little white bear, and it's holding a heart. The duct tape covers its arms, so it's hard to tell if the heart says anything on it. "Happy Valentine's Day," probably. I wonder, briefly, what the bear is supposed to be for. Is it supposed to be a gift to comfort Josh when he comes back from whatever ordeal has made him disappear? Is it an offering, a hope that he'll be able to get back whatever childhood is taken from him while he's gone?

If Josh came back and saw that white bear, what would he do with it? What use would a traumatized eighteen-year-old have for that little plush toy?

I stroke the bear's paw with my fingers, vividly remembering how Roya's skin felt when I did the same thing just yesterday. Remembering her fingers brushing that sudden bruise away from my leg.

I wish I could have had a dream about that. I didn't realize how much I missed dreaming about Roya, until I stopped.

"You must really miss him."

I snatch my hand back as though the bear has burned me. "What?"

When I turn around, Gina Tarlucci is standing behind me with her arms folded over her camera. I almost never see her when we're not in class or at the soccer field making awkward small talk. She's wearing a pink-and-gray floral dress that makes her look like something out of a 1950s movie about surfers. She looks down at me with sad, sympathetic eyes. "I just meant, this is probably really hard for you." She gestures at the locker. "You guys were a thing, right?"

My reaction is immediate and visceral. "What? No. No, we—*no*, we were *not* a thing. I barely even knew him." I wince. "Know him. I don't even *know* him."

Gina's eyebrows shoot up. She plants a hand on one ample hip and purses her lips. "Um, okay, well, that's interesting."

My phone is buzzing in my pocket again, but I ignore it. I don't like the way she says "interesting."

"I don't think there's anything interesting about it," I snap. "It's just the truth. Ask anybody."

"So, I guess what I saw at prom was just some friendly making-out between strangers?" she hisses. I glance up and down the hallway—thank goodness, we're alone. When I look back at her, I can tell that checking to see if anyone could hear her was the wrong move. A triumphant smile is spreading across her face. She starts fidgeting with her shiny brown braid. I fight the sudden impulse to give it a sharp yank and run away as fast as my legs can take me. "What, was it supposed to be a secret?"

"I don't know what you're talking about. You must have mixed me up with someone else," I say, gritting my teeth.

"Um, no. You two almost sat on me," she says. "I'm still finding glitter from your dress on all my stuff. Trust me, I know who I saw." She looks at his locker, and her brows draw together. "Why don't you want people to know that you were a couple? I won't tell anyone, but . . . I mean, it's weird. Everyone would probably want to support you."

Two freshmen walk through the hall. Gina and I stand silently, trying not to look like we're waiting for the freshmen to be gone before we finish talking. My mind is racing. *Gina saw*. A knot of terror forms in my gut.

I think back to prom night. Josh and I made out in the kitchen for all of five minutes before I whispered in his ear, asking him where his bedroom was. I'd thought we were alone. I'd been irritated about it. People at parties were supposed to linger in the kitchen—they were *supposed* to see us, talk about the fact that we were climbing all over each other. The gossip was supposed to get back to Roya. But there hadn't been anyone else in the kitchen to see his tongue in my mouth. I remember being annoyed, but also not wanting to make out with him for longer than was strictly necessary, so I just figured I'd get it over with.

But Gina must have been there after all. I try to remember, but . . . I can't. I remember Josh, and his hands moving from my waist to my butt, and the too-soft, too-wet way he kissed me. Tongue-first. I remember my heart pounding. I remember opening my eyes and trying to see past his nose, trying to see the rest of the room, trying to see if anyone else was there. I remember the way he nodded when I asked if we could go upstairs—two short, sharp twitches of his head, and then he was grabbing my hand and leading me out of the kitchen.

But I don't remember seeing Gina at all.

Shit.

"Look, we weren't a . . . a *couple*," I say in a low voice once the freshmen are gone. "It just kind of happened. It's not a thing. I don't want people to know because . . ." I hesitate—then inspiration strikes. "Because I don't want to take the attention away from people looking for him." It comes out in a rush.

Gina frowns at me. "Well . . . I mean. I guess that makes

sense," she says slowly. "But you should at least tell the police that you saw him that night, right?"

"Oh yeah, totally," I lie. "I talked to them already."

"I mean, maybe what you did to him has something to do with why he disappeared," she says casually. She shifts her weight from one leg to the other. Her head tilts to one side. "Don't you think?" I walk to my locker without saying anything, trying to buy time. Gina follows me. "What was it?" she asks softly. "A love potion?"

I pull my locker door open too hard, and the bang of the metal echoes through the hallway. "What are you talking about, Gina?" I snap.

"Well, if you guys didn't know each other at all, I'm assuming you did some . . . you know." She wiggles her fingers at me. I stare into my locker, not seeing the contents. I've temporarily forgotten what lockers are for, what books are for, where I am. Behind me, a few people are filtering into the hallway.

"You're assuming I did some *what*?" I whisper.

"Some magic," Gina whispers back. I look at her, and she's smiling at me. It's a little smile, a secret smile, like we're sharing something. Like we're friends. She's too close. I can smell her lip gloss.

"Some magic," I repeat slowly.

"You know. Like, how you and your friends do things."

I come to my senses. It's like someone's thrown a bucket of cold water over my head. I laugh, a loud, bright, hard laugh that makes Gina flinch. "Wow," I say, shoving things from my backpack into my locker at random. "You're hilarious, Gina. I mean . . . I didn't take you for the dark humor type, but honestly, that's just way too funny."

She's looking at me very strangely. "I don't get you," she says. "You know I'm not joking. You can tell me."

I shake my head at her and close my locker. "Seriously, you're a riot," I say, grinning at her with all my teeth. I start walking toward the cafeteria. If I'm lucky, Marcelina will be in there and we can split a bagel and I can forget about this whole conversation.

Gina grabs my arm. "Stop!" She's too loud in the corridor, and the couple of other students who are crossing through the hall turn to look. She smiles at them awkwardly. I shake her hand off me. "Just stop," she says again. "I know about— Alexis, where are you going? Come on—"

She's trailing after me, but I can't stop walking. A kind of numbness is taking over my arms and legs. Everything looks gray. The edges of my vision are vibrating. *Gina knows?*

She can't know about the magic, too. She shouldn't know about Josh and me making out, but she *really, really* can't know about the magic. We've been careful. We all have.

Haven't we?

With a sick feeling, I realize that we haven't. We used to be so cautious. We all know that we're different, that we have something people want. We've never needed to swear each other to secrecy because it's obvious to us what the consequences could be if the world found out about our powers. We've seen enough movies and read enough novels to understand what happens to magic girls. But lately, we've gotten . . . comfortable. I think of Maryam doing my nails in class. I think of myself at the reservoir, drying Roya off with a thread of power. I think of all the little things—the ways we've fixed each other's hair and mended each other's damaged clothes, the ways we've grown so comfortable with each other that it's second nature to expend a little magic helping each other out. I realize that anyone who was watching us closely would know right away what we are.

And apparently, Gina's been watching.

"Look, I don't know why you're so freaked out about this," she says. "I just want to talk to you about it. Unless you and your witch-friends did something *wrong*—"

I stumble. It's a little thing—my feet betraying me, tripping over nothing at all. The sole of my sneaker makes a loud squeak against the linoleum. I turn to see Gina holding a hand out, as if she's going to catch me. A small trickle of red oozes out from one of her tear ducts. My fingertips are burning.

Behind her, Iris stands frozen in the hall, watching us. She's holding her How Does Magic Work journal in one hand and a highlighter in the other. She's backlit by one of the fluorescents that's actually turned on, and her hair forms a halo of orange curls around her face.

"Oh my god," Gina breathes. "Wait . . . did you do something to him? You and your . . . your friends? Did you do something?"

"Of course not," I reply sharply. I don't know what the right reaction is. How would an innocent person answer this question? My phone is still going off, and I make a mental note to put my text notifications on silent. "I don't know what your problem is, but this is honestly the most ridiculous conversation I've ever had." Over Gina's shoulder, Iris stares at me with wide eyes. "I don't even know you, but you, what? You think you're Veronica Fucking Mars? You think you know all these big secrets about me?" I take a step toward Gina, and she steps backward. "This is seriously the most we've ever talked, and you're accusing me of—" The word "murder" sticks in my throat. I shake my head instead. "I don't know what your deal is, Gina, but this conversation is *over*."

Gina brushes her fingers against her face as if there's a bug on her cheek, then does a double-take, noticing the redness on her fingers. She touches her cheek again. The tiny smear of redness there spreads into a garish stripe. She's not bleeding any more than that, but it's enough to put panic in her eyes. "I don't think so," she whispers. Her voice is shaking, and I can't tell yet if she's mad or scared. "I don't think it's over until we've talked to the police."

"What are you going to tell them?" I ask. "That I'm Harry Potter? That I cast some kind of *magic spell* on Josh?" I wiggle my fingers at Gina the way she wiggled hers at me. She flinches away from me, but then she squares her shoulders and looks at me with a grim frown.

"No," she says. "I'm going to tell them that you were the

last person who saw him on prom night. I'm going to tell them that I think they need to talk to you and your friends about whatever it is you're hiding."

My entire body flushes hot, then cold, then hot again. I think I whisper "no," but I'm not sure, because at that moment, Iris drops her notebook.

Gina whirls around with a little yell. Iris has both her hands raised high in the air. She says "Alexis, help," and without thinking, I throw my magic at her.

I can't see the dark-bright light of my own magic, but Gina gasps. She's looking around with white-rimmed eyes, her braid flailing back and forth. She throws her arms over her head and half ducks like the ceiling is going to collapse on her.

Iris sweeps her hand through the air in front of her face, adding her own white light to the spell she's crafting. It circles Gina like a lasso. Then it tightens around her mouth.

All of us are perfectly still for a moment. Me, with my arms half-raised toward Gina, my mouth open as if there's anything I could say. Iris, her arms over her head, her hair frizzed out in a wild corona, her eyes still glowing like starfire. Gina, cowering, her mouth bound by light and power.

Then Iris drops both of her arms, and the spell vanishes.

Gina lets out a tiny squeak of a scream. In my pocket, my phone buzzes again. Iris stumbles into the wall.

I run to her. "Iris, are you—?" She waves me off with a weak smile, shaking her head, but I still press a hand to her cheek and search her eyes. No burst blood vessels in them, not this time. After what happened when she cast the spell in Josh's bedroom, I was so scared that something in her had broken. That she wouldn't be able to do magic anymore at all. But she just looks a little tired, a little extra pale under all those freckles. She's okay.

I turn to Gina, who's staring at her own hands in horror.

"What—what did you, how? No," Gina stammers. "No, no, no—you—"

"Shut up, Gina," I snarl, and her mouth closes fast. Her eyes are so wide, and she's breathing hard through her nose. A tear slips down her cheek, cutting a clear path through the drying blood that's smeared there.

"Am I going to die?" she whispers.

"No," Iris says. Am I imagining it, or is her voice a little shaky? I take her hand and give it a squeeze. "Or . . . well, I mean, someday, probably. But I didn't hurt you or anything."

"What did you do to me?" Gina asks. She's standing very, very still. Like she's afraid that she'll disintegrate if she moves too fast.

Iris looks askance at me. "I, um. Well. I made it so you can't say what you were threatening to say. About us."

"What do you mean?" Gina asks, her voice slowly regaining volume. "You mean I can't tell the police that you're all w—"

"No!" Iris shouts. Gina claps both hands over her mouth. "No, don't say it," Iris says desperately. "Look, I . . ." She looks around the still-abandoned hallway. "I made it so that if you tell anyone what you *think* you saw—which you *didn't*, by the way—if you tell anyone, something will happen to you. Something bad."

Gina's eyes are brimming with tears. She looks between Iris and me, still covering her mouth.

"What'll happen to her?" I mutter, and Iris grimaces.

"Her, uh, mouth will seal over," she says. "Temporarily, though. I think."

Behind her hands, Gina screams. I shake my head, trying to figure out how to make this right, but before I can say anything, she turns on her heel and runs. I hear the door to the girls' restroom slam open and then shut. She's probably hyperventilating. Or maybe the thought of what we are has made her sick.

It's making me a little sick.

"Jesus, Iris," I say. "That's . . . that's a lot." Iris shrugs, looking uncomfortable.

"It'll only happen if she commits to snitching. You gave me the idea," she says as she stoops to pick up her journal. "When you asked if she was going to tell the cops that you're Harry Potter, I thought of setting her up with a consequence. Hermione did the same thing to the girl who snitched about Dumbledore's Army, remember?"

I think back to the books. "I thought she gave that girl word-acne?"

"Whatever," Iris says, running her hands over her curls. "Close enough."

Jesus. Iris is always intense, but this is next-level even for her. "Iris. This is really messed up. I mean—"

"I just saved your ass, Alexis. Besides, I don't think you're in any position to tell me what's fucked up," she growls. I stop short and she walks a few steps ahead of me before stopping. Her shoulders rise and fall in an intense sigh. She lifts her hands to her face and scrubs the heels of her hands across her eyes before turning back to me.

She looks so tired.

"Are you okay?" I whisper. "You're . . . not really acting like yourself right now."

"I'm just trying to fix it all," she says. She sounds hollow.

I shake my head at her. "You don't have to fix it all by yourself. We're all together in this, you know?"

She gives me a grim smile. "I know. But I'm supposed to be the one with the big ideas, right?" Before I can say anything, she steps forward and pulls me into a stiff hug. "I'll fix it. I mean, I'll find a way to undo the thing with Gina. Don't worry."

I want to trust her. I do. But Iris doesn't really hug people, and something feels wrong. I ask the only question I can. "Do you promise?"

She steps back from me and holds out her pinky finger. "Promise."

I wrap my pinky finger around hers and we shake on it. The promise is sealed more tightly now than any spell could bind us—the pinky-swear is unshakable. And Iris might be turning into someone whose power I don't understand, but she's still my friend. I have to trust her.

I have to.

We head to the cafeteria together, weaving our way through the people who are slowly filling the halls. My phone goes off again, and I hear Iris's phone going off at the same time. "Do you know what's going on with Marcelina?" I ask. "She's been acting kind of off, and then those texts this morning—"

"Yeah," Iris interrupts. "I wanted to ask you about that. Have you noticed anything weird these last few days?" I don't say anything, letting the absurdity of the question hang between us. "Right," she says, "okay, that's fair. But like, have you noticed anything missing?"

"I don't know," I answer honestly. "I haven't really been looking, though. I've kind of been thinking about . . ." *Roya, Josh, body parts, the monster I might secretly be*.

"Well. Start paying attention," she says. She shakes her head at me. "I'm not just being mysterious and annoying," she says. I'd think she was reading my mind, but irritation is probably written all over my face. "I just . . . I'm not totally sure what it is, but I think I have an idea."

"What is it?" I say, and I can hear how brusque I sound, but I can't be bothered to apologize. It's been a long morning.

"There's a pull on the spell I cast on prom night," she says softly, pushing open the cafeteria door. "I don't know how to explain it. It's just like . . . a little tug on the threads of the magic."

My annoyance at her information-hoarding evaporates. "You can feel the spells you cast?" I ask, incredulous. She's cast so many over the years, while we were all experimenting with our magic and learning what we can do. I can't imagine having to be aware of all those spells, all the time.

"Not forever," she says. "And not all of them. But this one was really big, and I'm kind of . . . aware of it." She shrugs and pulls out a chair at one of the little round cafeteria tables. I sit across from her and rest my head on my arms. I'm so tired already. "My connection to the spell is going away, but it's not fading evenly like it usually does," she continues. "It's like it's getting split off, one chunk at a time. And I think something weird is happening when you guys do whatever you do to make that split happen." I stare at her, my chin digging into my arms, and try to do a mental inventory to see if I've felt anything "weird." I can't figure out what's weird enough to stand out and what's insignificant. "Try not to worry about it," she says, all business. "Stay focused on . . . on trying to bring Josh back."

A flash of irritation—does she think I'm not focused enough on bringing Josh back? Does she think that's the problem, my *focus*? I clench a fist and then immediately force myself to relax, because I'm afraid to get angry. Because I don't know what I'm capable of anymore. I can't let myself hurt anyone else.

I'm enough of a problem already.

She doesn't notice my anger or my fear, or any of it. She's in her own world, trying to fit all of our problems into boxes. "Just let me know if you notice anything, okay?"

"Sure," I say. "If I notice anything abnormal about any part of my life, I'll definitely tell you. There is one thing, though, and I don't know if they go together or—"

"What?" She's staring at me with intense focus, and the part of me that's worried about her strobes again. I ignore it.

"The heart," I mutter. "You know how it's wrong?"

"Yeah, and then that thing where it—" She flexes her fingers in a pulsing cardiac rhythm.

"Right." I nod. "It's beating. Just a little bit right now, but it happens more every time someone . . . splits off a chunk."

She grimaces. "Yeah, we should find a better way to phrase that. So, you think the heart is, what? Coming back to life?"

"I don't know," I answer. "We should talk to everyone about it, right?" The truth is, that's exactly what I think. I think that the heart is coming a little bit back to life every time we get rid of a piece of Josh.

Which would mean . . . what? Roya was panicking about it when we tried to bring Josh back to life, when all those hawks fell to the ground around us. She was afraid that we would be able to bring him back to life bit by bit, but that we wouldn't be able to put him back together, and that we would make everything worse with whatever we tried.

I don't know if his heart beating is making things better or worse. I don't know if we're solving the problem or if we're just hurting ourselves in order to put unearned life into a dead organ.

I don't want to be the one to say that Josh's heart is coming back. I want to throw it out there as an idea and let someone else pin it down, lay claim to it as a fact.

"Sure. We can all talk it over." Iris nudges my foot with hers. "Hey, do you want a bagel? I'm going to go grab one. I'll see if I can eat half of it before Roya gets to school."

My stomach growls. I unzip my backpack to grab my wallet. "Yeah," I say, digging through the things that didn't get blindly shoved into my locker, "let me give you some cash—" I freeze as my hand comes into contact with something that isn't a book, a binder, or a thousand loose pens. It crinkles under my fingers. "Actually, I'm good," I say. Iris nods and walks over to the tiny window in the side of the cafeteria kitchen where you can buy chips and bagels and uncooked instant noodles. As she walks away, I pull the brown paper bag out of my backpack. I'd meant to stow it in my locker, but between Gina's detective work and Iris turning into some kind of magic supervillain, I guess I got distracted.

I run my thumb across Dad's blue handwriting. *Alexis!* it says, exclamation point and all. I remember hugging him in the hall. Warmth fills my chest, and I eat a ham sandwich for breakfast as the rest of the girls arrive at school. For all that I didn't want it in the first place, it's actually a pretty good sandwich.

Guilt gnaws at me, because in spite of how I know I should feel, I'm actually . . . happy. I should feel like everything is falling apart, and I should be terrified for Gina, and a little scared of Iris, and worried about everyone else. But as I eat that sandwich with my sleepy-eyed friends, as we all talk about whether or not our magic is bringing a dead boy's heart back to life, I can't help feeling overwhelmed by how lucky I am.

I love my friends, and I love my life, and even though I know how easy it would be for all of it to go away—for my life to end for no reason at all, other than a little slip of someone's magical fingers—in that moment, I feel unbreakable.

10.

I AVOID GINA FOR THE REST OF THE DAY ON Tuesday, or maybe she avoids me. I skip study hall so I won't have to see her. I stop thinking about how she looked in the half-dark hallway right after Iris finished casting that spell on her, though. Hunched, and weak, and afraid. So afraid.

Afraid of *me*.

There's a little part of me that wants to feel powerful because of that fear. It's a part I don't like, a part I don't trust. A part I can't listen to. But it's there, saying, *So what if she's afraid? If she's afraid of you, she can't hurt you. If you can make people afraid of you, then maybe you don't* have *to be special. You wouldn't have to earn their love if you had their fear.*

I can't listen to that part, though. That's not the person I am. What happened to Josh was an accident. The little ways that people around me seem to keep getting hurt—those aren't about me. They aren't my *fault*. I don't want those things to happen.

I'm not the kind of person who wants people to be scared of her.

That's a fact that's driven home when I get to school on Wednesday morning. Gina is standing by my locker. She's wearing jeans and a worn T-shirt, and she looks like she didn't sleep last night. She's staring at the ground with her brow all scrunched up, like she's trying to decide something hard. I hesitate, because I don't know what the right thing to do is. I know I have to talk to her. I have to apologize, to tell her that we're going to find a way to fix it. I move toward her—but when she sees me, she spooks like a cat and walks away fast.

That's when I know for sure that I'm not the kind of person who wants Gina scared of me. Because in that moment, all I want is to tell her how sorry I am. All I want is to make things right. I don't want to see her scurrying around with her head down, trying not to get hurt by something that I can't even control.

I'm not the person she's afraid I am. But I have no idea how to show her that.

When I walk into the cafeteria at lunch, everyone's at the usual table. I keep glancing over at them as I buy food. Roya is stealing something from Maryam's lunch, and Marcelina is doodling on her arm with a felt-tip pen. Paulie and Iris have their heads bent together. Iris is gesturing wildly, her long pale fingers describing patterns I can't follow. Paulie looks totally absorbed in whatever they're talking about—but then, as I bring my burrito over to our table, I catch her eye. She says something to cut Iris off. They both look up at me: Paulie expectant, Iris guilty.

"I can't figure out how to take the spell off Gina," Iris says without preamble when I arrive at the table. From the way nobody else reacts to this statement, I guess she's filled them all in, and I guess they've been listening to her try to figure it out for a while. "Not without getting her to hold still for at least thirty seconds, and she bolts whenever I get near her."

Now it makes sense, why Iris and Paulie would be so sucked into their conversation. They don't usually ignore everyone else at the table, but this is a Paulie-and-Iris situation. Paulie is the only one of us who could *really* help Iris with this problem: while the rest of us more or less stick to the magic we're good at and only occasionally branch out, Paulie is a great experimentalist. She tries new things constantly. She approaches magic with a kind of courage I'll never have. She's not afraid of failure, not afraid of embarrassment.

"I still think that we wouldn't be in this situation if we'd all put a little more effort into figuring out how this all works," Iris says. Her tone tells me that the argument has been going on for a while, and she's hoping I'll take her side, now that I've arrived.

Paulie rolls her eyes. "It doesn't matter," she says. "We should just try something out and see how it goes."

She's like Roya running off the rocks at the reservoir, except half the time, Paulie doesn't know where she'll land. But she jumps anyway. She's always figuring out new things that she can or can't do, new ways that her magic can move and change and create and destroy. A month before prom, she showed up at my house and showed me that she'd figured out how to make soap bubbles turn into glass. She does stuff like that all the time: *hey, check it out, I tried this thing and it worked.*

She's pretty amazing. Iris is more driven, and has more book smarts, but she doesn't know how to take risks the same way Paulie does. I would have thought that the two of them together could unravel any problem. So it's kind of scary to think that even with both of them working at it, there's still not a solution.

I stall by taking a bite of my burrito. If I were Roya, I'd snap at them to figure it out. If I were Maryam, I'd pat Iris's arm and tell her that I believe in her. If I were Marcelina, I'd ask what ideas they already had, and then I'd help them put something together. If I were Iris or Paulie, I'd . . . well. I guess I would come up with something brilliant and dangerous and say *go*.

But I'm not any of them, and I have to figure out for myself what to say.

It's so much easier to think about my friends than it is to think about myself. It's so much easier to predict them than it is to predict me. What does Alexis say? What's the right answer? What does Iris need to hear right now? She and Paulie are both staring at me. Iris has a waiting-face on. Paulie is looking at my mouth and I wipe it with my thumb, thinking I must have rice sticking to my chin or something. I realize that the table has gone quiet: everyone is looking at me, waiting. I swallow my mouthful of burrito and clear my throat.

"We'll all help you however we can." I say it without thinking, and once I've said it, I know it's the right answer. I reach out and grab Iris's hand, giving it a firm squeeze. Relief floods her features. "You're not alone," I add, and I'm surprised at the tears that fill her eyes. "You know that, right? You know you're not all by yourself in this?"

"Yeah," she whispers, but I wonder. I think back to what she said yesterday, about being the one who's supposed to have all the big ideas. Iris has always put a ton of pressure on herself, but I wonder if maybe we've been putting some pressure on her too—making her feel like she has to be the smartest, the most put-together out of all of us. I squeeze her hand again. She looks away.

"I mean it," I murmur, low enough that it's just between the two of us. "You don't have to have all the answers."

"I don't really have any of the answers," she says. She taps twice on my knuckle with her thumb, and then she lets go of my hand and pretends to rummage in her backpack. "I mean, I still haven't figured out why we can all do what we do, and I've been doing research for years now. Besides, I'm not the one who figured out about the heart," she says, not looking up.

"You—did you tell everyone about . . . ?" Everyone's eyes are still on me.

"I think it's worth a shot," Roya says.

"What's worth a shot?" I ask. My burrito suddenly feels strange in my hands. I pass it to Roya.

"Getting rid of the pieces to bring back the heart," Maryam says softly. "Your idea."

I shake my head and look to Iris as if she'll give me answers, but she's still pretending to rummage through her backpack. This doesn't sound like what I said—but it makes sense, sort of. As much as anything does. "So, you guys think that if we get rid of all the pieces of Josh—"

"Maybe his heart will come all the way back, and then we can bring him back to life from there," Paulie finishes. "Yeah."

"We should try, right?" Maryam says. "I mean . . . it's still worth trying to make it right, obviously. This method is better than nothing." She's got her hands folded neatly on top of the table, and everything about her looks carefully constructed to seem calm.

I wait for Iris to look up. When she does, I catch her eye, and she frowns.

"It makes the most sense," she whispers. "And every time you guys get rid of a piece, except for when Roya did the arm—I feel better every time. Like the thing that's wrong in that spell is slowly easing off."

"It feels like we're setting things back where they're supposed to go," Roya says through half a mouthful of my burrito. "So, yeah. Let's go with it, huh?"

"What about the arm?" I ask, and Iris shakes her head.

"She didn't actually get rid of it. She just hid it," Iris says. "She's gotta go back and get it out of there, get rid of it the right way." The way she says it, I can tell that they already talked about this part. Without me. They figured it all out already.

Roya rolls her eyes. "Fine, yeah," she says. "I'll do it again. Alexis Rules: we have to get rid of the piece all the way, for keeps, before the heart comes back to life. Right?"

Alexis Rules? I'm not used to being the one credited with the big plans, and I'm so afraid that someone will be angry with me if this goes wrong too. "What if it doesn't work?" I ask.

Maryam unfolds her hands to drape an arm across my shoulder. "Then we'll figure it out. Together. But we have to try."

"Maryam's right," Marcelina says. "This keeps getting harder and more complicated, and you all know I'd rather run away, but . . . I don't think this is a thing we can run away from, and either way, I can't live the rest of my life knowing I didn't at least try to do the right thing."

"You're not alone either, you know," Paulie says with a smile. Before I can say anything, the lunch bell rings.

We all get up to head to class, but Paulie grabs my arm. "Hang on a minute," she says, running her free hand through her hair. It's a femme day for her, and she's wearing her hair long and loose. It falls past her shoulders in perfect waves. She sees me looking and winks. "Maryam helped me out with it this morning," she says. "She's been practicing on me. I told her that I'd let her if she promised to stop feeling bad about how she can't really help with the Josh project." She tosses it back and forth in a goofy parody of a *Baywatch* babe. "I think it came out pretty great, yeah?"

Pretty great is an understatement. She looks like something out of a shampoo commercial. "It's amazing," I say. "She's so incredible. Damn." I feel myself smile, and I realize it's the first time I've smiled today. I love seeing the things my friends can do. I love being impressed by them. "I didn't know Maryam was doing hair . . . stuff," I say. I glance around to see if anyone is listening to us.

"It took her like thirty seconds," Paulie whispers. "She grew it longer, even. This morning it only came to here." She holds her hand flat about four inches above the ends of her hair.

"Wow," I breathe.

"Yeah," Paulie says. She reaches out and touches my wrist with one hand. "So, I was thinking of going for a drive. Do you want to come with?"

"Uh, sure," I say, distracted by the way her fingers are brushing mine.

"Cool," she says. "Let's go."

"What, *now*?" She laughs and starts walking. I stand where I am, confused for a couple of seconds, before jogging to catch up with her. "What about fifth period?" I ask, like a total square.

"What, do you have a test or something?" she asks, pushing open an emergency exit door. No alarm goes off—they never do. I wish I could credit Paulie's magic for that, but it's really just that the school deactivated all of them because they were tired of alarms going off all day.

"No, I just have study hall," I say, blinking in the sunlight. "But . . ." I trail off. But what? It's a gorgeous day, and there's hardly any school left, and Paulie wants to go for a drive. What am I gonna miss? A bored teacher trying to get through their grading so that they can actually have a night at home without piles of half-assed essays to mark up? A room full of seniors trying to decide if they can get away with napping?

Besides, if I leave now, I won't have to spend study hall trying not to make eye contact with Gina. I know I should face her, but I don't think I'm brave enough to do it just yet.

I don't say anything else, and Paulie doesn't wait for an end to my sentence. She walks ahead, shoulders pulled back in that perfect cheerleader posture. She moves like she knows I'll follow.

And of course, I do.

11.

PAULIE DRIVES FAST AND BRAKES HARD. I BUCKLE in and spend most of the drive trying not to grab the dashboard. Every time she accelerates, her cheeks dimple with a held-back smile. She keeps the windows up and weaves in and out of traffic with even more precision than usual.

"Where are we going?" I ask. She said "for a drive" before, but she's driving like someone with a destination in mind.

"Barclay Rock," she says. I laugh.

"Are you trying to make time with me, Paulie?" I tease. She laughs too, and wiggles her eyebrows at me. God, it feels good to be laughing right now. It feels normal, and I realize I haven't laughed like this since I killed Josh.

Barclay Rock is the premier make-out spot in town. It's on the other side of the hill from the reservoir. When you're up there, you can see clear to the horizon. It's a pretty classic destination for anyone who's hoping to get some action, but there are also some decent picnic spots if you don't mind getting harassed by aggro squirrels with no fear of humans.

Paulie slows down for the switchbacks that climb the hillside. I lean my head back against the seat and stretch my legs out, resting my feet on the dashboard.

"Are you gonna miss it?" I ask, thinking of the conversation I had with Roya at the reservoir.

"No," she says flatly. I roll my head to the side to look at her. She's got her I'm-fine face on—a careful kind of casual disregard that doesn't suit her at all. I stare at her, waiting, until finally she rolls her eyes. "What is there to miss?" she asks. "It's a small town with a lot of small people in it."

"Do you think New York will be better?" I ask. I try not to feel the sting of "What is there to miss?" I know she doesn't mean she won't miss *me*, but it's hard to tell that to the flinching feeling of dismissal that came in the wake of her words.

"Yes," she says with absolute certainty. "Definitely."

"You won't be lonely?" I ask, completely failing to rise above the fear that she'll forget about us. That she'll forget about me.

She grabs my hand without looking, sliding her fingers between mine. She rubs her thumb over mine, and a wash of blue glitter passes over my arm, shining brightly before it fades. "I'll miss you," she says softly. "And all the girls, and the cheer squad. But I'm going to be so much *more* there than I am here, Lex. There's going to be so much more room for me to be me, you know? The pressure will be off and I'll have the space to figure out who I am when I'm not . . . here."

I realize all at once what she means. "You mean away from

your mom and dad?" I ask. She nods. Her mom and dad are great, but they smother her. A lot.

Here's why: Paulie had a little brother who drowned when he was four and she was seven. I found out about him the first time I slept over at her house—I walked into the kitchen in the middle of the night to get a glass of water, and her mom was at the kitchen table with an open bottle of wine and a photo album.

"What are you looking at?" I asked, and she invited me to come sit at the table with her. I was fourteen and felt awkward every time I talked to my friends' parents, but I sat, and Paulie's mom showed me the pictures of Paulie and her little brother. Pictures of them in the tub together. Pictures of them playing. Pictures of them wearing matching outfits.

The next morning, I'd asked Paulie about it, and she'd shrugged. "She gets like that sometimes," she said. "I think she was kind of like . . . made to be a mom to two kids? And now she only has one, and I'm not always enough for her to put all her mom-ness into." I remember watching her brush her hair into a high, smooth ponytail. I wondered, at the time, what it must be like to have too much of a mom. After that, I took to asking Paulie's mom for advice every now and then, letting her teach me things I already knew. Anything to give Paulie a break. Anything to give her mom an outlet.

"They love you a lot," I say to Paulie as she parks the car. She shrugs.

"I know," she says. "I love them too. But I want to be

someone other than the kid that lived. I don't care how awful it is."

"It isn't awful," I tell her, and something taut in her face relaxes.

"Thanks," she says. She slaps her hands on the steering wheel briskly, then unbuckles her seat belt and launches out of the car. Paulie has this way of rocketing from thing to thing—once she's done with a conversation, it's over, and there can be no lingering. I kind of love that about her. I've never had an awkward silence with Paulie.

By the time I'm out of the car, Paulie is rummaging around in the chaos of her trunk. It's crammed with clothes and cheerleading stuff and water bottles and textbooks. She holds an arm out behind her, clutching a sweater I thought I'd lost months ago. I take it, and she returns to digging through the debris with both hands. She emerges from the trunk after a few more seconds, triumphantly holding a duffel bag aloft.

"Is that—" I start to ask.

"Yep," she interrupts. She unzips the bag and pulls out Josh's severed leg. It doesn't look different from how legs usually look, although it's covered in a surprisingly thick layer of blond hair. I wish I had something in my memory to connect it to Josh. I wish I could say I knew it was his leg because of the birthmark on the knee or the scar on the shin. But I wouldn't know his leg from any other random dude's leg out there.

I only know it's his leg because Paulie has it in her trunk.

"Wait," I say as she starts to zip the bag back up. "What about the arm?"

"She'll only be able to take one," Paulie answers, and I don't ask. I just hold the leg as she puts the duffel back into the trunk. I'm holding it in both hands like a baseball bat. Or maybe more like a lacrosse stick. It's warm in a way that makes me uncomfortable, but I rationalize that it's probably just the heat of the trunk. They don't smell. I wonder queasily if the summer heat has been cooking the leg and the arm.

"Hey," Paulie says, snapping her fingers in front of my face. "Anyone home?"

"Yeah, sorry, what's up?" I say, and I realize that the trunk is closed and she's probably been trying to get my attention for a minute or two.

"We gotta go before someone drives by and sees you holding a leg," she says. "Come on."

I follow her away from the car, away from the overlook. She leads me across the road and into the trees that sparsely cover this part of the hill. She's wearing a dress with a long striped skirt, and her bare shoulders are already turning a little pink in the sun. She brushes her hands across them, and I see a spark of magic fly over her skin, and then the pink is gone.

"What did you do?" I ask.

"Sunscreen," she answers.

"When did you figure that one out?"

"Last night."

I can't help it. I laugh, delighted at the way she just *discovers* things. "Teach me how?"

She aims a grin at me. "You know it."

Once we're far enough from the road that we can't hear cars, she finds a tree stump and sits down. She pats it and I squeeze in next to her.

She leans her head on my shoulder, her blond hair spilling across the front of my shirt. She holds her hands out in front of her like she's pushing something away, and a net of blue erupts from her palms. The net flies out into the trees, taking a long time to fade from view.

This magic, I know. I know it because I taught it to her. I've tried to teach the other girls, but they never really got the hang of it the way Paulie did.

"Who ya callin'?" I ask, tilting my head to rest it on top of hers.

"A friend," she answers.

"Anyone I know?"

"Yeah, probably," she says. "If you don't know her yet, you guys will get along great, though."

"Cool," I say, and we wait in the quiet. I listen to the birds that stopped singing when we crashed into the trees—they're slowly coming to accept that we're here, and their conversations are starting up again.

"Can I ask you a question?" she says, and I can feel her jaw moving against my shoulder.

"Of course."

"What were you doing with him?" Her eyelashes brush over my collarbone and I suppress a shiver.

"I think that's a conversation you should have with a grown-up, Paulie," I joke, and she jabs me in the ribs with a knuckle.

"You know what I mean. Why would you try to climb on top of Josh Harper? Of all the people in the whole world? Of all the people in the whole school? Hell, of all the people at that party?" She lifts her head from my shoulder and looks at me, her face uncharacteristically still. Why does she have her I'm-fine face on? "Why him?"

"I don't know," I say, picking bark off the edge of the stump. "It was stupid."

She doesn't let me get away with that, though. "You're not a stupid person," she presses. "You don't do stupid shit like trying to lose your virginity to Josh Harper."

I flinch. "I don't really need you judging me right now," I snap. "I get that I shouldn't have done it, but I did, so just let it go, okay?"

Paulie stares at me. She pulls her hair up into a ponytail, then nods at me. "Okay," she says. "If you want to talk about it, we can. I don't mean to push it. I just want to know that you're okay." She's looking into my face and I feel like there's something I'm missing, something I don't understand, but then I say that I'm okay and she nods and rests her head back on my shoulder, and whatever it is that I was missing will just have to stay missed.

"Sorry I was a bitch just now," I murmur into her hair.

Paulie pats my thigh. "It's okay," she says. "It's okay to be upset at upsetting things."

I'm struck by the sentiment. "It's okay to be upset at upsetting things," I repeat, and Paulie taps her fingers on my knee in a pattern I don't follow.

"Yeah," she says. "I learned it from the therapist Mom and Dad took me to after Drew died. I kept apologizing for being mad or sad or whatever. She told me that it's okay to have feelings, and that it's okay to be upset at things like my brother dying. It helped a lot."

We sit and listen to the trees and the birds and I think about it. I wonder why nobody's ever told me that before: *It's okay to be upset at upsetting things*.

I think about what it would have felt like to be a little kid and have Nico disappear.

I've talked about it with Roya before a couple of times—both of us have younger brothers, although Nico is closer to the age Drew would have been if he'd lived. I try to imagine letting myself be upset about something that enormous, and I can't. I grab Paulie's hand and send a thread of magic into it, the same way she did to me in the car. I can't see the glitter, but she smiles, and I know it's there, dark bright purple or whatever the hell Roya meant. She squeezes my hand and then clears her throat.

"So, while we're out here—there's something I've been kind of wanting to talk to you about," she says. She's turning my hand over in hers and looking at the lines of my palm.

"Are you going to tell my fortune?" I ask, and she smiles down at my fingers before biting her lip.

"Not exactly," she says.

"Wait," I say, staring into the trees. I could have sworn I saw a shadow—"There," I whisper, pointing. Paulie looks up and follows the line of my finger with her eyes. The line of her neck is rigid.

"Say hi," she whispers back to me without moving her lips.

"What?"

"Say. Hi," she repeats through clenched teeth. "I called her, but I don't know how to say hi to her."

I look into the trees and see the shadow again. It's completely silent, moving toward us in fits and starts. I say hi.

The shadow doesn't move.

I tell it that it's come to the right place; that we have something to share. I tell it that we're not a threat, but that we're not to be trifled with either. I tell it without words, using the language I've known my whole life without knowing how.

"Paulie," I breathe as the shadow steps out from around a tree. "Is that a coyote?"

"Holy shit, yes," Paulie whispers. "It worked. Oh my god, it *worked*."

She's smaller than I expected her to be. I guess in my head, I always thought coyotes were just brownish wolves, but she's small and skinny. Her tail and head are low, and her hackles are raised. I repeat that we aren't a threat, but she still walks toward us slowly, pausing every few steps to stare at us with suspicious golden eyes.

Paulie's got a tight grip on my fingers. "Is she, uh, nice?"

"She's a fucking coyote, Paulie," I mutter.

"Right, but is she a *nice* coyote? Ask her if she's a nice coyote."

I grit my teeth, but . . . it's not like I have any better ideas. I ask her if she's a nice coyote, and she freezes. She lifts her head, cocks it to one side, and sits. Just like a dog. It's so bizarre, because she's *not* a dog, but everything in my brain is screaming DOG and I don't know what to *do*.

I stare at the coyote. She stares at me.

"What's wrong with her belly?" she asks, and I drag my eyes away from the coyote's. Her belly is droopy, slack. Tented.

"She's nursing," I answer. "She's got pups somewhere." I raise my hand slowly and point to the leg. The coyote's gaze follows the movement, but she just stares at my fingertip, uncomprehending. I tell her to look, and she glances between my eyes and my finger with an expression that clearly reads as *What does it look like I'm doing?*

I stand so slowly that my thighs tremble. She mirrors the movement. Paulie stays where she is, quiet enough that I think she's probably holding her breath. I move forward, pausing with every step, until I'm standing over the leg on the ground. The blond hairs on Josh's shin glint in the sunlight that filters through the trees. I point at the leg.

The coyote steps toward me so slowly that I almost don't see her moving. It takes her at least a full minute to reach me.

The top of her pointed ear comes up to my knee. I don't move as she raises her head to look up at me, lifts her snout to smell my fingertip. One of her ears droops slightly in an expression I can't read.

For you, I try to tell her. She cocks her head, and I hesitate for a few seconds before reaching out a shaking hand and resting it on top of her head.

The flood of communication is instantaneous, if garbled. *Who what smell pups far meat who touch why?*

I swallow and try again. *Meat for you*, I tell her. *Meat for your pups*. She shakes my hand off and takes a few steps away. I walk backward until my heels knock into the stump, then sit down and grab Paulie's hand.

"Did it work?" she whispers. "Is it gonna work?"

Before I can say that I have no idea, the coyote ducks her head. She takes the leg in her jaws and drags it backward into the trees, and by the time I can think to say anything, she's gone.

"Jesus," I breathe. Paulie starts laughing, these huge gulping laughs, and I want to be furious at her for calling a coyote and expecting me to deal with it, but instead I start laughing too. We lean into each other and laugh way past when we should stop. We laugh the entire drive back to my place, and when I get out of the car and turn around to say goodbye, she leans across the front seat, reaches out the window, and presses her palm to the top of my head. She doesn't say a word, but I say, "You too," and I can hear her laughter streaming out the open windows of her car as she speeds away.

Later that night, I send her a text. **Hey I just remembered you wanted to talk about something?**

Nah, she replies. Then, a minute or two later: **I honestly don't even remember lol**

It rings false, which is strange, because Paulie is scrupulously honest. I want to follow up. But I get distracted, because Dad taps his knuckles on my bedroom door. I look up to see him and Pop filling the doorframe. They look grim.

"What's up?" I ask, trying to ignore that gut-clench of dread that comes with knowing, somehow, that I'm in trouble. *It's probably nothing,* I tell myself. *They don't know about Josh. They couldn't possibly know about Josh.*

But they're looking at me like they know every awful thing I've ever done.

I've done some pretty awful things lately. Dad steps into the room and I know that this is going to be bad.

"Hey, bug," he says, unsmiling. "We need to talk."

12.

"GOOD DAY AT SCHOOL?" POP ASKS. THE LIGHT from my desk lamp is reflecting off his head, but his eyes are shadowy under the stern line of his thick brows.

I clear my throat and set my phone down. "It was fine," I say slowly.

"Anything interesting happen?" Pop says, and he's definitely using his overly casual lawyer-voice on me. My stomach twists again.

"Not . . . really?" Careful, Alexis. Careful. This is torture, because we all know that they've got *something* to talk about, but I have to pretend like there's nothing it could possibly be until they decide to drop the hammer. They stare at me with identically unreadable expressions. I clear my throat and raise my eyebrows. *Get it over with.*

"How was fifth period?" Dad asks.

Not *what did you do to Josh*. Not *we know you buried his head in the woods*. Not even *what the hell is going on with Gina*

Tarlucci and why is she terrified of you. None of those things. No. It's *how was fifth period?*

I'm dizzy with a sudden combination of relief and guilt. I want to laugh, and I also know that I should be feeling the dread that comes with getting caught cutting class, but it just feels so small. I can't muster the contrition that I know they're looking for.

"I didn't go today," I say. They look at each other, and I can't tell if they're surprised that I fessed up or satisfied that they got me to cop to skipping.

"Why not?" Pop asks.

Shit.

I can't tell him that I was with Paulie feeding a dead boy's leg to a coyote. I scramble, and I come up with a very, very good lie.

"I was with Iris," I say. "Her boyfriend cheated on her again. She was really upset and needed someone to talk to about it."

This lie should smooth everything over. Iris does indeed have a boyfriend—or rather, she did until a few days before prom. A boyfriend who went to another school, and who the entire gang hates. He kissed another girl last year, and even though Iris forgave him, the rest of us were prepared to be forever suspicious of him. Our suspicions were confirmed, obviously.

I'm pretty sure Dad and Pop don't know that, though. As far as they know, Iris and her loser boyfriend are still together. And they're always understanding of my need to support my friends. They don't get mad if I have to go out late or if I'm on the phone at midnight when one of the girls is having a crisis. They've both told me a few times that they think it's great that I have such a strong "support network," whatever that means. This lie should make everything better, should make Pop's heavy brows do a dance of sympathetic approval. But for some reason, they're both looking at me like I just told them I skipped fifth period to enjoy a late picnic lunch on the surface of the moon.

"Try again," Pop says, and he holds up his phone. He angles the screen toward me, and I see a text message.

From Iris.

Hey sorry to bother you but is Alexis ok?

My father's response: **Yeah, how come?**

Oh just haven't seen her since lunch and didn't know if she was sick or something, sorry, thanks

"I called the school to find out if you'd been in class, and they said you were absent for fifth and sixth period." Dad sits on the edge of my bed and I feel completely trapped. He runs a hand through his thick hair, leaving it all on end. "Why weren't you in class?"

I shrug, which is the direst mistake I could possibly make.

"What does that mean?" Pop asks.

"It means . . . I don't know," I say.

"You don't know what you were doing during fifth period?" Dad asks, leaning toward me. He's close enough that I can see the patchy places where his new beard isn't filling in yet. Pop rests a hand on his shoulder and he leans back again. I wonder if they've been talking about strategies for dealing with their wayward children.

"I mean . . . I know what I was doing, I just don't want to talk about it," I mutter. This isn't going well, and I don't know how to fix it. I look up at Pop, desperately hoping that he'll smooth things over somehow. He's good at smoothing things over. But he looks concerned, and I realize that he's not an avenue of rescue at all. Concerned-Pop is way more of a problem for me than Angry-Pop would have been. He never stays angry for long, but if he's worried about me? He won't let up until he's figured out the problem and engineered a solution.

"What's going on here?" Dad asks. He fidgets with a loose thread on my comforter. "You know you can tell us anything, right? Even if you're in some kind of trouble? But we can't help you if we don't know what the problem is."

Sudden anger flares in my chest—a pure, hot weightlessness that makes me feel like I'm ten feet tall. I don't even know what I'm angry at—my dads aren't saying anything that's wrong. They're trying their best. But I'm furious. It's not fair, but I'm angry with them for not knowing me like they think they do. I want to yell, and slam doors, and kick things. I want to tell them that I can't tell them everything because there are some things that are just too much to tell. I want to tell them that they can't help, *period*.

Instead, I take a deep breath. I let them see that I'm taking a deep breath. I let them see that I'm calming myself down, so that maybe they'll give me a little room to exist before they start trying to fix my life for me.

"Alexis," Pop says softly, his hand still resting on Dad's shoulder. "Your dad told me about the party you went to on prom night."

I feel my brow knit and try to smooth it out but fail. I'm not surprised that Dad told Pop. Not exactly. But part of me feels betrayed, like when Dad and I talked about the party, things were fine and it shouldn't ever have come up again.

"O . . . kay?" I say it in the shittiest teenager voice ever. I want to slap myself at the sound of my own voice. I don't talk like this, especially not to my dads. They always do their best to listen to me, to let me be whoever I am and let me feel whatever I'm feeling, and in exchange I try not to be an asshole to them even when I'm *feeling* like an asshole. It's a deal we've never discussed, but I know that's the trade: I try not to be awful, and they try to let me figure myself out. But that weightless anger is still expanding in my chest, and it's hard not to let it out. That snide tone I just used with him is the best I can do right now. Pop gives me a look that says he's letting me get away with it this once. For a soft-faced bald guy, he's really good at expressing "don't try that again" with a single glance.

"We know what kinds of things go on when you're a teenager and you're about to leave for college and . . . everything," Dad says, reaching up to rest his long fingers over Pop's short, blunt ones. My heart sinks. This isn't the talk I was expecting. "And we get it. We do."

No you don't, I don't say.

"But if you're sneaking off with some boy—" Pop starts, and I can't help it. I burst out laughing. Technically, I am sneaking off with some boy. Not a whole boy, but . . . some of him. My laughter comes out bright and mean. They both look startled, and I suck the laughter back in. "Or girl," Pop adds slowly, an edge to his voice. "Either way. If you're sneaking off with *someone* . . ." He trails off, and he and Dad both look at me expectantly.

"If I'm sneaking off with someone, what?" I ask.

"So you are?"

"No, Dad, I'm—look, it was a nice day and I wanted to be outside, okay? It's not a big deal, it's not like I missed anything important." I'm talking too loud and too fast. The balloon behind my sternum is still expanding, and I feel like I'm made of sharp edges and smooth, hot metal. I glance down at my hands to make sure that they aren't glowing. *Shit*. My nail beds are luminous. I tuck my hands under my thighs and hope that I look natural. People sit like this all the time, right?

"How do you know you didn't miss anything?" Dad presses. "You weren't there."

I roll my eyes. "I know because the last month of school doesn't matter!" Pop's eyebrows shoot up, but I act like I didn't see the clear warning sign. Those eyebrows mean *turn back*, but I steam on ahead anyway. My palms are hot and tingling, but the more I talk, the less they burn. "It's all worksheets and crap and we're not learning anything anymore, and honestly,

I'd be amazed if any of my teachers even noticed that I was gone. I'd be amazed if *anyone* even noticed that I was gone!"

I exhale, feeling like the balloon in my chest has suddenly deflated. I can hear my own heartbeat in my ears. Or at least, I hope it's my heartbeat, and not Josh's heart beating under my bed. I'm so tired. My hands hurt, and there's a smell like cut grass in my room that wasn't there before. I feel light, clean. Empty.

I look up to find Dad and Pop watching me. Dad's eyes are wide, but Pop—Pop is incandescent. His face and his bare scalp are both bright red, and he's got one hand over his mouth like he's holding himself back from screaming. His eyebrows are raised so high that his forehead is creased by bloodless white lines.

Dad looks up at him and notices.

"Bill, why don't I take it from here?" he says softly.

Pop shakes his head. His hand is still over his mouth, and he's not looking at me. He's staring through the wall. Not at the wall, not at anything on the wall—through it, like on the other side of it there's something that requires his complete attention. He finally lowers his hand, crossing his arms. "I can't believe you," he growls.

"What?" It comes out as a whisper, and I look at Dad to see if he understands, but he's watching Pop and I feel like there must be some mistake.

"This is the most selfish goddamn thing you've ever done," Pop says in that same low, furious voice. "We raised you to be more thoughtful than this, Alexis." He's holding his own elbow in a white-knuckled grip that looks like it will leave bruises in the morning.

"I don't understand," I say, but some part of me must understand because my stomach lurches like I'm at the peak of a roller coaster hill, right before that first big drop. I want to throw up. I want to run away. I want to be anywhere but here.

And then Pop looks at me, and the roller coaster drops. His eyes are shining and red, and he's looking at me like he's never seen me before. I've certainly never seen him like this before—furious, horrified, on the verge of tears. "One of your classmates is missing," he hisses. "Nobody knows what happened to him, nobody knows if he's even *alive*, and you think it's okay to disappear for an afternoon without telling us where you are? Because you want to go *outside*?"

"I just—"

"*No*," Pop says, "you don't *just* anything! You have no idea what the hell it feels like to get a text message that says nobody knows where your daughter is, Alexis. You have no *idea*—" He doesn't yell, just speaks at full volume, but I still flinch. He closes his eyes and takes a deep breath.

"Bill," Dad murmurs, "we said we'd listen, right?"

"I can't, I'm sorry," Pop says, running a hand over his scalp, his eyes still closed. "She's sitting there laughing and talking about how none of it matters, and I can't." He opens his eyes and looks at Dad as he talks about me like I'm not here, and I realize his hands are shaking. "I can't."

He walks out of the room without looking at me. Dad and I are sitting on the bed, and I feel like I should go after Pop, but I also don't know how to pursue one of my parents when he's too upset to see me. I look at Dad. He's staring at the open door to my bedroom, and he's rubbing his half-grown-in beard with one hand, and he looks small.

"I'm sorry," I whisper. "I didn't think about it that way."

"I know you didn't, bug," Dad says. He runs his hands through his Nico-hair again, making it stick up in the opposite direction from where it was pointing before. "But maybe you should, next time. People care about you, you know? You can hurt them just by forgetting that."

"That's not fair." I chip at my nail polish, scarring one of the little hearts Maryam gave me.

"It's how it is, though," he says. "You scared us. We love you, and you scared us. And that line about nobody noticing if you were gone?"

"I didn't mean it like—"

"What you meant doesn't matter," he says. He's being firm, but still gentle, and the gentleness stings more than it ought to. "What you said is what matters. Your impact matters more than your intentions, kiddo, and those words were maybe the worst ones you could have said to someone who spent his afternoon worrying about whether you were going to come home."

"If you were so worried, why didn't you come in here sooner?" I mumble.

"At first, we figured you just cut class. But then you didn't get home until the sun was going down. You breezed in through that front door and headed to your room right when we were about to call your cell and tell you to get your ass home. By then we were too upset to come talk to you right away," he says.

"You mean Pop was too upset?"

"No, I mean *we* were too upset," Dad says. I look up at him, surprised. He smiles. "I'm still upset, bug. I'm angry and hurt and surprised. But I understand, too. You're a good kid, and this is pretty minimal mischief compared to what you could get up to." I flinch, thinking of all the things he doesn't know. "But *you've* got to understand how frightening it is to think even for a second that you might be disappearing." He nudges me with his shoulder. "Just don't do that to us again, okay? We're old guys. Our hearts can't take the strain."

He's not old. They're not old. But they make jokes like that sometimes, and I know Dad is only doing it to make me feel better. I smile weakly and nod, feeling like a little kid. Feeling like an asshole. "What about Pop?" I ask.

"Well, he's pretty upset too. In some ways that I'm not. He'll need a little space, I imagine," Dad says. "Talk to him tomorrow. Apologize. He loves you more than he's mad at you." He gives me a squeeze and stands up. "I'm going to go check on him. It'll be okay, though."

"Okay."

"I mean it," he says in that same painfully gentle voice. "It'll be okay."

He kisses the top of my head and walks out of my room, leaving the door open just a crack behind him. I wait until I hear his footsteps disappear down the hall before I close it the rest of the way.

I'm a huge jerk. The other day, when Dad made bag lunches for Nico and me, I could tell that he and Pop were worrying because of the thing with Josh. I could tell, and I even said something to Nico about it—I told him not to hurt Dad's feelings. And then I turned around and acted like I could do whatever I wanted without making my dads worry about me, even though it's my classmate who's missing.

I didn't even think about it. And I wouldn't have thought about it at all, if not for Iris. I scroll way back in the group thread, and there it is: three texts from Iris asking where I am, and nobody answering her. No wonder she went to my dads.

I text Roya, needing to talk about it, needing to hear that I'm not a terrible person—but she doesn't answer. She hasn't answered any of my messages all day. I mentally start scanning through our previous interactions, trying to figure out what I could have done to make her angry, what I could have done to drive her away and make her ignore me. I feel like I'm standing at the rim of a very deep hole, a hole too deep to climb out of. If I keep just *thinking* about Roya and my dads and Josh and everything, I'm going to fall in.

I have to do something.

I lean over the edge of my bed and reach under it, far as my arms can get. The lip of my bedframe digs into my armpit hard, and I press into it, savoring the pain for just a moment.

Just before it starts to hurt too much, my fingers find fabric, and I've got the bag. I haul it back up onto my bed and tug at the zipper.

Josh's heart is inside. It's warm, and it's just a little soft under my fingertips. It's heavy, still, heavier than it should be. It beats in my hands, hard brutal spasms, still slow but faster than before. I stare at it, willing it to be surrounded by a living boy.

Nothing happens, of course. That pit yawns wider, the hole I mustn't fall into, the place where I'll lose hope and give up and stop trying to bring Josh back.

Maryam is right. I can't stop trying to fix this thing. No matter what I lose in the process—no matter how scary it is, not knowing how I'll change—I can't give up. Because giving up feels like admitting that the dark thing inside me, the thing that can use someone up and kill them by accident, is more powerful than the rest of me. That's what's at the bottom of the hole I'm trying to stay out of: the knowledge that the worst part of me is the strongest part of me.

I stand at the edge of the hole, holding that slowly beating heart and wishing I knew how to fix it, and I feel myself starting to fall.

Just before I topple over the edge, Paulie calls me.

"You have perfect timing," I say in lieu of *hello*. My voice is shaking. I press the phone between my shoulder and my ear as I slide the heart back into the bag.

"I know," Paulie says. "I'm pretty much perfect in every way."

I don't quite smile, but I can feel the bottom of the hole getting farther away. "You're also the humblest person I've ever met."

"I'm the best at being humble. No one on this earth is better at being humble than I am," she says, and I laugh. It feels good to laugh—some of the deflated, constricted feeling in my chest subsides. Paulie is always great that way.

I tell Paulie about what happened with my dads, and with Iris. She's immediately pissed on my behalf. "What the fuck?" she hisses. "Why would Iris snitch on you?"

"I don't think she thought she was snitching," I say tentatively. Paulie doesn't get angry easily the way Roya does—but unlike Roya, she doesn't let things go easily either. Once she's mad, it can be dangerous to get between her and the object of her ire. "I think she was just worried, you know? I mean . . . we did kind of vanish. And she's been under a lot of stress lately."

"Oh, boo-hoo," Paulie snaps. "We've all been under a lot of stress—that doesn't mean we get to start tattling on each other. What if she feels the need to unburden herself further?"

"Did you just say 'unburden herself further?'"

"Shut up," Paulie says, but I hear the smile in her voice. "I've been studying for the ACTs for like . . . four hours."

"You dropped me off at home two hours ago," I tease.

"Okay, but it *feels* like four," she says. "The point is, Iris shouldn't have done that. I'm sorry about your dads."

"It's okay," I say, even though it isn't, because it's easier to say "It's okay" than to keep trying to dance between mad at Iris and *too* mad at Iris and mad at myself and sad about hurting Pop. "I don't want to talk about it anymore," I add, because that's more true.

"Okay. Anyway, it's been a weird time over here. Want to hear about it?" Paulie asks, brightening.

"Absolutely. Wait, I thought you've been studying?"

"Well, yes, okay, but not the whole time I've been home."

"Oh my god, have you actually opened a study guide tonight at all?"

"Shut up," she says, and then "hang on," and I hear rustling and a click as she gets up to close her bedroom door. "Okay, so, I got home and my mom was being *totally bizarre*," she says in a soft voice. "I walked in the front door and she was sitting in the kitchen and drinking wine and looking through this photo album, right? But get this: I went to look in the album over her shoulder, and it was all pictures of me."

"Uh, okay? How is this weird?" I ask, lying back on my pillows and trying, in some corner of my mind, to remember the last time I talked on the phone with someone for this long. Usually I just text with all the girls, but it's kind of nice to be hearing Paulie's voice. I can picture the way she chews on her thumb when she's thinking about how to phrase something.

"I mean, it's a little weird because she's drinking wine by herself in the kitchen. But then, check this out, extra weird-factor: she was looking at pictures of me, but this other kid was Photoshopped into like . . . all of them." She pauses for a moment. "Yeah, I know, it's totally bananas, right? She was acting like I was supposed to know who this kid was, and I was like 'I don't get what you're trying to do,' and she got *really* upset. She acted like I was being mean or something, I don't even know." Paulie sighs into my ear.

"I don't get it," I say. "Who was the kid?"

"I don't know, some little boy," she says. "It was like she added him into my entire childhood, like she was writing fanfiction about me or something. How did she even find the time?"

I frown. "It wasn't Drew?"

"Who?"

I feel hot and cold all at once. "Drew," I repeat, sitting up slowly. "Your little brother, Andrew."

"Ha," she says, a humorless parody of a laugh. "Yeah, okay, sure."

"What?"

"Did my mom put you up to this? And if so, can you please tell her it isn't funny?"

"Why would you think that?" I ask. "I don't talk to your mom. Paulie, are you feeling okay?" I'm about to ask her if I should come over, but then I remember Pop's face, and I know that I have to be at home tonight. Even if he's still mad at me . . . I shouldn't leave.

"I'm fine," she snaps. "I just don't get what you and my mom are trying to do. She kept talking about 'Drew' too and I don't get the *joke*, Alexis."

"There's no joke," I say softly. I feel dizzy. "Andrew was your little brother's name. He, um. He died a long time ago. When you were both little kids. I wouldn't mess around with you like this. I'm telling the truth. I . . ." I hesitate. "I pinky-swear."

She knows I wouldn't swear to her on a joke. She has to know it. There's a long pause on the line, long enough that I ask if she's still there. "I'm here," she whispers. "I have a little brother." Her voice is strange, distant—it sounds like she's underwater.

"*Had* a little brother," I correct softly, because I think she needs it.

She's silent for a long time again before she says, "What happened to him?"

I swallow hard and pull one of my pillows to my chest. "He drowned," I whisper. "When you were seven and he was four. Your babysitter wasn't watching him and he fell into your swimming pool. That's why your dad had it filled in."

There's a loud, hard sniff. "He died," she says evenly. "My little brother died."

"Yeah," I say, my eyes starting to burn.

"I can't remember," she says. "I try to remember and I can't. Why can't I remember?"

"You mean like . . . like he's fading or something?" I say it knowing that's not what she means, but hoping, desperately hoping, that it is.

"No," she says, her voice cracking. "I mean I can't *remember him*, I can't—it's like there's a hole there, I can't remember anything about him, I can't—oh my god, my mom."

"Paulie? Are you, I mean—obviously you're not okay, but—"

"I have to go," she says, sniffing again. She sounds far away. "I'm sorry, but I have to go, I have to talk to my mom, I have to look at those pictures—I don't remember him, I have to remember him—"

"It's okay, go, go, go," I say. "I'll see you tomorrow, I love you, call me if you need to, okay?"

"I will, love you bye," she says in a rush, and then she hangs up and I'm sitting in my bedroom, alone in the silence.

How could she forget Drew? How could she forget him between the time we left school and the time she got home?

My phone lights up. It's the group text. I check it, and even though the latest messages aren't from her, Iris's voice chimes in my memory. *Have you noticed anything weird these last few days? Have you noticed anything missing?*

Why, yes, I think to myself. *I have noticed something missing.*

I stare at my phone for half an hour or so, not doing anything, just waiting to see if Paulie texts me to say that it was all one big misunderstanding or some kind of very inappropriate joke. But she doesn't—all the messages that come in are from Maryam and Marcelina, who are planning some kind of hair tutorial video for Maryam's channel.

Eventually, I realize that Paulie is probably not going to be getting in touch with me tonight. She's probably sitting with her mom and relearning everything she's somehow suddenly forgotten about Drew. I take my phone off silent and put it on vibrate, tucking it into my bra so I'll know if she tries to reach me. I could leave it behind, but I don't want to miss a call from her. Not right now.

Then I walk out of my room and down the hall. I knock on Nico's bedroom door. He opens it and stands in the doorway with his hair mussed and one headphone in, wearing pajama pants and a ratty T-shirt with a band I hate on the front. I grab him and hug him tight enough that he grabs me back.

"You okay?" he says, sounding less weirded out than he could.

"I'm okay," I reply. "I just love you, is all."

He pushes me away and looks into my face. "Are you crying?" His eyes are wide. "Are you okay? Did something happen?"

"Nothing happened, Nic," I say, but I wipe my eyes on the hem of my shirt. "Sorry I got your shoulder all wet. When did you get tall enough for me to get your shoulder wet, anyway?"

He grins at me. "Like . . . a week ago? All my bones hurt." He laughs, and I laugh, and then I hug him again and he hugs me back. I cry on my too-tall, growing-up-fast little brother until I stop being scared to let him go.

13.

ON THURSDAY MORNING I WAKE UP TO A DOZEN texts from Iris. **I'm so sorry, can we talk, call me, call me, call me.** A thousand sad and embarrassed emojis.

I don't know how to feel about Iris talking to my dads. On the one hand, I know I shouldn't be mad. She wasn't trying to get me in trouble—she was just worried. I probably would have done the same thing, and hearing about how I made Dad and Pop worry by going AWOL makes me understand even better why she would be so stressed by my disappearance. Besides, I'm not even grounded. The only thing that happened was that my dads got upset and I had to apologize, and then I had to apologize again to Pop this morning and have a whole big talk with him. And I spent last night feeling guilty. But that's about my thoughtlessness, which isn't Iris's fault. It's nothing to be upset about, really. That's obvious and reasonable.

But on the other hand . . . I know I'm *supposed* to be mad. I know that's what a girl in my situation is expected to do. If

I watched a movie where this exact situation played out, the girl playing my role would be outraged that her friend got her in trouble; she would make it a huge thing, force Iris to apologize, hold it over her friend's head as relational leverage. *You owe me*, she'd say later, and she would use that for as long as she could.

I know that I'm supposed to be angry with Iris. I'm supposed to not speak with her, and I'm supposed to start a lot of turmoil about it. I have a free pass right now to be pissy and dramatic, and I know it's what everyone expects from me. Not because of who I am and how I act, but because that's how these situations go. She got me in trouble. I'm supposed to pitch a fit.

But I'm just *not mad at her*. I know that she did the right thing, even though it got me in trouble. I keep looking for any part of me that might be angry with her, but it's not there. I completely understand where she was coming from, texting my dads, and even though I wish she hadn't, I get it. And I bet I would have done the same thing, if Roya or Paulie or Maryam or Marcelina or Iris had vanished without notice.

It would be easy to just feel what I feel and not be mad at her, except for the guilt. I feel so awful for making Dad and Pop worry, for making them think that I didn't care about their feelings. I was an asshole to them—there's no way around that. I didn't consider them, the fact that they love me and notice me. I got so wrapped up in my own world that I basically forgot about them altogether—these men who devoted their lives to raising me and loving me. I forgot them. And I feel so awful about it, and it would be *so much easier* to blame it all on Iris instead of feeling awful.

But Dad and Pop raised me right, which means that I recognize the way I'm looking for an out, which means I can't really take it. Right?

I'm all tangled up. I think about it all morning instead of texting Iris back. I zone out in more than one class, trying to figure out if I'm mad at her or not. I think about Paulie's reaction to what happened, and it feels like an open door to doing the wrong thing. *Why would Iris snitch on you?*

Every time I replay last night's conversation in my head, though, I stop thinking about Iris altogether. I think about Paulie every time I come back around to the talk we had—her forgetting her brother, her finding out that he was dead. Every time I think about her, I send her a check-in text. She doesn't respond. She's not in school and she's not posting on social media. Between classes, I ask Maryam if she's heard from Paulie, and she says no.

"I haven't heard from her *or* Roya since yesterday," she says, tucking her hair behind her ears. "But I'm sure they're okay. We would have heard if they weren't."

I chew on my lip. "I don't know if Paulie's okay. Can I tell you what's going on with her? I promise it isn't gossip."

Maryam purses her lips for a second. She doesn't listen to gossip. It's something that's important to her—a principle she stands by, no matter how hard it can be to navigate high school without tuning in to rumors. Ultimately, though, she trusts me enough to nod.

I tell her about Paulie's lost memories of Drew. Her eyes go wide.

"That's messed up," she says softly. I nod, biting my lower lip. She pokes my chin with a manicured finger. "Stop it." I stop biting my lip, then immediately start again. Maryam rolls her eyes and pulls a dark red tube out of her purse. She holds my chin while she applies the contents to my lips with an expert hand. "If you don't leave it alone now, you'll have lip stain on your teeth all day," she mutters.

"Are we sure Paulie's even in school?" I ask, trying not to let my lips touch while the stain sets. She shakes her head.

"I'm not sure who's here right now," she says. "That cop from the cafeteria has been pulling people out of my classes all day."

"What? Shit." I didn't notice it happening. I was too busy trying to figure out what my stupid *feelings* are, when I should have been paying attention to the goddamn police investigation. "Shit. Is Roya here today? You guys have bio together, right?" I ask.

"She's not here," she says, laying a gentle, magic-warm hand on my arm. "We usually have bio, but she's out sick or something. Don't worry about her."

"I'm not worried about her," I say, too fast. Mercifully, she ignores me. She keeps her hand on my arm, though, sending a wave of calm through me.

"Have you talked to Marcelina?"

My stomach twists with guilt. "Not for a few days," I say, and Maryam frowns at me.

"Are you guys fighting?"

"No," I answer truthfully. "I guess I've just been really distracted, and I haven't seen her since lunch the other day."

"When Iris went with the cop?"

"Yeah. That cop. I don't know, Maryam." The bell rings, but we both ignore it. All around us, people are hurrying, scooping up backpacks and shoving past each other to get into classrooms, but Maryam is frowning at me, so I don't budge. It's her "I don't know how to say a thing but I want to say it but what if you get mad at me for saying it" frown. It's a frown I've been seeing from her a lot lately.

"What's up?" I ask gently.

"You should talk to Marcelina," she says, her eyes sliding away from mine. "I think she needs you right now."

"Why?" I ask, but Maryam shakes her head.

"She's having a hard time," she says. "But it's not my news to share."

We hug each other tighter than usual and then head off to class. While the teacher hands out the day's worksheets, I sneak my phone under my desk and text Iris.

Meet you after school? Soccer field?

Her response is so immediate that I wonder if maybe she had her own phone under her desk—if she was about to text me again.

Yes yes yes.

I also text Marcelina, asking if she wants to hang out soon, telling her that I miss her face. She doesn't reply, because Marcelina never has her phone out during class. I still wait, though. I wait, and I fidget, and I try not to bite my lip.

At the end of the class, I turn in a blank worksheet. I don't even put my name on it. Roya's not here. Paulie's not here. Something's going on with Marcelina. It feels like things are falling apart.

I just don't know *why*.

I slip out of fourth period five minutes early by telling the teacher I need to use the restroom. She waves me off without a hall pass. I wait outside of Marcelina's class and catch her as she's walking out the door.

"Hey, are you okay?" I wince even as I'm saying it, but then again, Marcelina's never been one for subtlety.

"No. Definitely not," she replies. See what I mean?

"What's up?" We walk toward the senior lockers and I grab her textbooks so she can use both hands to open her sticky combination lock. She bangs on it twice with her fist before it pops open.

"I'm all fucked up, Alexis." Her voice is calm, but one of her eyes is twitching. She's hardly wearing any eyeliner at all, and she's only got four earrings in each ear. She looks like half of a Marcelina. "Like, really fucked up."

"What is it?" I hand her books over and she shoves them ungently into her locker. She braces herself against the shelves.

"I wasn't sure until this morning, but now I've definitely got it figured out." She looks up at me and I notice the heavy layer of concealer under her eyes. The thick makeup has settled into creases, making her look older than she is. "I can't forget anything."

"What?" I feel like I've misheard or misunderstood, like I missed a stair. "What does that mean?"

"It means," she says slowly, "I can't forget *anything*. I remember everything that's happened to me in the last . . ." She counts on her fingers. "Five days."

"I don't get it," I say. I move out of the way of her locker-neighbor. Marcelina slams her own locker door shut and spins the lock, and we start toward the cafeteria. She's walking fast, not looking at anyone we pass. Her eyes stay on the linoleum like she's watching for landmines.

"Normally you forget like . . . half the things that happen in a day, right?" she says, her voice low and urgent. I shrug. I guess I know what she means, although I never really thought of it that way before. "Well, I can remember it all. In like . . . really intense detail. Everything. Even my dreams, Lex. Not just the highlights, like when you describe a dream to someone and you jump between the good parts. I can remember every moment of every dream I've had in the past week. Every feeling. Every person who appeared in the fucked-up situations my brain invents while I'm asleep." She shakes her head hard. "All of it. I can remember all of it."

"Your—wow," I say. I think back over my own past five nights with a growing sense of unease. I haven't had a single dream. Not even the kind that I don't really remember but that leaves a lingering cloud of emotion for me to wake up to—not even that. "That sounds intense."

"Iris thinks it's the spell," she mutters. "She said that 'every action we take has a reaction, like ripples in a pond,' and that she can 'feel the ripples running back along the threads of the spell every time we sever one.'" She says it all in a perfect imitation of Iris's voice. The pitch and cadence are unmistakable: it's Iris's voice coming out of Marcelina's mouth.

It's eerie.

"Whoa," I whisper. "That was . . . interesting."

"I know," she says in her normal voice. "I guess when you can remember every single inflection of how someone talks, it gets easier to do impressions."

I loop an arm around her shoulder. "I'll talk to Iris, okay?" I tell her. I try to imagine what Maryam or Roya would say to make her feel better. Not to make her feel like things are solved, but to make her feel better about the fact that everything is messed up. "We'll figure it out."

"She's already trying," Marcelina answers, but her voice is a little softer. Her face is a little calmer. She bumps her hip into mine and almost smiles. "You don't have to fix it, you know. We're already working together. All of us."

Oh, I think. *They've been talking about it. Without me.* I try to push aside the pang of hurt. Of course they talk without me sometimes, that's what people do. They talk to each other without me sometimes. That's normal. It doesn't mean that they're excluding me. *Be normal about this*, I scold myself.

"I know," I lie, then redirect. "Are you okay?"

"No. I'm freaked out and I didn't sleep last night because I didn't want to remember my dreams all day. But . . . we'll figure it out," she says, echoing me in an exact imitation of my voice.

"Okay, but you can't do that voice thing. I can only handle so much weirdness in a day," I say, and she lets out a small laugh.

"That's the least-weird part of this whole thing," she says. "You're just gonna have to deal with it."

14.

"I'M SORRY I'M SORRY I'M SORRY I'M SORRY—" I hear Iris long before I see her. It's after school and I'm sitting in the grass at the edge of the soccer field, watching the endless practices. Boys' JV, Boys' Varsity, Girls' JV, Girls' Varsity, and Junior Leaguers all practice on various parts of our high school's gigantic field. I can never tell which team is which—unless my brother's one of the people kicking the ball. He's not at practice today, because of something to do with a chemistry project he's trying to finish at the last minute. As a result, I'm watching the various soccer practices with a kind of removed disinterest. It feels a little like watching waves crashing at the beach: there's movement and noise and things I don't quite understand, but I can spot patterns and pretend I get it.

Iris skids onto the grass next to me, still apologizing, and there it is again—that uncertainty. I know what the right way to respond is, and I also know how I *could* respond. I could give her the cold shoulder, make her explain. I could yell at her that *sorry isn't good enough*. I could do it, and then I wouldn't have to face my mistake. I could blame her.

But then I look up and see her stricken face, and my conscience kicks me hard in the gut. She doesn't deserve that shit from me.

"Hey, it's okay," I say, and I wrap my arms around her. "I'm not mad."

"Really?" She pulls back and wipes at her eyes, smearing mascara stripes across her freckled cheeks, and my conscience kicks me again for even considering lashing out at her.

"Yeah, really," I say, smiling. She smiles back, her relief palpable. "I get it. You were worried. It's okay. I didn't even get in that much trouble."

"I just . . . I didn't know where you were," she says, "and with the police around and everything. I was scared that maybe they were talking to you, or maybe . . ." She looks around and closes her mouth abruptly.

"I get it," I say. She's doing that thing where she's been going over what she should say all day, and my saying that I don't need to hear an explanation doesn't change the fact that she needs to explain. She doesn't need to do it for me, but for herself.

"Can we go somewhere else?" she asks. I raise my eyebrows, and she stands up, brushing grass off her butt. "I want to talk about stuff, but I don't want to talk about it here." Her voice is soft—she's not being the bossy Iris I know and love. She's being hesitant. She's still worried that she did something to make me angry with her, so she's being something less than what she usually is. I hate it. I hate that she thinks she can't be everything she always is, just because she thinks I might be mad.

And then I follow her eyeline, because even if she's being gentle with me, it's not like her to avoid eye contact. She's usually aggressive as hell about eye contact. I turn to look where she's looking, and I see what she's seeing, and then I want to leave too. Because it's the cop—the one with the short gray hair and the long nose. She's standing at the edge of the soccer field, maybe halfway across the grass from us. The sun glints off her handcuffs. She's got her arms folded, and I can't tell if she's watching the players or if she's watching us.

Either way, she's too close for us to talk about what we need to talk about. She's way too close.

We walk together, looking over our shoulders the whole time, and wind up behind the school in one of those spots that seems built for skulking. There are no windows looking out into this little alley between the classrooms and the chain-link fence that marks the boundary of the campus. Cigarette butts litter the ground, and there's a used condom just on the other side of the fence. I look away from the condom, but it lingers in my mind, bumping up against memories that I'd rather not relive.

"What's up?" I ask Iris. She lets her backpack thud to the ground.

"Okay," she says, and then she takes a deep breath and says it again. "Okay."

"Okay?"

"Okay, so, something's going on."

I lean against the fence, bouncing against the chain link. "I know," I say. Iris gives me a confused look. "I mean, I know about one thing that's going on. Maybe it's not the same thing you mean? But I know about Paulie and Marcelina."

"And Roya," Iris adds, and now it's my turn to be confused. She looks uncertain. "Did she not tell you?"

"Um, no?" There's my asshole-voice again. I don't know where this is coming from, this anger. I could let it trip me up, but instead, I cross my arms and just try not to feel embarrassed at my ignorance. I try not to wonder why Roya didn't talk to me about whatever's going on. I try not to wonder why she talked to Iris instead.

"Well, anyway, I figured it out this morning," Iris continues, blatantly ignoring the uncomfortable moment. She's not going to tell me what's happening with Roya, then. I usually really admire how Iris and Maryam both refuse to gossip, but right now, it's the most annoying thing about either of them. I just want to know what's going *on*.

"I went over some of my notes and I realized that there's a correlation between some of the—well, okay, let me back up. See, after I cast the spell on the, um." Her voice drops to a whisper. "The body? I felt like I was being pulled in a bunch of different directions. It's gotten a little better every day, and at first I thought that I was just getting used to it. You know, like. Getting stronger or something." She looks uncomfortable. “I guess I wanted to believe that I was growing, somehow. Getting more powerful. But then I started talking to everyone and I realized that every time I was feeling better, someone else was feeling worse.” She clenches her fist as she talks, but her voice stays low. “And then last night, I got a text from Paulie right after you guys got rid of the leg, and I realized that I wasn’t just getting used to feeling bad. I really was feeling better. Because you got rid of one of the parts.”

I shake my head at her. Poor Iris—she’s so ambitious. The idea that she thought she was getting better when she really wasn’t is kind of heartbreaking. “That doesn’t make any sense,” I whisper.

“It does, though,” she says. “See, my magic is what’s holding all the pieces of Josh separate. And it’s a lot, you know? That spell was a lot. I’d never done anything like that before. It’s . . . it’s all of us, all bound together, stretching one spell to its breaking point to try to make someone *disappear*.” She rolls her wrist across her hip, pushing a rubber band from her wrist onto her fingers. She stretches it out tight. “Like this but a million times more complicated.”

“Okay, that makes sense,” I lie.

“Shut up, no it doesn’t, but just. Listen.” She holds the rubber band up and stretches it as far as she can. “Here’s what I think is happening. When you get rid of one of the body parts, my part of the spell is over, and the magic kind of . . . breaks. I can feel it. It pulls really tight, and then it *snaps*. And then the recoil hits us.” She flicks her thumb, and the rubber band snaps against her palm. Her pale skin reddens immediately. "This is a really powerful spell, and it's connected to all of us, and it's super volatile. When one of us gets rid of a body part, I think we sever our connection to it. The magic breaks, and snaps back on us. I think we're all losing things because the spell is doing something to each of us every time we break part of it."

I shake my head. "That's never happened before," I say.

"We've never done anything like this before," she answers. "We've never . . . we've never killed anyone before." She can't look into my eyes, and I know what she isn't saying.

It's not that *we* killed someone. It's that *I* killed someone.

I used someone. I lied to him. I pretended that I was ready for something I wasn't, and I pretended to be someone I'm not. I took the part of me that knew I was only going to hurt myself by making myself do something I didn't want to, and I pushed it so far down that it turned into this. It turned into Josh being dead.

I used him, and I lied to him, and I killed him, and now all of my friends are dealing with the consequences. An awful thought occurs to me: What if my friends weren't helping deal with the consequences? What if all the losses weren't distributed across our group? If I had tried to use magic to get rid of the body all by myself . . . would that magic snap right back and kill me, too?

And is it worth it to risk that recoil if it means saving my friends?

I decide to think about that later. I can't put that on Iris. It's a decision I'll have to make on my own. But there is one thing I should tell her about, no matter what I decide. "There's something else that's been going on," I say, and she waits while I figure out how to explain it. "I think I've been . . . hurting people?"

"What do you mean?"

I tell her about the girl with the nosebleed in the cafeteria, and my bruise at the reservoir, and the blood that oozed from Gina's eye. I tell her about a half dozen other moments I've noticed—moments when I'm not sure if someone is just having an accident near me, or if I'm causing them injury somehow. "I'm not doing any of it on purpose. It's just kind of *happening*," I explain.

"Okay," she says. She tugs on one ginger curl. "Well, that makes sense, with all the tension."

"You think it's stress-induced?" I ask doubtfully.

"No, no, not like that. The magical tension. Maybe because you did the original, uh . . . thing?" I'm grateful that she doesn't say "murder." Iris doesn't usually mince words, but she's being gentle with me. She's being careful. "All of the magic that's being used to hold the body in pieces is pulling on me, right? Well, it's got to be pulling on you, too. And that recoil is probably hitting you really hard."

She pulls on the rubber band around her wrist again, harder this time than before. I flinch as it snaps against her skin. The place it strikes her turns red, but then she pulls the whole thing off and shows me the red mark it left on the opposite side of her wrist, where it dug into the skin as she pulled on it. She continues with her explanation, running a finger across the red welt the rubber band has left. "The tension and the recoil are both going to be hard on you, and something in that has to be making you do stuff by accident. I mean. That's all just a theory, but you've definitely got a lot of"—she gestures vaguely—"a lot of residual magic pulling on you. It looks like you're getting yanked in a bunch of directions all at once. Have you been hurting anyone on purpose, or is it like, when you're stressed and not paying attention?"

I remember how I tripped before hurting Gina. I remember giving myself the bruise while I was thinking about Roya, and watching the cop when that poor freshman got the nosebleed. "Stressed and not paying attention," I answer. "Definitely that one."

"Well, there you go," she says authoritatively. "The parts of the spell that are tangled up around you are tense as hell. It's snapping when you get stressed out, and it's hurting people around you by accident." I would be skeptical—after all, we don't really know how *any* of this works—but then, it's Iris. She's bossy and overbearing sometimes, but she's brilliant and she understands magic better than I do. And I trust her, and she sounds certain.

"I don't want you to feel like you have to have all the answers," I say, hesitant. "But we should try to figure out how to fix this."

Thankfully, she nods. "I don't think we can prevent everyone from losing things as they get rid of pieces. But we *can* keep your problem from escalating. For that, it just stands to reason that we have to get rid of all the pieces as fast as we can. There'll be consequences for the rest of us, but there were always going to be consequences for us. At least this way you won't, you know. Slip up." She nods, and I nod back, and with that, we agree to stick with the crappy answer for now.

"So what do we do?" I ask softly.

With a grim smile, Iris unzips her backpack and pulls out two gallon-sized ziplock bags. Each one contains one of Josh Harper's hands.

"What do we do?" she repeats. She drops the ziplock bags to the ground and then looks back up at me. "We make sure."

When Pop and Dad met, Pop was trying to make it as a musician. He was the lead singer for a prog-rock band called WYLDFYR2. I guess they were supposed to be called WYLDFYR3, but the guy who printed their T-shirts messed up and they stuck with it. I've never known him to be anything but bald, but before I was born, he had long wavy hair down to his butt and these big hair-sprayed bangs. He wore eyeliner and stuck his tongue out a lot in photos. Dad met Pop after a show and told him that when you say "WYLDFYR2" out loud, it sounds like "wildfart" and Pop couldn't stop laughing and I guess the rest was history. Even though there are tons of pictures, I still have a pretty hard time imagining Dad at a show *or* Pop onstage.

Even harder to imagine? Pop drove a van. Technically, he lived in the van, although he also talks a lot about crashing on people's couches and doesn't like it when I say, "Pop lived in a van." The van had this amazing airbrushed mural on the side—it was a wizard standing on top of a mountain, doing battle with a dragon, and a half-naked Viking-god was riding the dragon. It was awesome. In the pictures I've seen of the mural, the wizard has his arms over his head and lightning is shooting out of his staff and one of his hands is holding a big fireball.

That's kind of how Iris looks now. She looks like the wizard, except instead of fire and lightning, she's got a thousand threads of magic. Honestly, I think she'd beat the wizard. I love it when she does this. Her magic is always really showy, so she doesn't do it all that often. She's the only one of us who can see her own magic, and I think it embarrasses her to use it in front of people. It doesn't really bother the rest of us to use ours, because we can't see how flashy it is, so it feels small and subtle and private more often than not. But Iris gets flustered. She sees something huge inside herself, and instead of embracing it, she looks away.

But when she does embrace it—man, it's awesome. Literally awesome. Not awesome like "cool" or "big" or "loud," but awesome as in, it puts me into a state of *awe*. Wonder. She circles her hands over her head and as she does it, blazing threads of white gather around her spread fingers like cotton candy. They cling to her arms too, sliding up around her shoulders like a bright mantle. Her eyes are bright white, and she watches her hands with her lower lip between her teeth as a fat spool of crackling white builds between them. When she's got exactly enough for whatever she has in mind, she lowers her arms in front of her like she's about to throw the spool of white power at the ground. But she doesn't throw it; she holds it there, like a ball of lightning between her fists. The magic is still, static. The air feels heavy. She twists her fingers just so, and the threads shift into some subtly different configuration. She nods, satisfied.

I wonder what it would be like if I could see my magic. Would I be able to do the amazing things Iris can? She has so much control, so much strategy, whereas I just kind of feel things out as I go. She can fine-tune so many little details, all because she can watch what the threads are doing before she uses them. But she's also obsessed, because she can see everything she makes.

Still, I can't help admiring both her obsession and her control. If I could see my own power, what could I achieve? What would I become?

Iris interrupts my train of thought by swinging both of her arms in a shallow arc, stretching her magic wide. Then she aims her power at the hands that are spread out on the ground in front of her, and she lets go.

Her magic falls onto the hands in a deluge of electric

white. A wintry smell fills the air, like snow and ice and lightning. As I watch, the pink flesh of Josh Harper's fingers turns pale, then gray, then black. Goose bumps rise on my arms as cracks spiderweb across Josh's palms. Frost spreads across the ground between us. Iris doesn't stop until the hands are unrecognizable.

"Whoa," she says, staring down at the fruits of her labor. A sheen of sweat has broken out across her forehead.

"Are you okay?" I ask, and she nods. "Do you feel . . . different?"

"Not yet," she says. "But I'm not really done yet, am I?" She wipes her forehead and gestures to her backpack, which is closer to me than it is to her. I grab it and reach inside.

Textbooks. Notebooks. Her journal. Graphing calculator. A loose pen.

A hammer.

I haul it out. There's tape across the handle. Iris's last name is written on it in blue marker. "Is this yours?" I ask.

"It's my dad's," she answers. She holds out her hand, and I give her the hammer. She stares at it for a moment. "Well," she says to the hammer. "Here goes."

She crouches in front of the hands, lifts the hammer, and lets it drop. The super-frozen flesh of one hand shatters into a million pieces. She smashes the other hand, one finger at a time, and then she falls backward onto her butt with an *oof*.

"How do you feel?" I ask, and she takes stock before answering.

"Normal?" She shrugs. "I don't know. Better than I did a few minutes ago, to be honest."

I gingerly step over the pile of Josh-shards and sit next to her. We stare at the shattered flesh on the ground for a few minutes before I break the silence. "I'm sorry to have gotten you mixed up in all this," I say.

She shrugs again. "You're my best friend. I mean, you all are. I know every one of you would do the same thing for me." She looks up at me. "Hey, what about you? Have you noticed anything different? Missing?"

I nudge a half fingernail with the edge of my shoe. "Kind of," I say hesitantly. "I wasn't sure if it was anything. I mean, I'm still not. It might just be a coincidence. But . . ." I hesitate, and she nudges me, and I just say it. "I haven't had any dreams."

"Since when?"

"Since I buried his head in the woods. So . . . three days ago?"

"And you're sure that you're not just forgetting them?" She grimaces as she says it, knowing the answer already.

"I'm positive," I confirm. "It almost doesn't even feel like I'm sleeping. I just close my eyes and then when I open them again, *hours* have gone by."

"Roya can't cry," she whispers. I look up in surprise. "And you can't dream, and Marcelina can't forget."

I'm about to ask her about Roya—what does that mean? She can't cry? But my breath catches in my throat. I'm looking at Iris, but she looks . . . different.

"Iris." My voice breaks on her name. "Your freckles."

"What?" She frowns at me. "What about them?"

I swallow hard. I don't want to tell her. But she's going to see for herself soon enough. "They're gone."

Her face goes pale, and it's so much more drastic than usual because there's nothing, nothing at all, covering her cheeks. She grabs at her backpack and roots around inside it until she finds a compact. She opens it up and looks at her face in the palm-sized mirror.

She drops the mirror and uses her fist to muffle her own scream. "No," she says, "no, no, no, they can't—no, they can't be *gone*?!"

I'll admit it: my first thought is that she should calm down. I get that her freckles are important to her, that she's spent a long time learning how to love them. I get that they're basically her defining feature, and that her face looks completely different now and that's scary. I get it. But I can't help thinking that it's kind of a mercy, that she's only losing freckles when everyone else has lost things that are so much bigger. I immediately regret the thought: if my entire face changed, I would be freaked out too. But whether the thought is right or wrong, I still think that she's lost something smaller than everyone else.

But then she lifts a hand to her face. She's still looking in the mirror. Her hand starts to glow, and power sparks between her fingers wildly. She looks between the mirror and her hand, shakes her fingers. The magic grows until it's almost too bright to look at.

"What are you doing?" I ask her.

"I'm trying to fix it," she snaps. "But I must have drained myself freezing the hands. I can't get my . . . you know. I can't get it to go."

I squint at the bright nimbus of her hand. It's blinding. When I look away, spots dance in my vision. "Iris, what are you talking about? You're holding the freaking sun over there. Can't you—*oh.*"

For the first time in our friendship, I figure something out before Iris does.

She can't see it.

She can't see it, and she's spent so long relying on seeing it that she doesn't know how to just *feel* it.

"Iris, stop pushing," I say softly. "You've got a lot of magic around you right now, and you're going to hurt yourself if you don't stop."

"No," she says, her voice cracking. "No, I'm—there isn't any—I'm not. I can't." She won't look at me. She's surrounded by a bright halo of magic, and she's pushing more out around herself every second, and not a single freckle has reappeared.

I reach over and gently, carefully, gingerly wrap my hands around hers. I close her fingers into fists and force myself to look into her starbright eyes. "You have to stop," I whisper.

Her magic fades, and she stares at me with wide, desperate eyes. I can't believe I thought, even for that brief moment, that she hadn't lost all that much. Even if she could still see her magic—even then, she would have lost something that tells her who she is, that helps her anchor herself.

Iris leans forward and her head drops onto my shoulder. I'm still holding both of her fists as she lets out the first sob. She shudders against me. She weeps on me with a desperate kind of loss I don't know how to contain; the only thing I can do is be there for her to lean against, so that's what I do. I hold her as she chokes on her own tears, and I watch over her shoulder as the pieces of Josh start to melt away.

15.

ROYA SLIDES INTO THE SEAT NEXT TO ME ON Friday at lunch as if everything isn't broken. Her eyes are on the door to the cafeteria, where the gray-haired police officer is standing, watching the room. She makes a disgusted noise in the officer's direction, then grabs my burrito with one hand and a few of Iris's fries with the other. "I'm starving," she says through a mouthful of rice and beans.

"Me too," I say, and take the burrito back. She makes puppy-dog eyes at me, and I hiss at her like a pissed-off cat. "Eat your own lunch first, you vulture."

"Come on," she whines, half-serious. "I'm starving. I'm a starving athlete. I need your carbs."

"Get your own carbs," I say, holding my lunch out of her reach.

"She's desperate. Coach has been brutal lately," Iris says, dousing her fries in ketchup and getting some on Roya's reaching fingers. Her voice is flat in a way that sounds like more than just exhaustion. I search her face, which is heavy with foundation. She won't look at me.

"It's your last meet tomorrow, right?" Maryam asks, and they both nod. Iris looks a little sad about it, but Roya looks thrilled. She's an amazing swimmer, but she kind of hates being on the team. I think she'd like it if she were a little more passionate about it or if the coach were a little *less* passionate about it—but as it stands, she's ready to be out of the water. Still, it's her last meet, and we shouldn't miss it. "I'll be there," Maryam says. "Alexis, want me to give you a ride?"

"Sure," I say, even though I had been planning to walk. I know how to drive, but I don't have a car and I'm not allowed to drive the family car since an incident involving a closed garage door that I thought was open. I'm at the mercy of my friends to get me from A to B. It sucks, but also, it's nice to ride around with them. It's nice to have time together like that.

"Me too, me too, me too," Paulie sings as she tosses her salad onto the table. Maryam rolls her eyes and throws up her hands.

"Fine," she says. "I'll drive both of you. But, Paulie, you gotta be at Alexis's house when I get there. I'm not playing bus driver, okay?"

"Sure thing, Mom," Paulie says sweetly, sliding into the last empty chair at the table and giving Maryam a squeeze and a kiss on the cheek. She's giving off greaser vibes today with her slicked-back hair, white tee, and boyfriend jeans; the moment her butt lands in a chair, Maryam leans forward and starts touching up her brows, muttering about how they need to be darker and fuller to complete the look. Paulie sits patiently, but she peeks at me out of the corner of one eye and gives me a wink.

"I wish I could go," Marcelina mutters.

"It's okay," Roya says, wiping her ketchup-fingers on a napkin with a grimace. "We'll come by the Crispy Chicken after to give you the play-by-play." Marcelina smiles at her, even though missing the meet isn't exactly what's bothering her about having to work a Saturday-morning shift at the Crispy Chicken while the rest of us are cheering by the pool.

"I'll hook you guys up with curly fries," Marcelina promises. Her eyes slide from Roya to Iris, and they linger. Roya and I follow her gaze. Paulie's eyes strain even as she tries to hold still for Maryam's brow touch-ups.

Usually, we let Iris be. When something's wrong, we let her decide when and if she wants to talk about it. We don't push her the same way we push each other, because she's got so many different levels of thinking and feeling and analyzing going on below the surface, and she has to sort them all out before she can talk about things. Most of the time, we let her come to us.

But this is bigger than the usual stuff she goes through. And we've all been exchanging glances and hoping that someone else would bring it up first. Marcelina is watching Iris eat french fries, and we're all watching Marcelina watch Iris, and nobody says anything for a long beat. Marcelina purses her lips and I can see her deciding that enough's enough.

She clears her throat. "So. Iris." She trails off awkwardly, then gestures to Iris's face. The foundation there is matte, thick, and heavy. She's not wearing any other makeup. She's just . . . hiding.

"We gotta talk about it," Roya says bluntly.

Iris picks up five french fries and shoves them all into her mouth, then makes a helpless series of gestures that translate to *alas-I-can't-talk-my-mouth-is-full*. It's a blatant Roya move to get out of answering, one that doesn't fit right on Iris. Roya can get away with using gross humor to deflect us, because it's kind of her thing. On Iris, it seems like a grotesque masquerade. Roya's brow furrows. She chews on her lower lip for a moment, then catches Maryam's glare and switches to chewing on a fingernail.

"We *gotta* talk about it," Paulie echoes. Her voice is muted because Maryam still has a grip on her chin, but everyone hears her loud and clear. I try very hard to be invisible.

"I think so too," Marcelina says softly. "I think we have to talk about it because if we don't, I don't know what will happen, but I'm pretty sure I'll explode."

The bite of burrito in my mouth turns to cement. I swallow hard and pass the rest of my lunch to Roya. I know Marcelina didn't mean "explode" like how Josh exploded, but still. My appetite is gone.

And they're right. We have to talk about this.

Maryam releases Paulie and raps her knuckles on the table. "Out with it, all of you. Enough of this. We don't keep secrets from each other."

"Fine," Iris says, her voice taut. "Fine. We'll talk about it."

She steeples her fingers on the table, not looking directly at anyone. She goes into tutor mode, neatly sidestepping the question of what's going on with her face. She explains the whiplash effect that she told me about the day before—the way that the magic is moving, taking things. Finally, when she can't talk around it anymore, she holds a hand out to Roya.

"Roya, take it off," she says. She grits her teeth as Roya grabs her hand. A glow suffuses their clasped hands, and then the thick foundation on Iris's face is thinning, thinner, vanished.

The other girls gasp. She doesn't look that different from how she looked with the foundation—maybe a little less orangey—but still. I don't think any of them really realized what she looked like without her freckles. I know I didn't, not until I saw it for myself.

She's blank. She's still gorgeous, but she looks empty—not just in that her skin is an unbroken expanse of cream. There's something missing in her eyes, too. She looks miserable, like she knows that the thing she loves most about herself is so far out of reach that there's simply no hope of retrieving it.

"Oh no," Roya whispers. "Oh god, Iris, I'm so sorry."

My fault.

The tears fall, but Iris holds her chin high, and when she speaks, her voice is steady. "It's fine," she says. "It's not fine, that was a lie, but . . . it'll be okay."

Paulie looks at Maryam. "Can you . . . ?"

Maryam shakes her head. "I tried. I can't put them back. I can make them show up, but they fade right away."

Iris squeezes Roya's hand, then lets it go. "I, um. I should tell you guys about the rest of it too."

And then she looks at me. She's not saying anything, but her lips are white and her eyes are wide and her nostrils are flaring and I can see it, I can see the cost of saying it out loud. I can see the toll it will take on her. I raise my eyebrows and hesitate because maybe I'm misunderstanding—but then she nods at me.

"Please," she whispers.

I look around the table. "She can't see her magic anymore," I say. My voice is shaking. I make myself meet all of their eyes, make myself see their horror at Iris's loss.

"I'm going to have to relearn it all," Iris says. Her hands are knotted together in front of her, the knuckles stark white. "I'm going to have to figure out how to do it all without looking. I can't do anything right now, hardly. Last night I figured out how to warm up my hands, but I burned myself a little." She shows us a red patch on her palm.

Paulie takes a deep, shuddering breath. "I lost my memories of Andrew," she says. She doesn't say that she'll be fine, and I'm oddly grateful that she's not trying to pretend it's okay. Roya and Marcelina look surprised. Maryam doesn't.

"I can't forget anything anymore," Marcelina whispers. "My head is so full. I'm learning how to deal with it, but . . . it's so much, you know?"

My fault, all my fault.

"I can't cry," Roya says. She says it casually as she's finishing my burrito, but she won't make eye contact with anyone. "I went back to the reservoir like we talked about, and I dove down and got the bag with the arm, and I got rid of it for real. With my magic. And then afterward, I was fighting with my mom because I got home after curfew, and I felt like crying, and I *wanted* to cry, and I couldn't. So I went online and found one of those videos that always makes me cry? And I *couldn't.* I felt all the feelings, but I couldn't *cry.*" Her voice breaks and I wonder if she wants to cry now. "This sounds stupid. It sounds like it's not a big deal, but it feels like a big deal."

"I mean, if anything sounds like not a big deal, it's fucking *freckles,*" Iris says, and everyone laughs, but Marcelina and Maryam both shake their heads at the same time.

"It's a big deal," Maryam says. "It's all a big deal. You all lost things." She looks at me. "What about you, Alexis?"

I shake my head. "It's not important."

"It's important," Roya says, and when I look at her, she's staring at me with eyes that would be crying.

"I think, um. I think I can't dream." I say it to everyone, but I'm looking at Roya. She closes her eyes for a second, and when she opens them again, they're still dry, and she looks stricken by it. "I go to sleep and it's like I close my eyes for a few seconds and then open them again and it's morning. And I can't tell if I'm tired or not? I don't know," I finish awkwardly. "I—I don't know."

We sit under the weight of all the things we've lost. We look at our hands and we look at our food and we look at the scratched surface of the table. We look at those little things, because it's too much to look at each other and see the magnitude of what's happening to us.

"This is so fucked up," Paulie whispers. "This is really *bad*."

My fault, my fault, my fault.

"So what do we do?" Marcelina asks.

I straighten my back like Iris does before she says hard things. I clench my jaw like Roya does when she's being brave. I summon the certainty that Marcelina brings to every word she says. I imagine that I have even a tenth of Paulie's courage and confidence. I will myself to speak with Maryam's quiet authority. If I can be anything like my friends, I can do this.

I can do this.

"Here's what you do," I say. "You give it all back to me. I know that I can't fix what you've all already lost, but I swear to god I wouldn't have let any of you help me if I'd known this would happen, and I can stop it from happening more, so. Give it all back to me, and I'll get rid of all the . . . pieces. On my own." I look each of them in the eye, making sure that they're listening. "I'll deal with whatever happens as a result. It's my mess, and I really appreciate you guys trying to help me clean it up, but it's hurting you. And I'm not going to let it hurt you any more than it already has."

They look at each other, then back at me. Maryam's got her hands folded in front of her on the table, neutral but still present, ready to be here for us. Her fingernails are silver today, and so is her eyeliner, and I know she must have been up late perfecting her technique to make them match so perfectly. It's comforting to see something beautiful that she did with her magic, just because she loves it.

That's what I think, instead of thinking about the thing I just committed to doing. I think of Maryam's fingernails. I can't be scared as long as I'm thinking of her fingernails.

Paulie clears her throat. "No."

"'No' what?" I ask, still watching the light play over the shining silver of Maryam's nails. There are little sparkles in the polish that I didn't notice before.

"No, I'm not giving you my piece," Paulie says. Behind her, someone drops their lunch tray. People laugh and do the whole sarcastic-clapping thing, but none of us look. "It's mine. I took it and I don't have to give it back just because you say so."

"Me either," Roya says sharply. I look up to find her glaring at me.

"Same," Marcelina says. She pops a french fry into her mouth and levels a challenging stare at me.

"Yeah," Iris says. "I mean . . . I already did mine, but I wouldn't give them back if I still had them."

"You guys, come on." I try to make my voice sound like Pop's voice does when he's being lawyer-y, but it doesn't quite work. "This is hurting you. It's hurting you all so much, and it's not going to hurt you anymore. It's time for me to handle my mistake on my own."

"Fuck that," Paulie spits. "We aren't going to let you kill yourself to protect us."

"I don't think—"

"Yeah, and screw you for thinking we would," Roya says, and she sounds just as mad as Paulie.

"You idiot," Marcelina says. She gets up and stands behind my chair, wrapping her arms around me. She feels soft and strong and furious. "You big stupid jerk, why the hell would you even say something like that?"

I awkwardly squeeze her elbows, then extricate myself. "I don't think it'll be that bad," I say, and they look at each other like I'm being willfully ignorant.

"It would probably be that bad," Maryam says. "I mean, look at the combined effects so far. Imagine if just *one* person lost what you've all lost. Their old memories, their dreams, their tears, their ability to forget new things, *and* the person who they've come to understand themselves to be." She looks at Iris on this last note, and Iris's eyes turn glassy. "And that's only half of the changes," Maryam continues. "Whatever else happens . . . all of it together would turn you into a completely new person, wouldn't it?"

"It's like a Ship of Theseus," Iris whispers.

"A what?" Roya asks.

"Yeah," Marcelina says, nodding fast, excited. "Yeah, it's totally like that."

"What is that?" Paulie asks.

"It's this thing," Iris says, looking at Marcelina for confirmation that it is indeed a thing, "where you have a ship, right? And you replace the sails, but it's still the same ship. And then you replace some of the planks, but it's still the same ship. And then you replace all the oars, but it's still the same ship. And then you replace some of the other planks . . ."

"But it's still the same ship?" Paulie interjects dryly.

"Is it?" Marcelina asks, grinning. Paulie's brow furrows. "It's like a thought experiment. When does the ship stop being the original ship and turn into a whole new ship? Is it when there's just one old plank left? Or two? Or three? Or is it the second you replace the sails?"

"I think I get it," Roya says. "So . . . we're all still *us*, even though we lost things. But maybe if Alexis took this all on herself like a big stupid *idiot*, she'd lose too many things, and then she wouldn't be herself anymore."

"Okay," I say, half-annoyed. "I get it, you think I'm wrong."

"We think you had the worst idea in the history of ideas," Marcelina corrects me. "We think you're the most wrong that anyone has ever been."

"But we still love you," Roya adds. "And we still want you to be *you*. Not whatever might be left of you after you try to take this whole thing on by yourself." She bumps her shoulder against mine, and I feel heat climbing my neck.

"This sucks and it's really hard, but we're in it together," Iris says, and her voice carries a firm finality that settles over the group like a thick fog. "Right?"

"Right," we all say, sort of together. I feel like I'm going to cry, so I reach out my hands and let a tiny spark of my magic go out to each of the girls in turn. It's not much, but it should give them a little bit of energy, a little bit of joy, a little bit of warmth. They each smile at me as they feel it.

"Besides," Iris says, "we're going to bring him back, right? Once we've gotten rid of all the pieces and the heart is beating again, we can bring Josh back, and then maybe we'll all get the things we lost back too."

"Oh shit, yeah," Paulie breathes. "That might work, huh?"

"I don't know, guys," Maryam says, her brow furrowing. "It's not like bringing him back is going to undo what you did. It's just going to—you know what?" She interrupts herself, shaking her head. "Never mind. It could work. It could totally work."

"It could totally work," Marcelina whispers.

"It could totally work," Roya echoes. "And then we can all go back to normal. Now, do you think I have time to get another burrito from the burrito-lady before the bell rings?" As if to answer her, the lunch bell drones, and the cafeteria is filled with the sound of scraping chairs and sneaker-squeaks and voices shouting about where to meet after school. "Damn it," she mutters.

We all say goodbye, and a moment like this should feel fraught and tense, but it doesn't. It feels comfortable. It feels like things are going to be okay. Like they're really, actually going to be okay.

Although, I have to admit, I don't think I'll ever go back to feeling normal again.

Roya gives me a hug before she goes, and I can smell her hair and her body wash, vanilla and mint. My fingertips tingle. I squeeze her close, and she doesn't let go of me either, and for the space of a caught breath I wonder if maybe she wants to hang on as badly as I do. I wonder if maybe—

But then she pulls away, and she says "See you tomorrow," and then she's stepping past me, and her hair is brushing my shoulder, and something in my chest aches.

"See you," I call. I don't turn to see her go, because even though things feel okay—even though I know I'm not alone—I don't know if she's going to look back at me. I'm so scared that she won't look back.

When I get out of my last class of the day, Paulie is waiting for me. She's leaning against a locker with sunglasses on and a lollipop stick between her teeth, and she looks so much like Danny Zuko that I stop dead in my tracks and start laughing. She grins, which makes it even worse, and then she looks over her sunglasses and winks at me, and there are tears streaming down my cheeks by the time I manage to catch my breath.

"Are you grounded?" she asks once I've regained my composure.

"No, why?"

"Because I want to finish what we started the other day," she says. "Vis-à-vis the thing in my trunk."

"I can probably go. Let me text my dads," I answer, even as

I'm trailing her out of the school and to her car. We stand outside the car with the doors open, letting the oven-hot interior air out for a couple of minutes. By the time it's cool enough to get inside without melting, I've already gotten a reply. Have fun, thanks for checking in, love you! from Pop, and Be home by ten from Dad. I send them a string of kissy-face emojis and we get into the car. Paulie blasts the air-conditioning, and I buckle up and brace myself for another traumatizing ride.

"How'd today feel?" I ask, and she shrugs.

"Good," she says. "Comfortable."

"Think you'll do this one again?"

She shakes her head, hesitates, then nods. "Probably. I mean, I look handsome as hell." She waggles her eyebrows. "Don't pretend you didn't notice."

"How could I miss it?" I laugh, and she gives me another wolfish grin.

We talk about college, and about New York, and about whether she'll stick with female pronouns when she leaves our little town. We talk about State, and about the apartment I'm going to share with Roya and Maryam, and about how hard it is to believe that there are only three weeks left until summer.

"I meant what I said last time we talked about this. I'm going to miss you a lot, you know," she says, no grin this time. I put my hand on her shoulder and she clears her throat. "All of you guys."

"We're going to miss you too. But we'll come visit you in

New York, and you'll show us Times Square and all the best restaurants and clubs and stuff."

"Yeah," she says with a small smile. "Yeah, that'll be great."

We spend the rest of the drive talking about how scary all of this is—how awful it is to be losing pieces of ourselves as we get rid of the pieces of Josh. It feels like we all just started really understanding who we are, and now that's all changing, and it's awful.

Talking about it doesn't make it better. But it's good to tell someone I'm scared. It makes it easier, knowing that I'm not alone.

We get to Barclay Rock and lapse into a heavy silence. Paulie pops the trunk and hands me Josh's arm. We walk into the trees and find the tree trunk we sat on last time. Paulie casts a net of magic out into the tree line, and then she spreads out a little blanket on the ground, and we sit on it and pick at the crunchy grass and wait.

"Do you think I can touch her this time?" Paulie asks.

"I don't think that's a great idea," I answer. "She's a coyote."

"*You* touched her," Paulie mutters. I glare at her and she holds her palms up. "Okay, okay, I was just asking."

When the coyote finally shows up, she pauses and smells the air for a full minute before approaching us. She looks a little less ragged than she did last time we saw her. A little less bony.

She sits near the edge of our picnic blanket and cocks her head. Her muzzle is brown, muddy-looking, and I wonder if it's dirt or dried blood I'm looking at. I hold out a hand and she growls, a low rumble in her throat, but she lowers her head and shoves it against my palm.

More meat for you and your pups, I tell her.

Why what smell who meat smell good meat why

I point to the arm, and she smells the full length of it before grabbing the wrist in her teeth and using it like a handle to tug the arm.

Wait, I tell her. *Come back?*

She looks up at me with golden eyes and drops the arm. She steps toward me and waits, her body tense.

I grab Paulie's hand. Her fingers shift under mine, trying to lace into the spaces between my knuckles, but I turn her hand over so her palm faces down. Out of the corner of my eye I see her look at me, but I don't take my gaze away from the coyote.

Slowly.

Slowly.

Easy now.

Careful.

I lift Paulie's hand to the top of the coyote's head.

As her fingertips land on fur, I let my thumb brush against the coyote's head. *Still, stay still, it's okay, she's good*, I say, as quietly as I know how to talk in this language that isn't talking. The coyote is unmoving, but rigid. Her ears twitch. *Thank you thank you thank you*, I say, and the coyote licks her chops, and I pull Paulie's hand away. Her fingers twine between mine, and I can feel her trembling.

The coyote is gone before we can say anything else. She takes the arm with her. Paulie lets out a long, slow exhalation. She's still got my hand in hers, and she's staring at the tree line with a look on her face that I've never seen before. She looks scared, and excited, and *full*.

"It's amazing, right?" I say.

"Yeah," Paulie answers. "It's totally amazing. I tried to talk to her the way that you do, but I couldn't figure it out. It's—her fur was softer than I thought it would be?"

"Yeah, she's been shedding her undercoat a lot lately, and probably hanging out with her pups a lot, so she hasn't been out roaming around. But I didn't know she'd feel like that either," I admit. "I didn't know she'd be so small."

"I can't believe I just pet a coyote," Paulie says, and then she doubles over laughing, the kind of breathless laughter that comes after you do something incredibly stupid.

"You did it, kiddo," I say, laughing with her. She sits up and looks at me, and the laughter on her face changes. The I-can't-believe-we-did-that grin softens. It turns into something that's still a smile, but different. It's between the two of us. It's a smile that's only for me.

I realize that she's still got my hand. Her thumb is tracing an arc from the back of my wrist to the inside of my palm. Her gaze flicks from my mouth to my eyes, and she bites her lip hard enough that if I were Maryam, I'd yell at her.

Part of me knows what's coming. And part of me wants it. We've been flirting for years, even during times when I've had a girlfriend and she's had a boyfriend, or the other way around. Part of me knows that it would be so easy, so nice. Part of me wants to make Paulie happy. Part of me thinks I could be happy too. Maybe I could.

She leans forward and lifts her free hand to my cheek. Her fingers slide back across my cheekbone, along my neck, her thumb brushing my earlobe.

And then she's kissing me.

Her hand is in my hair, and her mouth is on mine, and our eyes are closed and I can taste the tip of her tongue, soft and a little sweet. She's kissing me, Paulie is kissing me, and I'm kissing her back, and she shifts her weight a little and drops my hand and grips my waist and it's good, it's so good but—

It's wrong.

I pull back and keep my eyes closed. "I'm sorry," I whisper. It's the worst thing I could say, but it's also the only thing I could say.

"I'm not," Paulie whispers. I open my eyes and she's a few inches from my face, smiling like she can't help but smile. She leans forward to kiss me again and I let her because I'm a bad person, because it feels good and because I like it a lot when she kisses me. I let her kiss my mouth, and I let her trail kisses along my jaw to my throat, and I press my lips to her collarbone. Because I'm weak. Because it's easy to give in when someone makes you feel good. And oh god, she feels good, and her hands and her mouth feel good, and her thigh is sliding between mine and her hair is in my hands—

But then my back is against the blanket Paulie brought, and I have to stop because it's wrong. What I'm doing is *wrong*.

"I can't do this," I whisper against Paulie's hair.

"Yes you can," she whispers against the bent-back cup of my bra.

"No, I mean—I can't do this," I say again. "I'm sorry. This is—"

She looks up at me, her thumb pausing just below the undone-button of my jeans, her hair tousled in a way that makes my breath catch in my throat. "Please," she says. "I know I'm not the one you want, but—I need this right now."

I take a deep slow breath, and my conscience battles with the feeling of her breath against me. I could do it. I could make this decision with Paulie, a choice we both know is a bad one. Not bad because of what it is, but bad because of *who* it is. Her eyes search mine, and in that frozen moment, I can feel the tug of the wrong decision, pulling at me like a tide.

I could do it. I could sleep with Paulie, and it would be great, and I wouldn't even start to feel guilty until the next time I saw the person I really wanted.

I could do it.

But I won't. She deserves better than that from me.

I scoot out from under her. She sighs and sits up, leaning her back against the tree stump and scrubbing her hands across her face.

"I'm sorry," I start to say, but she holds up a hand.

"Don't," she says. "I know."

"No, I—it's not you," I say, and I feel like a cliché, like

an idiot. "Honestly. You're amazing, and I would totally—I would be so into this. I really would. But it wouldn't be right. I made this mistake with Josh." I bite my lip too hard, flinch, keep talking. The words come fast. "I think that using him like that, and lying to him about being okay with it, I think that's what made my magic go all crazy. I think that's why he died. And I wouldn't feel right about using you the way I was using him. I don't know if you would get hurt the same way, I mean. I don't know if you would get hurt physically? But it was wrong, the way I used him. Even if you would survive it, I couldn't do that to you."

"Yeah," Paulie says. "I get it. I'm great, but I'm not *her*. This isn't news."

The words take a second to sink in. "Wait, what?"

"I'm not Roya," Paulie says. She runs her hands through her hair and grimaces at the pomade that comes away on her palms. She wipes them on the dry grass at the edge of the blanket. "It's okay. I shouldn't have put you in that position."

I half smile. "It was a pretty decent position to be in," I say, and she lets out a grim laugh. "Wait, so—how do you know about me and . . . ? I mean, not that there is a me and Roya, but how did you know that I—"

"That you're fucking crazy about her?" Paulie asks. "Are you looking for a reason other than 'It's the most obvious thing in the goddamn world'?"

"Yes . . . ?" I fidget with the blanket. "But we don't have to talk about it. Paulie, I'm really sorry if I gave you the idea that—"

"You didn't," she says sharply. "I just . . . Things are really fucked up right now and I needed an outlet, okay? It didn't mean anything." I flinch, stung, and she revises quickly. "I don't mean it that way. I just mean—look, I'm not heartbroken that you said no, okay?"

I can't tell if I believe her or not. It would be so egotistical to think that she was *desperately in love with me* or whatever, but also, I don't want to go the easy route and take her at her word. I want to trust her, but I don't want to do the wrong thing if she doesn't really mean what she said. I don't know what to say. I don't know what to do. I hate this.

"Really," she adds, scooting closer to me and draping an arm around my shoulder. "I just thought you looked really hot and I was getting a little bit of a vibe and the coyote thing was *awesome* and I thought maybe we'd have fun. But I don't want to do anything that will leave you feeling guilty or messed up. And our friendship is more important than how great of a kisser I am." She plants a very wet kiss on my cheek, and I wipe it off on my sleeve, laughing.

"Are we okay?" I ask.

"I think so," she says. "Are you sure you don't want to make out just a little, now that we both know where we stand?"

I look over at her with no idea how to say *yes I want that a lot but I can't because it would be wrong but I want to do that a LOT*—and I see the wolf grin waiting for me. She cackles at the look on my face, and I shove her over. "You're an asshole," I laugh.

"You're fucking smitten." She cackles. "Holy crap, Alexis, you've got it *really* bad. I knew you liked Roya, but *yikes*." She wipes her eyes and props herself up on her elbow. "If I'd known you were this crazy about her, I would never have tried anything," she says more seriously. "I promise."

"I know." I stand up and hold out my hand. "Thanks for understanding."

"Of course," she says, taking my hand and pulling herself up. "And hey—Roya's going to be a lucky gal once you two finally make out. You're a damn good kisser, Alexis."

I blush so hard that she starts laughing again. She cracks jokes until we're a few blocks from my house. At the driveway, she puts the car in park and rubs the back of her neck awkwardly.

"Would, um . . . would you mind not telling the gang about what happened tonight?" she asks softly. "It was awesome and I'm not embarrassed or anything, but I don't want them to think I'm pining after you or anything."

"Of course not," I answer. "And . . . no weirdness. Between us, I mean. At least, not on my side of things."

Paulie cups my chin in one hand and presses a gentle kiss against the tip of my nose. "I know," she says. "I might be sad for a minute or two, but . . . no weirdness."

"Hey, Paulie?" I ask.

"Yeah?"

"What do you think you lost this time?"

She looks blank for a second before she remembers. She

forgot. I did too—we both got so caught up that we almost forgot about what we've been losing of ourselves. "I don't know," she says. "I'll find out, though."

"I hope . . . I hope it's not too bad," I say softly.

"It'll be fine," she says, giving me a tiny smile. "Whatever I lose, there's no way it'll be as bad as what I lost last time. And besides, it's only temporary. We'll bring Josh back, and I'll remember my brother again, and you'll dream again, and we'll all be fine. It'll be over before we know it, yeah?"

I nod. Dreaming again. I don't think I realized how much I missed being able to dream, but I find myself tearing up at the idea of getting my dreams back. "Yeah."

"Yeah." She ruffles my hair. "Now get out of my car."

"Love you," I call out over the squealing of her tires, and she throws a hand out the window. Her pinky, index finger, and thumb are outstretched in the sign-language symbol for *I love you*, and my heart swells with our friendship, and what could have happened, and the reasons why it didn't happen.

It's totally obvious, she said. I can't help but wonder if it's that obvious to Roya, too.

I head inside and slip into my room without getting intercepted by anyone. I tug the backpack out from under my bed—the one with the heart in it. I unzip it slowly. Part of me doesn't want to check on how it's doing. But I haven't looked at it since before Iris got rid of Josh's hands, and I hadn't realized that Roya had taken extra measures with the leg she dropped in the reservoir, and now Paulie and I have taken care of the other leg—if getting rid of pieces of Josh is bringing the heart back, I figure it'll be obvious by now.

As soon as I unzip the bag, I know I'm right. The heart inside isn't quite flesh, but it's softer than it was last time I touched it. It's cool to the touch, like Maryam's hands first thing in the morning.

I cup it in my palms. It's still heavy, but lighter than it was the last time I held it. It beats and the sudden spasm is startling, nothing like the soft, occasional throbs of the morning we all tried to bring Josh back. The way the heart moves now—once every thirty seconds or so—is so violent and visceral that I almost drop it. The whole thing jumps in my grip. It feels wrong to put something so clearly alive back into the backpack, but I do it anyway. Between heartbeats, I lower the heart carefully into the bag. I zip the backpack shut and push it under my bed.

It's working. We're getting rid of pieces of Josh, and his heart is coming back. If we do this right, everything will go back to being the way it was.

If we do everything just right, the whole plan will work.

I lie back on my bed and try not to listen for the sound of the dead boy's heart beating underneath me.

16.

ON SATURDAY, A BAREFACED MARYAM PULLS UP to my house in her brother's spotless car. It's already sticky outside, the kind of warm early-morning air that portends either a thunderstorm or a hellaciously hot afternoon. I'm in a tank top and shorts, and I'm still plucking at the fabric where it sticks to my back and thighs. "Paulie texted me a couple of hours ago," she says as I slide into the front seat, the bare skin of my legs squeaking on the leather. "She's not feeling well."

"Hope she's all right," I mumble, avoiding eye contact. "You doing okay? You're naked." I gesture to her face.

"Fine. Just indecisive today." Maryam grabs one of two metal thermoses out of the cupholders between us and hands it to me. I take a sip—it's iced tea, I think, but it's cool and squashy and weirdly sweet, and I can't tell if I love it or hate it. I hold it up and give Maryam a what-the-hell-is-this face.

"Cucumber strawberry mint iced tea, I think?" She shrugs. "I don't know, my dad's been on a Pinterest binge lately. He told me to have you try the tea so I could report back. He thinks I'm being 'unfairly critical of his efforts.'" She drums her fingers on the steering wheel, fidgets with her earrings.

"What happened?" I ask.

"Last night he made miniature quiches in a muffin tin and I told him my opinion."

"How'd they turn out?"

She gives me a look. "Wet."

I offer a sympathetic grimace. Maryam's dad has been on a journey into the world of creative cooking for a few years now. Sometimes he succeeds. Other times he has what he calls "learning experiences." Lately he's been doing a lot of "learning." I sip the tea again. "It's . . . good, I think? It's different. It's good."

"I'll tell him you said so," she says grimly. She turns into the school parking lot, which is already crowded with minivans and SUVs. She pulls into a space, cracks the windows, and turns the car off. She flips down the mirror on the driver's side, pursing her lips at her reflection. "I can't decide what to do. I was almost late coming to get you because I kept putting different colors of liner on and then deciding they were wrong."

"Want help?" I ask, and she tugs at her earring again, considering her reflection.

"Mmmmm . . . yes," she says, and I nod. We both unbuckle our seat belts and turn to face each other. I settle my tea in the cupholder and hold out both hands. Maryam rests her fingertips on mine and lets out a long, slow breath. She closes her eyes. "I feel lost," she starts, and then she's off. It's something we've done for years, since our shared drama class where the teacher made us do all these bonding, trust-fall types of exercises. I think the teacher secretly wanted to be a guidance counselor. None of us came out of the class wanting to be thespians, but it was a good class. It taught us how to listen to each other.

I can't give Maryam advice on how she should do her makeup—that would be like Nico trying to give soccer tips to Mia Hamm—but I can listen while she figures things out for herself. She talks about the different colors she tried, and how they all felt too juvenile, too trendy, too pop-star. She talks about how everything looks the same after a while. She talks about how worried she is for all of us, that this thing we're trying to do will break us or change us into people we don't want to be. She talks about trying to find a new line so her brows will feel interesting, and feeling stuck in the same looks she's been exploring for years. Maryam isn't telling me what she wants her face to look like—she's telling me how she feels now, and how she *wants* to feel when her makeup is on.

After a few minutes, she lets out another big breath and she opens her eyes. I sit quietly, keeping my face as neutral as possible. She looks at me for a long time, then nods. "Okay," she says. "I think I know what I'm gonna do." She smiles at me, and as she does, magic washes across her face like the glow from a flashlight. This is Maryam's magic: subtle and suffusive and luminous. Her lips go dark, plummy, and a gradient of grays spread over her eyelids. Her brows fill in, sculpted and long, higher and thinner than usual. By the time she's finished, she looks like an older version of herself—regal. Imperious. She doesn't check her work in the rearview mirror; instead, she looks at me. "What do you think?"

"Brilliant."

She smiles, a tucked-in kind of smile that gives her deep dimples. "I know."

The swim meet is already in full gear by the time we walk into the pool complex. It's open-air, but surrounded by high concrete walls so that people can't get drunk and sneak in and make out in the pool at night. The pool is enormous and blue-bottomed, with long strings of white buoys separating the water into lanes. The crowd is a sea of swim caps and sun hats, goggles and sunglasses. A long line snakes away from the tiny concession stand, where a student volunteer is selling Costco snacks and off-brand sodas to the families of the competitors.

Maryam and I climb all the way to the top of the bleachers, where we won't get splashed by swimmers or deafened by overzealous swim-moms shouting encouragement to their kids. We look for Roya in the crowd—it's hard to tell the swimmers apart when they're all wearing caps and goggles, but she always stands out. To me, at least.

"There," I say, pointing, and Maryam stands up to wave.

She flings both arms over her head and flails them around, trying to get Roya's attention. I cup my hands around my mouth and shout "GOOOOOOOO ROYAAAAAAAAA," and half of the people in the complex turn around to stare at us. It's worth the dirty look I get from the swim-dad in front of me, just to see the way Roya's head tips back as she laughs at us. We cheer until she does a strongwoman pose for our benefit, her arms flexed in different directions to show off her biceps and triceps, which are rippling from the grueling hours of extra practice she's been through in the past few weeks.

The coach points at Maryam and me and gives us an over-the-sunglasses death glare. We shut up before our hollering gets Roya in trouble. Her smile doesn't fade even as the coach leans in and says something to her—probably telling her to keep her head in the game and not let her weirdo friends distract her. She's only got one event at this meet, and I'm sure the coach wants her to make it count.

Maryam slides on a pair of huge sunglasses and leans her back against the railing behind us. Her brows arch over the top of the enormous dark glasses. She looks like a movie star. I tell her so and she flashes that deep-dimpled smile again. "Thanks for listening to me in the car," she says. "It helped a lot. You're a really good listener."

It's hard to tell because of the sunglasses, but I feel like she's staring at me. She's talking like there are layers of significance to her words, but I can't begin to untangle what they might be, so I pretend not to notice. "Anytime."

A whistle sounds and a group dives into the water. We watch them, even though neither of us can really tell what's happening under the white froth of the water, and we can't tell who any of the swimmers are, and we don't really even know what they're trying to accomplish other than *go fast* and *don't drown*.

"You know I'm always happy to return the favor, right?" Maryam asks as the swim-dad in front of us stands up, blocking our view. He's shouting something about shoulders. Does he think that his kid can hear him in the water?

"Yeah," I say, but I don't look at her because I don't know. I mean, I know she would listen if I asked. She would listen to me talk about whatever I need to talk about. I know she would probably give me good, kind advice.

But I don't know if she'd be happy to do it. Maybe it would just be annoying to listen to me complain. I don't know if it would burden her—or any of my friends—to hear about my insecurities, my worries. Aren't I already asking enough of them all? They're hiding a body for me. I can't help but feel like I should deal with my emotions about it on my own. And if that's hard, well . . . don't I deserve to be alone with it? With what I've done? With what I feel?

But that's a lot to say to someone, and if I told Maryam I was feeling that way, she'd probably try to comfort me, and that would just make it worse. So I say "yeah" one more time and stare at the chipped hearts on my fingernails.

Maryam looks at me and opens her mouth like she's about

to say something, but she's interrupted by another loud whistle and swim-dad's defeated groan. The bleachers shake and rattle with the footsteps of people going down to the pool to comfort or berate swimmers.

"Excuse me."

I look around Maryam and realize that the rattle of our row of bleachers wasn't an overinvolved parent. It was Gina Tarlucci, walking along our row. She has a long lens on her camera—she's probably here to take pictures for the yearbook. Her dress is green with white flowers, and her hair is in some kind of 1940s-ish style that would make Paulie's jaw drop if she saw it. Maryam tucks her legs to one side to allow Gina to pass, but instead, our row rattles again as Gina steps down to the bench in front of us. She plops down onto the spot where swim-dad was sitting until a moment before. She looks pissed.

"Are you in on this whole thing too?" she asks Maryam.

Maryam looks at me, inscrutable behind her movie-star sunglasses. I shake my head. "No, Gina, she doesn't have anything to do with any of your crazy conspiracy theories. Please leave us alone."

Gina drums her nails against the metal, and the sound echoes across our section of the bleachers. "Well, does she know what you *are*?" she hisses.

"I don't care what she is," Maryam says smoothly, looping her arm through mine. There's a note of warning simmering in her voice. "She's my friend."

"Oh, are you sure about that?" Gina's eyes narrow and she

looks at me with such hate that my heart jumps. "Because you might like to know that she's a—"

"Enough," Maryam growls, her fingers tight on my arm. She whips off her sunglasses with her free hand, then leans forward and looks into Gina's face. Maryam's eyes spark with furious fire. "That is *enough*. I will not tolerate whatever hateful garbage you think you have to say. Alexis asked you to leave us alone, because she is a good and kind person. I am not asking you to leave us alone." Her voice is low and dangerous, and the colors on her face are sharpening with every word. The shadows under her cheekbones seem to grow a little deeper. Her eyes flash, not with anger, but with the light of growing magic. "*I. Am. Telling you.*"

A breeze ripples between us, and Gina bolts upright. She's gone before Maryam's got her sunglasses all the way back on. She shoves someone aside to tear away down the bleachers. The wind continues behind her, pushing at her back, whipping her hair into her face.

I notice that the people she passes don't seem touched by even the slightest of breezes.

I look at Maryam. She's back in movie-star mode, her face exactly as still and unreadable as it was before Gina showed up.

"Did you do that, just now?" I ask Maryam. She gives a single nod, pursing her lips. "You can do wind?"

"I try not to," she mutters. "But sometimes when I get angry . . ."

"Remind me not to mess with you," I intone.

She looks at me over the top of her sunglasses in an uncanny impersonation of Roya's swim coach. "If you don't know that by now, I can't help you," she says sternly.

I laugh and give her arm a squeeze. "You're amazing. That was amazing. I can't believe she thought you didn't know—or that she didn't think you were also—that was amazing."

"You can tell me, you know," she says.

"What?" I can't see enough of her face behind the sunglasses to know if she's even looking at me.

"Whatever it is that Gina was going to say."

"What do you mean?"

"You're entitled to your privacy," she says softly. "But I'm here to listen, and I'll still love you no matter what. You don't have to be worried that I'll, I don't know. Disapprove. Or whatever."

The bleachers are digging into my thighs and I shift, but I can't get comfortable. "I'm pretty sure she was talking about magic."

Maryam purses her lips. "What else, though?"

"I mean . . . you know everything about me. Pretty much everything."

She's still not really looking at me. "I don't," she says. "I know the stuff you tell me, but there's stuff you hide, too. And that's okay. I'm not hurt or anything." I don't know if I believe her. She says that she's not hurt with a breeziness that rings false. "I just want you to know that you're not the only one who can listen."

"I know you can listen," I tell her. "I just feel bad. I keep making you guys listen to my problems and clean up my messes and it's not fair to you, you know? I'm starting to think maybe I should just turn myself in."

There's another shrill whistle-blast. Swim-dad stomps back up the bleachers. He sits in front of us with his arms crossed, shaking his head. I wonder if his kid even likes swimming. He adjusts his cap, blocking my view of the pool. But then his elbows drop, and I look down to the water, and there she is.

There's Roya.

She's standing behind one of the starting blocks, shaking her hands out by her sides. She squeezes her fists tight, then shakes out her fingers three times, then rotates her wrists, then starts over from fists. She's nervous. It's her only event at her last meet and she's nervous.

I want more than anything to send the thinnest thread of magic her way, just something to say that I'm here and it'll be fine and she's going to do great. Just a little warm touch, the kind we all send each other all day long, checking in, making sure everyone knows that they're not forgotten and not alone. But she'd be furious—she made us all promise a long time ago that we'd never, *never* help her at meets. Even though I wouldn't even know how to use magic to help her swim, just the act of making her less nervous would probably count. She doesn't want any interference, and that means no magic at all, not even her own. She doesn't love swimming, but still—she wants to be amazing in her own right.

Not that she needs help.

She climbs onto her starting block and bends to grip the edge. My chest aches at the sight of her. I know that this event is the 100-meter butterfly, because that's all she's been talking about for a month. That's pretty much all I know about it, and that largely describes the end of my knowledge about the sport as a whole. I'm not a great swimmer. I can mostly just keep myself alive in the water and make my way across the reservoir. Roya, though—she might not use her power for help, but she doesn't need it. What she does in the water is its own kind of magic.

When the whistle blows, she shoots off the starting block like a finger of lightning jumping from one cloud to another. Her entire upper body arcs up out of the water, her arms meeting over her head and then driving powerfully backward. She moves through the water like a torpedo. When she kicks off the wall of the pool and turns around before anyone else has finished even half of a lap, I let out a whoop that makes swim-dad jump and turn to look at me. I ignore him, standing up to cheer.

She wins. Of course she wins—she's Roya. She's incredible.

Maryam and I yell ourselves hoarse, but we don't go down to congratulate Roya. Not now. She hates being talked to right after she swims. I did it once at the beginning of sophomore year, her first year on the team: I ran right up to her to congratulate her, offer a high five, and ask how it felt to kick so much ass. She was glassy-eyed and panting, her cap clenched in one hand, her hair in a tight braid that hung over one shoulder. I can still picture how the tip of her braid was dripping—I was surprised because I always thought the swim caps were there to keep your hair dry. She had goggle-lines around her eyes, and I remember being startled by the impulse to reach up and smooth them.

"You were amazing." I remember how I said it breathlessly, even though I hadn't been out of breath a second before. She looked at me like she didn't recognize me. She'd apologize later—explain about the adrenaline, the oncoming energy-crash, needing time to shake off the intense focus of an event. It was a perfectly sensible boundary for her to set, but at the time, I was stung. It was the first time I'd felt such a strong urge to be seen by someone, and at the time, she didn't seem to want to look at me.

"So," Maryam says as I sit back down.

"She killed it," I breathe.

"Yeah," she says. There's a heavy silence between us.

"Do you know when Iris is up?" I venture.

"Not sure," Maryam says. "I haven't spotted her yet." Her hands are shoved into the big pocket on the front of her hoodie, so I can't see if they're in fists or not, but her voice makes me think they probably are. I lean my shoulder against hers and try to decide if I should ask her what's up or if I should just give her space.

Before I can make up my mind, she huffs out a little breath and shoves me off her. I look over, startled. She's taking off her sunglasses. Her eyes are narrowed and she's looking at me like I'm an impossible derivation on a calc worksheet. "This week has been really hard on everyone," she says.

My stomach immediately clenches with guilt. "Yeah, I know," I say, "and I'm really—"

"No," she says, slicing her hand through the air. It's another of her mom's gestures, one that means you'd better shut up before you get yourself in even worse trouble than you already are. "Don't apologize. I've had enough."

"What do you—"

"I've had enough of you sitting there and feeling bad because all your friends love you," she snaps. "Just now, when you were cheering for Roya? It was the only time this whole week I've seen you look something other than guilty for your friendships."

"But—"

"No!" She slices her hand through the air again, and I feel like I've been caught sneaking in past curfew with a hickey on my neck and a bottle in my pocket. "We all love you, okay? Your friends all love you, and it doesn't matter if you think you deserve it or not because we love you anyway. You think it isn't fair to let us love you and help you? I'll tell you right now: the way you've been mooning around feeling bad about our friendship *isn't fair*. It puts the onus on all of us to make you feel okay about the fact that we're helping you and it *isn't fair*. And it would be *incredibly* stupid and insensitive of you to turn yourself in. Doing that? After everything those girls have sacrificed to keep you safe? Just because you don't think you deserve their friendship?" She shakes her head at me. "Honestly."

She huffs out a short, sharp breath. A couple of people near us have turned to stare. She got pretty loud by the end there. My eyes burn and my vision blurs and I feel my chin buckle in that little-kid way I hate. Maryam is still glaring at me. She's quiet for long enough that I think I'm allowed to talk. "I'm really—"

"*And another thing*," she interrupts. "It's really messed up that we all have to go around pretending that we don't know you're in love with Roya, and it's really extra messed up that you don't think you can tell *me* about it!"

With that, she shoves her sunglasses back on, crosses her arms, and turns back to the meet. Tears spill down my cheeks, but they're nowhere near as hot as the shame that roils in my gut. I look over at Maryam, then down at Roya, standing by the pool with a towel draped over her shoulders. "Did Paulie tell you?" I whisper.

"What?" Maryam snaps.

"Paulie—did she tell you about how I'm . . . how I . . . Roya." I can't look at Maryam, so I keep watching the way Roya's long wet braid is dripping over her collarbone.

"No. You talked to her about it, but you wouldn't talk to me about it? Who else? Gina Tarlucci?" She sounds like a pot of water that's on the edge of boiling over.

"No—never Gina, I don't—no. But Paulie talked to me about it," I mutter. "The same way you did, pretty much. Although she was a little less mad at me."

Maryam sighs, a big exhausted kind of sigh. She takes her sunglasses off again, tucking them into her pocket this time. "Look," she says, then goes quiet for a while. She seems so tired. Two whistles blow before she continues her sentence, but I don't dare interrupt. "It's just that there's only a few weeks until the end of school, and then summer is going to go by really, really fast, and then we're all moving in together at school, right?"

"If you still want to." I hate how petty and insecure I sound.

"So, are you really going to bring all of this with us? The pining and the meaningful glances and the frankly *unbearable* chemistry between you two? Because I don't want to have to clean up after the elephant."

"The what?"

"The elephant that's in the room any time you two sit next to each other," she snaps. I laugh before I can stop myself. She tries to look stern, but she laughs too, then wraps an arm around me and squeezes my shoulders. "You gotta do something about it," she says. "You can't keep torturing all of us like this."

"I will," I say, leaning into her. "I'll do something about it. I promise."

Maryam spots Iris and we cheer for her in the 200-meter

freestyle. She and one other swimmer finish at what looks to me like the exact same time, and there's some seriously poor sportsmanship on display from the other team as the coaches argue. Iris pinches the bridge of her nose to wait it out. In the end, they call it a tie. Maryam and I both boo, earning another dirty look from swim-dad.

I stifle a giggle, then nudge Maryam with my elbow. "So. Do you really think we have chemistry?"

Maryam rolls her eyes. "Are you seriously asking me that?"

"Yeah." I bite my lip, then stop before Maryam can catch me at it. "She's been kind of distant lately."

"Like, since prom?" She's tapping her fingernails, idly changing them from green to pink to blue.

"Yeah."

Maryam raises her eyebrows. Her mouth drops open into an O. She turns to me and lowers her voice to a barely audible whisper. "I wonder if . . . Do you think that could have anything to do with you trying to sleep with a boy you don't even like and then her having to lie to her *chief of police* mom about the fact that she knows exactly what happened to him? While also losing pieces of herself for reasons she doesn't understand and can't predict?" She manages to maintain a straight face for long enough that I'm not sure she's making fun of me until she starts chewing on her bottom lip and says, "I don't know, maybe you're right and she's acting strange because she *hates* you."

"Okay, I get it." I laugh. "I'll talk to her." The final whistle blows, marking the end of the last event, and the bleachers start to empty almost instantly.

"You'd better," she says. "Or else I'll yell at you again."

"I don't think I can survive another dose of Maryam Realness," I say to her back as she starts off down the bleachers. I stay where I am for a minute longer, pretending to collect my bag.

Really, I'm just standing there, watching as Maryam makes her way to where Iris and Roya are waiting.

She passes the gray-haired cop on her way down. The cop is talking to someone who's impossible not to recognize, even from a distance. She's talking to Gina Tarlucci.

As I look, Gina says something, and they both look up at the bleachers. They look right up at me.

I force myself to look away. I dig my phone out of my pocket and pretend to be taking a picture of Roya and Iris, down by the pool. They're both wrapped in towels, their goggles hanging around their necks. Iris still has her cap on. She looks so pale without her freckles that it takes me a moment to realize it's her—but then she looks up at me, standing there in the bleachers, and she sends a single gossamer thread of magic up to me. I feel it brush against my ear, cool as a drop of water, and I lift my hand to wave at her. I take the picture and put my phone away.

When I look over, Gina is gone, but the gray-haired cop is staring at me. She's looking from me to Iris and back. She starts lifting a hand to wave me over, and I pretend I don't see. I busy myself grabbing my bag and extricating myself from the bleachers, and then I take the long way down to tell my friends how proud I am of them.

Before we all leave, I look back at where the cop was standing. She's still there, watching me. Watching us.

She doesn't say anything. She doesn't unfold her arms from across her chest.

She just watches.

And I have no idea what it is that she sees.

17.

WE TAKE ROYA AND IRIS OUT FOR LUNCH AT THE Crispy Chicken. True to their word, they fill Marcelina in on the meet, with stroke-by-stroke recaps of each of their events. They devour two Crispy Chandwiches each and share a huge carton of Crispy Fries. Roya actually growls at me when I reach for one. Marcelina takes her lunch break with us, her paper hat sitting in the middle of the chipped Formica table. Maryam asks her how she got her matte black lipstick not to crack even after a full morning of running the drive-thru window, and they do a deep-dive into a sponge technique that sounds to me like some kind of advanced alien technology.

"So what'd you think?" Roya asks, sorting through the Crispy Fries to find the perfectly balanced soggy/crispy fry of legend.

"Of what?"

"Of my 'fly," she says, a smile curling the corners of her lips up like burning paper. "Did I kick ass?"

"You destroyed it," I say, finishing the last of my strawberry shake. "You absolutely demolished it. The water looked scared by the time you were finished."

She cackles and throws a fry at me. "Hell yeah it did," she says, then turns to Iris. "Can you believe that was it? That was the last meet we're gonna do." She sounds giddy.

"I'm never gonna be this hungry again," Iris says around a mouthful of Chandwich. "Or this tired. Or this chlorine-y."

"Okay, kids, I gotta go finish the shift," Marcelina says. She pats each of us on the head like we're her wayward ducklings, then pins her paper hat back over her shining black topknot. "Are my seams straight?" She turns around, flashing us the back of her red uniform pants, which are embroidered with a large rooster tail.

"You look like a supermodel, mama." Iris toasts Marcelina with her shake, and Marcelina gives her feathers a wiggle. Before she leaves, she turns and points at me.

"By the way, my house, tomorrow afternoon? I gotta do the thing."

I spin my empty shake cup between my hands. "Sure," I say, heat climbing my neck. I'm trying hard not to look like I feel bad about the thing I feel bad about. "I'll be there."

She gives my head one more pat, then goes back to work. I look at Maryam to see if I did a good job of not being guilty and terrible, but she's already busy experimenting with Iris's new contouring possibilities. I watch her fingers trace the lines of Iris's face, leaving behind different shades of pink and brown. "I don't know," she says. "You've got such fine bone structure already. I think adding anything at all might be overkill, to be honest."

"Well, feel free to keep trying," Iris says. "I've never used that stuff before, so I'm a whole new canvas for you to play with. You win at long last. Go nuts."

"I've gotta do the thing too, soon," Roya says to me. "Monday? After school?"

"Yeah," I say, still spinning my empty shake cup, watching Iris and Maryam so I don't have to look at Roya and think about the elephant that Maryam was talking about. "Sure."

"Great," Roya says, and I can see her watching me out of the corner of my eye. "Perfect."

Maryam drops me off at home after lunch and I walk inside feeling slightly sun-dazzled. It takes my entire body a minute to adjust to the transition from the bright, hot afternoon to the cool darkness of the house. I feel instantly sleepy and hyperaware of the sweat drying on my arms and back. I head to my bedroom, torn between taking a nap or taking a shower.

Thoughts of either leave my head the second I open the door.

"What the hell are you doing?!" I shout. Nico scrambles out from under my bed, one hand clutching a file folder, the other holding a bag.

The bag with the heart in it.

"Why are you in my room?!" I demand as I storm in, reaching

for the bag in his hand. A corner of the duct tape on the front is peeling back, and I can see the corner of the letter *J* peeking out.

He jerks it out of my reach. "Chill, okay, I was just—"

"Don't tell me to chill! What are you doing in here? Why were you under my bed?" My fingers are burning and my palms are prickling and I clench my hands into fists to stop myself from doing something I'll regret. Something I can't control. I can't keep the quaver out of my voice, though.

"I'm trying to tell you, I was—"

"You have *no right to be*—"

"Oh my *god* just let me *explain*, you don't have to be such a—"

"Don't you *dare call me*—"

"WHAT IS GOING ON IN HERE?"

We both turn to see Pop standing in the door, hands braced on the frame. His entire face is red, all the way up to the top of his scalp, and his eyebrows are a long, low furrow of what-the-hell. He's wearing his worn-out college sweater and a pair of cargo shorts, which is his sitting-in-the-office-all-day-reviewing-depositions outfit. If he could hear us all the way back in his office, with the door closed and his white noise machine going—we were shouting at each other at top volume. I'm out of breath. Shit. *Shit*. This is *really* bad.

Pop looks between me and Nico and the file folder in Nico's hand and the bag in Nico's other hand, which I'm still reaching for.

"Um," we both say, and Pop crosses his arms.

"Nico was in my room," I say.

"Alexis was being a total—" Nico starts, then catches the look on Pop's face and stops midsentence. He doesn't finish what he was about to say.

"Why were you in her room, Nico?" Pop asks, his voice strained with the *extreme* patience of a parent mediating between his kids. Nico's ears flush and he mumbles something unintelligible. "I beg your pardon?"

"I was looking for something," Nico says, just loudly enough to hear this time.

"What were you looking for?" I demand. "And why didn't you just *ask me* for it?"

"Because I knew you'd say no," Nico says, not looking at me. He brandishes the file folder in his hand. "I was looking for your final essay from when you had Nichols for English in your sophomore year."

Pop's brows were already low, but they drop even farther at hearing that. Nico looks like he wants to crawl under my bed and hide. "Why would you want her final essay?" Pop asks. I can't imagine that he actually doesn't know—maybe he's just trying to give Nico an opportunity to defend himself.

"He was going to copy from it," I answer. Nico's still holding the bag with the heart in it, and I'm trying to figure out how I can make sure he doesn't get so distracted by being in trouble that he takes it with him. I reach for it again, but as I do, he turns to me with a look of shock and betrayal.

"I wasn't," he says, but it's for Pop's benefit. "I just know how you save all that old crap, and I wanted to see what approach you took—"

"Oh *please*," I start to say. Pop cuts me off.

"Nico," he says in a level voice that's trying very hard not to be lawyerish, "isn't that essay due tomorrow?"

Nico looks miserable. "Yes. That's why I wanted help."

"I see. Let's go talk about this somewhere else." Pop gestures to Nico, who turns to trudge out of the room. They walk toward Nico's bedroom to talk about how much trouble Nico's in, and I hear Pop saying, "We both know that copying and 'getting help' aren't the same thing, young man," as he half closes the door to my bedroom behind him. As the door swings shut, I catch a last glimpse of the bag still dangling from Nico's hand.

"No no no no no no no," I moan, falling onto my bed and pulling a pillow over my head. Nico has Josh's heart. He's holding it. He's going to forget that he took that bag out of my bedroom, and then he's going to notice it and remember that he's pissed at me, and then he's going to decide to snoop. He'll open it and see what's inside, and how am I going to explain why there's a heart that isn't bleeding in there?

What am I supposed to say?

Sorry to leave you out of the loop, Nico, but your big sister is actually some kind of magical freak who accidentally killed a guy she barely knew because she was about to sleep with him for all the wrong reasons. Oh, and she keeps hurting people when she gets freaked out and she's pretty sure she would have hurt you if

Pop hadn't interrupted that fight. Please don't tell anyone?

And then I realize that if I can't get the heart back from him, I'll probably hurt people even more. That's what Iris said: the tension of the spell is what's making me accidentally hurt people, including myself. What if I can't get the heart back from Nico and then I lose control and kill someone else?

What if I hurt him? Or Dad, or Pop? I know I should feel just as bad about hurting anyone, because hurting anyone at all is awful, but . . . what if it's one of them? I'm already a murderer. What if I can't stop killing people?

What if I'm a monster?

I scream into the pillow.

I've never screamed into a pillow before. It always kind of seemed like a cliché. But now that I'm doing it . . . it's pretty satisfying. I scream into it again, so hard that my throat burns, and then again, and I'm just gearing up for another scream when I hear the door to my bedroom open.

"Did you impale an eyeball on something?" Pop asks, pulling the pillow off my face. "You know this thing doesn't actually muffle you that much, right?"

"Oh, um. Sorry," I mumble. "I didn't realize. Hey, that was fast." I scramble up to a sitting position and sit with my back against the wall, my legs stretched across the mattress. "Is Nico off the hook?"

"Far from it," Pop says with a wry shake of his head. "But Dad took over so I could come talk to you. Once we heard the wailing, we figured we should probably divide our efforts. And I thought you might want this back." He lifts his arm, and I realize for the first time that he's got my bag.

"Thanks." I grab the bag and drop it on the pillows next to me, trying to get that exposed *J* facedown. I want to shove the whole thing back under the bed, but that would look suspicious. Or maybe not doing it looks suspicious? I don't know what to do with my hands.

"So, we need to talk." Pop leans against the wall next to the doorframe with his hands in his pockets. He ducks his head, giving himself a little double chin. He's staring at the bag. I resist the urge to push it behind the pillows. "You're not in any trouble," he says quickly, probably seeing the blood drain from my face. "But Dad and I are worried about you."

"What? Why?" My palms tingle with a bloom of sweat. *Worried* is way worse than *mad*. "What's going on?"

"You're not yourself lately. Skipping classes was one thing, but shouting at your brother? What's that about?" He shakes his head. "You know we're not—"

"*—not a shouting family*, I know." I can't keep the annoyance out of my voice. Maybe I'm not trying very hard. Pop's eyebrows unify at the interruption, but he doesn't stop me. "You didn't see what he was doing, though, Pop. He was *under my bed*."

"It's not just about yelling, bug," he says gently. "You've been giving everyone a whole lot of bad attitude lately. Not just Nico. Me and Dad, too. What's that about?"

Oh, great. So this is a *you're-a-huge-jerk-and-nobody-likes-you* talk. I clench my jaw. "I don't know what you mean."

"I'm not trying to beat up on you here."

"Could have fooled me," I mutter.

"I just want to know what's going on with you. This behavior isn't like you at all—"

"Well, maybe you just think that because you don't know me." I let my hands drop to my sides, and one of them lands on the bag with the heart in it. "You think I'm not being myself because you have no idea who I am!" Pop takes a deep calming breath of his own, and for some reason, it infuriates me. The words pour out before I can stop them, my volume creeping up with every word. "You think I'm still some little kid that you can control, but I'm not, and I haven't been for a long time! And I'm dealing with all of this shit on my own and you have no idea what it's like, okay?! You have no idea."

My cheeks and palms are both burning. When I touch my face, my fingers come away wet. I tuck my hands under my thighs just in case they're glowing. They feel like they are, and for the hundredth time, I wish that I could see my own magic. I dig my fingernails into my palms hard.

I'm losing control.

Shit.

"I'm sorry I yelled," I whisper.

"Oh, sweetie," he says, and then he's sitting next to me with his arm around my shoulder. He's soft, and his ratty old sweater feels the same way it did when I was little. "I can't understand what's going on if you don't tell me. But I want to understand. I really do."

I want to lean on him and cry like a kid. I want to. But it just doesn't feel *right*. I shake my head, sitting up stiffly, and he takes his arm off my shoulder. I wonder if I hurt his feelings by not wanting the hug. I wonder if I'm just destined to hurt everyone around me. I clench my fists even harder, and try to focus on the pain so I don't lose control and ruin everything.

"It's just that I can't be who you want me to be, okay? That's not who I am anymore," I tell him.

"Okay," Pop says.

"I'm—wait, what?"

"I said okay," he repeats. "I believe you. But I want to know who you are. Your dad does too. Hell, I bet Nico even wants to know who you are, even if he doesn't really know how to show it." He shifts away so he can look at me, and maybe also to give me a little space. "Look, kiddo. Sorry, not 'kiddo,' I should stop calling you that." My chest hurts. I don't want him to stop calling me that. "*Alexis*. Whatever it is that you feel like you can't tell us . . . I can't force you to trust me, but I'm here to listen, okay? And no matter what's going on, I'll love you. I promise."

I look at my kneecaps, my nightstand, the pattern on my bedspread. Anywhere but at him. I take a few more deep breaths. I'm going to do something stupid. "Are you sure?" I whisper.

He hesitates. "Have I ever told you about what it was like when I came out to my mom?"

I shake my head. Grandma died when I was too little to remember her, and Pop barely ever talks about her.

"I wasn't that much younger than you are now," he says. "I felt a lot of the things you're feeling—like I wasn't the person who she thought I was. Like I was lying to her, but also like it was her fault that I couldn't tell her the truth."

I open my mouth to say that I don't think it's his fault I can't tell him, but then I close it. Because he's right. I do think it's his fault. I don't know why, but it's true—some part of me blames my dads for the fact that I've kept my magic a secret.

"When I told her," he continues, "she didn't say all the right things. In fact, she said a lot of things that really hurt. The very first thing she said was, 'I still love you, no matter what.'" He shakes his head. "That kind of hurt the worst, you know? It felt like she was saying she loved me in spite of something. It felt like she was saying it was hard to love me, now that she knew who I really was." He clears his throat. "She grew a lot over the years. By the time I met your dad, she'd figured out how to say things a little better. We adopted you. She got to be a grandmother for a couple of years before she passed. It was really amazing to see the way our family changed—but I never forgot how 'I love you anyway' felt."

"Wow," I whisper. I can't imagine how much that must have hurt.

"Yeah," he says. "But then, you remember when you were

really little and she passed? I had to go away for a couple of weeks to clear out her house?"

"Kind of?" I remember my dad's friend Patricia coming over to hang out with me a lot, and I remember eating macaroni and cheese for breakfast a couple of days in a row because we ran out of cereal and Dad kept forgetting to go to the store.

"I found her old journals while I was there." His voice is far away now, like he's completely lost in the memory. "I kept going back and forth on whether I should read them, but one night I cracked open a bottle of whiskey and went for it. I read all of them in one sitting. And I realized I had it completely backward that whole time."

"What do you mean?"

"She wrote pages and pages about how she could tell she was getting things wrong, and how she wanted to say the right things but didn't know how to. She kept writing about how she hoped I knew she loved me, even when she messed up." He smiles. "She wasn't saying 'I love you in spite of who you are.' She was saying 'I might screw this up a lot, but the biggest thing is that I love you. The most important thing in my heart is that I love you.' Does that make sense?"

"I think so," I say, although I'm not really sure if it does.

"The point is, whatever it is you think you can't tell me about, bug? I might not know how to say the right thing about it, and I might have questions. I might not understand right away. But I love you, and that doesn't change. That's the biggest, most important part of this."

"Are you sure?" I ask again.

"I'm sure," he says back.

My heart is pounding so hard that I can see the front of my shirt fluttering just a little. My breathing is too loud. I'm going to throw up. I'm going to black out. I can't do this. I can't do this. I can't—

"This is who I am."

I take my hands out from under my thighs and hold them out in front of me, palms up.

Magic.

I can't see the threads of my magic, but I can feel them. I can feel the power spiraling out of me. It feels like I'm exhaling a held breath. And there's at least one thing that Pop and I can *both* see.

Blood.

There are crescent-moon divots in each of my palms, dents from my fingernails. They open up slow, like sleepy eyes. Blood curls up out of the wounds. A tiny stream of red from each little crescent-wound, coiling together to form slender vines. Four delicate orchids bud and bloom along the lengths of them, each thumbnail-sized flower unfolding in perfect stop-motion synchrony with the others.

It lasts for only a few seconds. Then, realizing what I've done, I gasp and clench my fists. My fingertips sting the places where my palms are wounded. I squeeze my eyes shut against the pain. When I open them again, I peek at my hands to see how bad the cuts are.

They're gone.

My skin is smooth, completely intact. There's blood threaded into the creases of my palms, though, and four impossibly small, impossibly perfect dark-red orchids rest in each of my cupped hands. The petals, each the size of the white crescent at the tip of my smallest fingernail, curve across each other like the panels of a spread fan. I gently stroke one with my thumb. It feels like warm glass.

I made this. I made it with a tiny bit of blood, and then I healed myself. It didn't feel like it does when Roya heals me, though—it felt like something different. It felt like the blood was trying to come to me for a purpose, for a reason, and once that was finished, the healing happened by itself.

I look up at Pop.

He isn't doing so good. His lips are white and his eyes are wide and I'm not sure if he's going to pass out or not. Beads of sweat stand out on his scalp. He opens his mouth once like he's going to talk, and his jaw trembles and then snaps shut again. I've never seen his nostrils flared so wide. He glances up at me, then back down at my hand, and I wonder if he's about to say that he loves me anyway.

After a long silence, he opens his mouth again. "This . . . um. *This* is who you are?" he asks tentatively, reaching out to touch one of the orchids and hesitating with his fingertip an inch away from it.

"Well. I didn't know I could do *that*," I whisper. "But yeah. I guess this is who I am." He doesn't touch the orchid. He curls his finger back away from it. When I look up, he's got an expression on his face that I can't read. He's still wide-eyed and pale, and I can't tell if he's scared or angry or sad or . . . what. "Pop?"

"Yeah, bug?"

"Say something."

He starts nodding as if he's agreeing with something I didn't say. "We've got to show your dad," he says. My eyes fill with tears again. It's not a bad answer, but it's not a good one either. He looks up at me, and I see that his eyes are shining too. "We've got to show him," he says, "because, damn, kiddo. This is the most amazing, beautiful thing I've ever seen."

I blink back the tears hard. "Really?"

"Can I hug you? Is that okay? I'm sorry I called you 'kiddo' again, I just." He doesn't finish the sentence, and he doesn't blink back his tears. They start streaming down his cheeks one at a time, sliding along his jaw and dropping off his chin with loud *plops*.

"Yeah," I say, "that's okay." And Pop wraps his arms around me, and I finally let myself lean into him. The neck of his sweater is damp with tears. It's been a long time since I've let either of my dads hug me for longer than a few seconds, and it doesn't feel the same as it used to. When I was little, it felt like the only safe place in the whole world. Now it's nice, but also kind of awkward, like trying to fit into clothes that are just a little too small.

I'm so glad he didn't say that he loves me anyway. And as he hugs me and cries, something occurs to me that should have occurred to me a long time ago. That should have occurred to me while he was telling me the story about his mom.

The thing he was probably expecting me to tell him.

"Pop?"

"Yeah?" His voice is strained.

I clear my throat. "You, um. You know I'm not straight, right? I know we've never really talked about it, and I kind of assumed that you guys knew, but. In case I have to tell you. I don't totally know what the right word is for what I am, but . . . I'm definitely not straight."

He laughs in that way that you do when you're crying and overwhelmed and so, so, so thankful that there's something, *anything*, to laugh about. "Yeah, bug." He kisses me on top of the head. "I know."

"Is it okay that I don't want to talk about it?"

"Sure," he says. "But if you have a girlfriend or a boyfriend or any kind of partner-person, I'd like to know."

I hold back a smile. "I don't. Yet."

"Are you going to soon?"

"I don't know." I laugh, sitting up. "I don't even know if I should ask her out or not."

"Well, when you're ready to, know that you have my blessing," he says. "Roya's always welcome in our family."

"Wait, what did you—"

"Yeah," he says. He wipes his face on the hem of his sweater, then slaps his knees with both palms. "Now, come on. We've got to go find your dad and blow his mind."

18.

"I CAN'T BELIEVE YOU TOLD THEM." MARCELINA cups her hands around the pile of kindling she's crafted. "After all those years of arguing about whether or not any of us should tell any of our parents, I can't believe you're the one who broke first." Her fingernails are dark with dirt, and the smell of turned earth lingers in the air around us. The kindling forms a perfect pyramid, rising out of the hole we've dug in a far corner of her family's sprawling yard. I'm half lying down in the grass, damp with sweat from the digging.

I'm digging so much these days.

"Me either," I say. "It feels like a dream." I flinch as the words leave my mouth—I shouldn't use the word "dream" so lightly anymore. Just like the word "explode." They both have a new flavor now. A bitterness.

Smoke spirals up from the kindling. Marcelina doesn't move her hands, but her forehead creases with focus. "Bad dream or good dream?"

"I'm not sure. I mean, they took it better than I could have hoped. But at the same time . . ."

"Yeah," she says, nodding. I don't say anything for a few minutes, letting her concentrate on heating the kindling enough to get a fire started.

It's true—Pop and Dad both took the whole "I'm magic" thing shockingly well. They had a lot of questions, and what Pop said was right: sometimes, the questions kind of hurt to hear and none of them were easy to answer. Questions like "Did you do anything illegal to get this power?" and "Does it hurt you to do the things you're doing?" and "Have you ever used this power to hurt anyone?" That last one was really tough to answer, because before prom night, the answer would have been "no."

I didn't tell them about Josh. I told them about other stuff, like cheating on a test once (disappointed Dad-glares) and fucking with Nico by getting birds to chase him (poorly smothered laughter). I told them about how there are things I can do and things I can't do, and I don't know what all of those things are yet.

And, after a lot of thinking and a lot of hesitation, I told them that I'm not the only one. I didn't tell them who else is magic—I couldn't betray the girls like that. I told them that there are a ton of people in town who can do what I can do, and I told them that I bet there are also a ton of people out there in the world who can do it too. I told them that I don't think there's something about this town that made me the way I am, but that really, I don't know. None of us do. We don't know if it's genetic, or environmental, or just a fluke. We don't know if we're evolution or radiation or . . . or anything. We could be anything.

I didn't tell them who's magic, but I told them that I'm not alone. I told them that I found people like me, and that we support each other, and that I'd trust those people with my life. I told them about recognizing something different in each other, something special. Something magic.

I think they knew who I meant, but they told me not to tell them any names. They said that I shouldn't ever share someone else's secrets without their permission. They said that they were proud of me for honoring other people's identities.

My dads listened to me in a way that I don't think they've ever listened to me before—it didn't feel like they were waiting to give me advice or instructions, and it didn't feel like they were humoring me. It felt like they respected me. They took in everything I was telling them, and they asked questions as if I were teaching them things they'd never even imagined before. Which I guess I was.

Really, it couldn't possibly have gone better. Except that they talked to me like an equal, which means that they didn't really talk to me like they were talking to their daughter. They talked to me like they were getting to know me, which means that they didn't act like they'd known me my whole life.

I felt like a stranger. A stranger they respected, but still—a stranger.

"Okay," Marcelina says. She sits back on her heels, and when I look into the shallow pit we dug, there's a little fire going. It's small, but it's crackling and growing every second. It climbs quickly up the twigs and paper curls, and before long, it's leaping at the larger sticks she's stacked onto the outside of the pyramid of kindling.

"Wow, nice!" I sit beside Marcelina and admire her handiwork. As usual, she wastes no time preening—she starts carefully placing wood, building a pyre that looks like a little house for fire to live in. She directs careful loops of magic to the fire, twisting threads around the kindling like she's twirling a lasso.

"Paulie taught me this," she says without being prompted. "I have no idea how it works, but it always makes the fire hotter." Sure enough, it's not long before the fire is so powerful that we both have to back away from it. Sweat soaks Marcelina's black tank top, and she lifts the hem to wipe at her streaming face.

"Where did you get all this wood?" I ask. Marcelina's house doesn't have a fireplace, and I've never seen a woodpile around her place.

"I did it this week," she says, and she sounds breathless but proud. "I asked a few trees to drop any branches they didn't need, and then I directed the water out of the wood and into the roots to dry it out."

"You can do that?" I ask, impressed.

"I guess so," she says. "This was my first time trying it and it seems like it worked okay. Remind me to tell Iris so she can add it to her research?"

"Yeah," I say. "There's a lot she should probably add, at this point."

We sit and watch the fire grow. Marcelina is really good at tending to it—holdover Girl Scout skills, I guess, plus whatever experiments Paulie has been sharing. She blows on glowing embers to make them blossom into flames, and she nurtures those tiny petals of fire until they engulf whole logs. The woodsmoke smell mingles with the turned earth and summer air. The grass is soft and thick and the woods are quiet and everything feels as perfect as it possibly can. I breathe it in, try to hang on to the feeling of peace and contentment. I try to capture the moment in my mind, so that later, when I remember how much I've ruined everything, I can come back to it. *One peaceful minute.*

When she's satisfied with the size of the fire—or at least satisfied enough to trust me alone with it—Marcelina pushes herself upright and walks to the house. I stay behind to watch the fire. When she opens the door, Handsome and Fritz come barreling out to see me. They race across the grass, ears flapping, going fast for no reason other than that running is fun. Fritz gets to me first, skidding to a stop and slamming into my legs with nearly enough force to knock me over. I brace myself on his back, fingers buried in his fur, and wait for Handsome to knock into us both. When he does, I'm overwhelmed by the two of them. *Good outside good hot??? Good friend yes smells good smells.*

I sit on the ground and let them wash over me, all wagging tails and musty farm-dog smell. They tell me about the thing they found to roll in, and the mole that's burrowing underneath us right now that they can never seem to dig to, and the pig ears that Uncle Trev brought home for them. By the time Marcelina comes back, carrying the backpack with Josh's liver in it, I'm lying on the ground with a dog on either side of me, their noses next to my ears.

She laughs when she sees me. "You look like you just had a spa weekend."

"These guys always know what to say," I respond without lifting my head. Handsome *boof*s in my ear. "Also, Handsome needs the water warmer when you give him a bath tonight. It makes his hips hurt more when it's cold."

"I'm not giving him a bath—"

"Yeah, sorry, but you are. He's been rolling on a dead toad," I say. Marcelina glares at Handsome. "So has Fritz, but I think Handsome got to it first. He got the squishiest bits on him."

"You guys are gross," she says, patting Handsome on the rump. He wags his tail at her. "That's not a compliment," she mutters, and Fritz lifts his nose to see if he can get a pat too.

"I think the fire is ready," I say, pushing myself up onto my elbows. "I didn't touch it."

"Okay." She eyes the fire in the pit, which is high and bright and loud. She throws a few more pieces of wood into it, and there's a series of loud pops. The smell of burning pinesap fills the air, tinny and acrid. "Do you want to do this, or should I?"

"I think you," I say cautiously. "I think it'll be worse if I do it. Worse for you, I mean."

"Okay," she says. "Okay. Okay." She blows out a long stream of air. "Okay." She opens the backpack and pulls out the liver. It's shiny and taut, darker than I would have expected. Almost purple. She holds it in both hands and looks from it to me. "I'm scared," she whispers. "Like, really scared. I'm freaked out, Alexis." Her brown eyes are wide, and I can see her trying to be brave.

"I'm here," I say. It's the only thing I can say. It's the only comfort I can offer, and I know it isn't enough. "It'll be okay."

Marcelina looks back down at the liver. "What if I lose something really big?" she asks it. "What if I don't lose anything and someone else loses something instead? What if it's not okay?"

"Then we'll all be not-okay with you," I tell her. Her mouth twitches into the briefest of smiles.

"It's not fair when you use my own lines back at me," she says. Then she takes in a gulp of air like she's about to jump into a swimming pool, and she throws the liver onto the fire.

Nothing crazy happens. The fire doesn't change color, and a chill wind doesn't rustle through the trees. The liver sizzles and smokes, and a smell that's uncomfortably reminiscent of barbecue fills the air. Handsome and Fritz both lift their noses to take in the aroma.

"Okay," Marcelina says again. She takes her hair down and runs her fingers through it nervously.

"How do you feel?" I ask.

"I don't know," she says. "Fine, I think. Maybe it's not done yet."

She sits in the grass, leaning back on her hands and watching the fire. I sit next to her. Handsome and Fritz attempt to drape themselves across our laps, and there's a brief moment of chaos as we simultaneously try to push the two wriggling dogs off us. "You're *too big*," I tell them both, but they just wag their tails and pretend not to understand.

"So, you also told your dads that you're . . ." She waves her hands vaguely. "Whatever? What did you tell them? Bisexual?"

"Um, kind of. I told them that I'm still figuring out where I land, and I guess bisexual is the closest thing to true?"

She nods. "You've never really said it out loud before. It's okay if things change later, you know?"

"Yeah, that's what they said. And they both also said that they already knew and they thought I knew they knew? So it wasn't really a big deal, I guess."

"It's still a big deal, even if it wasn't a big deal," she says, scratching under Fritz's collar.

"Pop said something weird," I say as casually as I can. "I think he was just trying to be supportive or whatever, but he said that he thinks I should ask Roya out." I catch Marcelina rolling her eyes. "What?"

"What?"

"Why are you rolling your eyes at that?"

She does it again. I use a little spark of magic to tell Fritz to lick her in retaliation, and she tries to shove him away, but he nails her right in the ear. She makes an *euuuaaaghh* noise. "Gross, Fritz, you have toad-breath."

"Good boy, Fritz," I say, rubbing the hard-to-reach spot under his ear.

Not to be outdone, Handsome tries to shove his nose into her other ear. "Call off your goons, Alexis!" she cries, shoving at the big shaggy dog.

I grab Handsome by the collar and he settles for shoving his nose into *my* ear, which isn't my favorite sensation, but which isn't nearly so bad as getting licked. "You don't have toad-breath," I whisper, even though he kind of does.

"Look, I just think that it's sort of obvious that you should ask Roya out, isn't it?" Marcelina grabs a long, forked stick and pushes the black lump of liver deeper into the fire. "We all thought you were going to ask her to prom, but—"

"She wanted to go with Tall Matt," I say bitterly.

"Um, no," she says. "She *wanted* to go with you, but then you never asked her and Tall Matt did. They were there as friends."

"She was just saying that because she's afraid of commitment," I snap. Marcelina gives me an *oh hell no, how did you just try to talk to me?* look and I grimace. "Sorry. I didn't mean to snipe."

"Damn right you didn't," she mutters. "And you need to give Roya more credit than that. She wouldn't lie about not being into Tall Matt. She likes him as a friend. Did you even see them dancing at prom, or were you too busy getting groped by Josh? Who, I am delighted to remind you, *you* don't even *like*?"

"Didn't," I murmur. Her face softens.

"What were you doing with him, Lex?" She combs her fingers through Fritz's fur. His eyes close in contentment and he does some tiny tail-wags that tap against my thigh. "I know everyone's been asking you and you're super grumpy about it, but . . . it just doesn't make any sense."

"Why not?" I purse my lips, trying not to get snappy with her again. "I've dated guys too. What, just because I'm"—vague hand waving—"whatever kind of queer I am, I can't still hook up with dudes?"

"You're full of shit," Marcelina says mildly, still dragging her fingers through the long, coarse fur on Fritz's head. "You know that's not what I mean. And don't try to play it like you've ever slept with a guy before. We both know that would have been your first time." She shakes her head. "And it would have been with *Josh Harper*."

She's right. I am full of shit. I'm so full of shit that, even though I know the answer, I say, "Well what *do* you mean, then? Because it sounds an awful lot like you're trying to tell me who I'm allowed to sleep with."

Marcelina gives me another *oh you're really going to try this crap* glare. "What do I mean? What I mean is, it doesn't make any sense because you're clearly crazy about Roya. And you didn't know the difference between Josh Harper and Short

Matt until you were dancing with Josh at prom. What I *mean* is, it seems an "awful lot" like you were going to sleep with a guy you've barely exchanged two words with for no discernible reason. *What I mean is*, you're usually pretty smart and you almost did something so *monumentally stupid* that it made me wonder if you'd fallen and hit your head when I wasn't looking."

"I was going to sleep with him because Roya went to prom with Tall Matt!" I say it too loud, just on the threshold of shouting. Handsome startles and looks up at me with concern. I should probably reassure him, but I can't right now. I'm tired of feeling so many damn feelings all the time, and I'm tired of trying to calm myself down when I'm angry, and I'm tired of telling dogs that it's not *them* I'm upset with. "I was going to sleep with him because Roya went to prom with Tall Matt and she went to Homecoming with Kevin Ng and she made out with Karen Carter over the summer and I'm tired of waiting for her!"

I dig my fingers into the grass and yell. I yell with my voice, letting my exhaustion and frustration rip through my throat; and I yell with my magic, pushing all the wasted patience and lingering hurt into the ground, probably shocking the hell out of that poor mole. Handsome and Fritz jump up and run in panicked circles, trying to figure out why they can hear me yelling in two voices at the same time.

After a minute, warmth floods my face. I open my eyes and there's Marcelina's eyes, a few inches from mine. Her hands are cupping my cheeks, and she's whispering something in a low, steady stream that I can't hear but that I can feel lapping at me in steady waves. The warmth spreads into my throat and chest, and I feel like I've been dipped in honey. "Are you done?" she says softly, and I nod, taking a hiccuping breath. "Good."

She takes her hands away and sits back in her place in the grass. Handsome and Fritz slink over with their noses low and their tails tucked under their bellies. "Sorry I scared you, fellas," I say, stroking their heads and silently telling them that it wasn't their fault I yelled.

"I'm going to say something," Marcelina says. "And you aren't allowed to yell."

"I'm sorry I—"

"Shut up," she says mildly. "I didn't say 'You shouldn't have yelled.' I don't want your apology. I just want you to listen for a minute." I nod. She crosses her legs and rests her elbows on her knees, steepling her fingers. "First: I cannot believe you were going to do something so stupid as to sleep with Josh Damn Harper in order to make Roya *jealous*." I start to object, but she holds up her hand. "Nope," she says. "I'm talking right now, you're listening. Don't try to tell me that you weren't hoping you'd sleep with Josh and make Roya feel as jealous as you were feeling about Tall Matt, because that's a lie. And you can lie to yourself all you want, but you do not lie to *me*."

I bite my lip and wait for her to continue, even though I have a sinking feeling that it's only going to get worse from here.

"I cannot *believe* that you would do something so *monumentally, staggeringly foolish* as to put Josh Harper's penis inside you in order to *hurt Roya's feelings*," she says, ramping up fast. "I can't believe that you, of all the people in the whole world, would decide to *fuck a boy* over something as *petty* and *messy* as Roya going to prom with Tall Matt and making out with Karen Carter, who makes out with *everybody* and you know it!"

She hasn't moved an inch, but her eyes are blazing. I feel about an inch tall. When she puts it that way . . . I can't really believe that I was going to do that either. I knew I was making the wrong choice the second Josh's dick exploded, but I've been trying really hard not to think about it too much in the last week. Both because it's really awful to think about, and because I knew that if I looked too closely at what I almost did, I would be just as disappointed in myself as Marcelina is now.

"That was the first thing I needed to tell you," she says. Her eyes are glassy now—she's still glaring at me fiercely, but there's sadness there too. "The second thing I need to tell you is that the liver is done. It's gone."

I peer into the fire, but I can't tell one lump of black char from another. "How can you tell?" I ask.

"Because," Marcelina says in a whisper, "I lost the color green."

"What?" I look back at her. Her mouth lifts into a very small, very sad smile.

"That's what I lost," she says. She sounds terribly calm. "I can't see it." She runs her hand across the grass.

"What does it look like?" I whisper. She shakes her head.

"Gray." She swallows the word.

"Oh, Marcelina—"

"It's fine." She says it through clenched teeth. "Lots of people can't see green. I'll get used to it." Next to her, Fritz whines and rubs at his muzzle with a paw.

"God, I'm so sorry," I say, reaching out a hand to rest on hers. "But hey, there are only a few pieces left to go, and then we'll bring him back, right? And then you'll get to see green again, just like normal." She jerks her hand away.

"Sorry," she says. "I don't want to be touched right now. I just—I need a few minutes." She gets up and walks back into the house, carrying the empty backpack with her. I wait outside with Handsome and Fritz, watching the fire die and thinking about what she said. What she said about getting used to it, and what she said about me being an idiot. The dogs doze in the sun. After a while, I hear footsteps in the grass behind me. I look up, ready to do whatever Marcelina needs—but it's not her. It's Uncle Trev.

"Mind if I join you?" he asks, waiting a few steps away until I nod. He never sits with me unless I say yes.

"What's up?" I ask, watching the embers in the little pit we dug.

"I smelled smoke and wanted to see what was going on." He picks up Marcelina's forked stick and pushes a glowing log around. "It's awful hot for a fire."

"We had some stuff to burn," I tell him. It's out of my mouth before it occurs to me that I should have an answer ready in case he asks *what* needed burning, but he just nods.

"So, Marcelina's in the house crying her eyes out," he says mildly. "What's going on?"

"Um." I flip Handsome's floppy ear back and forth. "Nothing I can really share."

"Hmph." Uncle Trev chews on this for a minute, then shakes his head. "Look, I'm not going to get into her business. I just need to know that she's okay. She's crying like she just found out her best friend died. But I know that's not the case, because you're out here, and you're alive."

"I'm her best friend?" I blurt. I regret asking immediately.

"Far as I can tell," he says. "Are you *still* her best friend? You guys didn't just have a big blow-up or anything, right?"

"No, we're good," I say. "I mean, she gave me some real talk today, but nothing bad. She's just, um. She's going through a hard time right now."

"She's not hurting herself or anything, though, right?" He says it fast, so fast that I almost don't catch it. He pokes the crumbling log in the fire a couple more times, not looking at me. His face is set.

"No," I say softly. "She's not hurting herself."

"Can you promise me that you'd tell me if she was?" He looks at me and there's the feeling again, the one I had with my dads last night. Uncle Trev isn't talking to me like a kid right now. He's not asking me if I'm lying to him. He's trusting me to take care of someone he cares about.

"I promise," I say, and I lift my hand to hold out a pinky finger. But then I think twice, and I hold out my whole hand.

We shake on it.

He stands up, brushing grass off his butt. "I'm going to go back in and check on her," he says.

"She actually said that she wants space," I tell him. "She needs to be alone for a little while."

"Okay," he says. "I won't bother her or get into her space or anything. But I gotta make sure she's okay, you know? I'll leave her alone, but I can't leave her *alone*." He musses the back of his hair, frowning. "I'm the only adult around right now and I gotta make sure she's safe. Do you want to come with?"

I shake my head. "It'll make her feel ganged-up-on. When she asks for space, she really needs it, you know?"

"I know," he says, nodding. "I'll just poke my head in to make sure she's in one piece and then I'll leave her be. I promise."

He walks back toward the house with his hands deep in his pockets. He's a good guy. He's trying to do the right thing. I wish I could convince him not to check on Marcelina, but at the same time, I'm really happy that he's going to check on her. Because maybe she needs checking on. Maybe she needs someone making sure she's in one piece. I think I'd notice if she was feeling bad enough to need checking on, but then, there are lots of things I don't notice.

I'm glad Trev is here for her, is all. I'm glad that Marcelina isn't going to be *alone*-alone. I look around me at the green grass and feel a pang of something like emptiness, and even though I know I'm not *alone*-alone, I feel lonely. I pull out my phone and text Roya.

Hey.

She texts back so quickly that I wonder if we hit send at the same time. **Wyd?**

Getting slobbered on by Handsome and Fritz.

She responds with her favorite picture of Fritz, from his birthday party a year and a half ago. We'd filled a cupcake wrapper with peanut butter, and his snout was covered in it. Roya caught a photo of him in the exact moment that he was trying to lick his own eyebrow. It's a picture with a lot of tongue. She captions it **Tell him I said he's a good boy.**

So I do. I poke at the embers in the fire pit with a stick, and I tell Fritz he's a good boy, and I wait for Marcelina to come outside into the gray world.

19.

WHEN I WAKE UP ON MONDAY MORNING, THERE'S a text from Roya waiting for me. My heart stutters, then rights itself when I see that it's just a message on the group text. I squint blearily at the screen. When I see what she's written, my stomach drops.

Senior wing girls' room 1st period 911

It's the "911" that does it. That's a summons that means exactly what it implies: Emergency. Come right away. No questions, no arguments: *I need you.*

There's a long line of thumbs-up emojis from everyone else on the chat. It's the only acceptable response. I send one too, then put my phone down and stay in bed, listening to the sounds of the house and trying hard not to worry. Water is running in the bathroom—Nico's morning shower, which will last for about thirty minutes or until Dad pounds on the door to tell him to leave some hot water for the rest of us. Dad and Pop are murmuring to each other in the kitchen. I strain to hear what they're saying, a habit from when I was little and would try to overhear them talking about me. I wonder if they're talking about me now. About what they know, and what might need to be done about me.

I wonder if I was wrong to show them.

My alarm goes off again. I turn it off and stay under the covers. It feels like maybe if I lie still enough, everything will freeze around me and I won't have to face the day. I won't have to find out what the 911 is about, what today's disaster is going to be. I won't have to watch that gray-haired cop pulling people out of classrooms. I won't have to eat, won't have to have conversations, won't have to breathe.

But then I hear Dad's footsteps down the hall, his knuckles on the door to the bathroom. A few seconds later, they're tapping on the wall outside of my room.

"Hey, bug, time to wake up," he says to the door.

"I'm awake," I say, and the spell is broken. I can't stay in bed, and I know it. I become aware of the bad taste in my mouth and the way the covers are a little too warm.

Something bad is happening. I can feel it. I wonder if someone else lost something big, if something else is broken beyond repair, if something else is going horribly, horribly wrong.

The day is waiting. The 911 is waiting. The gray-haired cop is waiting. The worry is waiting.

And I have to face it all.

* * *

Maryam and I are the last ones to arrive at the restroom during first period. It's not that we have trouble getting hall passes—it's just that it's nearly impossible to make Mr. Wyatt look up from the earnest "Are you interested in dating a high-strung calculus teacher with a penchant for lavender ties?" profile he's in the middle of composing. He doesn't seem to notice that we're standing next to him until there's a knock on the door of the classroom. It's a freshman from the administrative office with a note for Mr. Wyatt—a summons for Angela Trinh.

Here is what I know about Angela: Her twin brother is on the lacrosse team. She does badly on quizzes but never seems stressed about her grades. She wants to be a singer. That's about it. Sometimes I wonder how it's possible, in a town as small as mine, that I don't know more about all of my classmates—but then, I've never really needed to learn more about them. I've always had my friends, and they've always been all I need. And by the time I started to really feel bad for not making more of an effort to get to know everyone, it was already senior year, and it felt like a waste.

Angela leaves slowly. Her eyes fill with tears as she picks up her bag. She could have been called to the principal's office for anything, but everyone in the classroom is thinking the same thing as she hesitates with her hand on the doorknob: she is going to be questioned about Josh.

Josh, who has been missing for over a week now. Josh, who still hasn't been found.

We trail Angela and the office messenger down the hall, walking a little slower with every step until we're far enough behind them to duck out of sight. We scoot behind some lockers and wait until we can't hear their footfalls. Until we can't hear Angela sniffling anymore. Maryam's face is calm, but she twists the hem of her shirt between her fingers.

"You okay?" I whisper.

"Yeah," she says. "Just worried about Roya. And everything."

"You don't have to come to this. It's probably about the thing, and the less you know, the less involved you are."

Maryam looks at me like I've slapped her hard across the cheek. "Of course I'm coming. It's a 911, Alexis. I'm not ignoring that."

"Okay, okay," I say. "Sorry."

She shakes her head. "I'm still here, you know," she murmurs. "Just because I couldn't—"

"I know," I interrupt desperately. "I know, I'm sorry, I know. I didn't mean it that way."

She lifts her chin. "Stop apologizing," she says. "Let's go."

When we walk into the restroom, Roya steps past me and locks the door. I raise my eyebrows as Marcelina checks all the stalls for occupants. "What's the big emergency?" I ask.

Roya leans against the sink with her arms crossed. She's wearing a flannel over ripped-up shorts today, and I have to work hard not to stare at the lines of muscle in her thighs. She's not looking at Paulie, and I can't figure out if she's just not looking at Paulie or if she's specifically *not looking at Paulie*. There's a major vibe. I try to catch Paulie's eye, but she's busy adjusting something in the back of her high-waisted skirt. Paulie is all business today: chignon, pressed blouse, a pen on a necklace. I try to parse what message today's fashion is sending, because there's always a message with Paulie. But my head is swimming, and I just can't. I can't decode my friends today.

"We have a problem," Roya says. Her voice is low, strained. She takes out her phone and pulls up a photoset. "Look."

She passes the phone around, and I watch as one by one, my friends see whatever it is that made Roya lock that door. Marcelina makes a noise low in her throat. Iris sways on her feet. I peer over Maryam's shoulder when the phone gets to her. Wordlessly, she hands it to me, and I am the last to see.

At first, I'm not sure what I'm looking at. They're pictures of photos. Photos of dry grass, little yellow plastic triangles, grid markers and rulers. A plastic bag with . . . something in it. Something that my brain can't resolve into a *thing*. It looks like a ham covered in jelly, or maybe the broken end of a baseball bat with paint on it. Or . . . no, none of that is right. I squint, and then, finally, the red pulp in the picture resolves itself into a recognizable shape.

It's an arm.

It's a half-eaten arm.

I drop the phone. It clatters across the tile and comes to a rest against the base of the already-full trash can. Roya stoops to pick it up and checks it for cracks before tucking it back into her pocket. "So," she says.

"What the fuck, what the fuck? What the fuck?" My hands are shaking. My whole body is shaking. Maryam wraps an arm around me and takes a few deep breaths, trying to make me match her rhythm so I'll calm down. Another trick Iris has taught us over the years. I struggle to breathe with her. My throat feels too narrow to admit all that air.

"They found it last night," Roya says. I look up at her and realize that she has the wide-eyed stare of someone who hasn't slept. Her hair is in a tangled bun, and the outline of yesterday's headband is still creased across the top of her head. I was so busy staring at her legs that I didn't even notice how exhausted she is.

I feel like an asshole. What kind of friend am I, to miss that kind of thing?

"I overheard my mom talking to my dad about it after she got home," Roya continues. Now that I've noticed how tired she is, I can hear the fatigue in her voice, too. "They got a call from someone who thought they'd found a body, but it turned out that it was just the arm. I guess it was chewed up by something. They matched a birthmark to a picture of Josh. I don't know about, you know. DNA or whatever. But there's going to be a search party. They're canceling classes tomorrow. You'll hear about it in fourth period."

The rest of the girls immediately start talking over one another, talking about the search party. About where it will be and what the searchers might find, and whether we should go. While they argue, I try to remember a birthmark. I didn't notice it. I was going to sleep with that boy, and I didn't even know about his birthmark. I fed his arm to a coyote, and not once did I look closely enough at it to see the damned *birthmark*. I swear, every time I think I couldn't possibly have screwed this up worse, I discover some new way that I'm a disaster.

"It's my fault," Paulie whispers. "I'm sorry."

"It doesn't matter whose fault it is," Roya snaps, making Paulie flinch. "We just need to fix it. What are we going to do?"

Someone tries to pull open the door to the restroom, then pounds on the metal when they realize that it's locked. Maryam shoots out a hand and, faster than gasping, the light of her soft, suffuse magic etches mascara trails down Marcelina's cheeks. Paulie and Roya wrap their arms around Marcelina, and Roya hisses "Cry!" as Iris unlocks the door.

"I just—can't—*believe*—he—said—" Marcelina is choking and sobbing, and the twin streams of mascara on her cheeks cover for the fact that her eyes are dry.

"Do you mind?" Roya snaps at the sophomore standing in the doorway.

"Oh god, I'm sorry," the girl says. "Is she okay?" Marcelina wails, and the girl holds up both hands like she can ward off the tears. "Never mind," she says. "I'll leave you guys alone. Um, I hope things get better soon?"

"And—then—he—said—" Marcelina puts a high wobble into her voice, and the girl closes the door fast. As soon as Iris has slid the lock home, Roya and Paulie straighten. Roya pats Marcelina's cheeks with her fingers, and the mascara trails vanish.

"You're amazing," Maryam says.

Marcelina grins. "I know."

Roya snaps her fingers. "Hey, you're both amazing. But we gotta figure out this arm thing, like, now." She's being Iris-levels of bossy, but nobody so much as glares at her, because if Roya being abrupt is ever warranted, now's the time.

"Can you get rid of it? Like, just grab the bag and throw it away?" Paulie asks, then shakes her head hard. "Never mind, that's stupid."

"Yeah, that's a terrible idea," Roya says. "If it goes missing, they'll know for sure that someone is trying to cover something up. I don't think that they are saying he was—" She stops short and looks at me with an apologetic grimace. "I don't think they're calling it murder yet. I'm pretty sure they're trying to figure out what happened before they make an announcement. But they *definitely* know that it's Josh's arm." Her mouth flattens into a grim line.

"We'll have to wait and see," Marcelina says. "Maybe it'll be okay."

"Maybe it'll be okay," I repeat. My lips feel numb.

"That search party," Iris whispers. "We have to go. We have to."

Marcelina whips around to stare at her with stark incredulity. "We can't do that, are you crazy? It'll look so suspicious."

Roya shakes her head. "No. They're canceling classes so that everyone can join. Everyone will be there. We *have* to go."

"We can't go," Paulie says, her face white. "Are you kidding?"

Maryam clears her throat. "You have to go." She looks around at everyone. "I mean, I'll be there too, but you guys really have to go."

It's Iris and Roya and Maryam versus Paulie and Marcelina. Normally, Iris and Roya on the same side of an issue means that the whole group goes with whatever they say. They're individually strong-willed enough that the two of them together feels indomitable. But this time, everyone looks at me. They're waiting for me.

This is my mess. I have to choose.

I nod. "Yeah," I whisper. "We gotta be there." I don't say that the reason we have to be there isn't because of suspicion, isn't because of who might be watching, isn't to try to prevent more bits of Josh from turning up. It's just because I can't imagine sitting at home, alone, waiting for more bad news.

If this is going to go wrong, it might as well go wrong right away.

Roya bites her thumbnail and looks at me. "It's settled. We'll go."

"Shit," Marcelina hisses. "Okay. I'll be there." She turns to Maryam to coordinate a carpool, and the conversation shifts to logistics.

Roya is still watching me. She lets her voice drop to a lower, more intimate tone. What she says next is just for me. "Don't do anything stupid, okay?"

"Like what?" I ask. She rolls her eyes.

"Like turning yourself in. Anything could happen from here. We have to stick together."

I close my eyes for a count of four. "I won't turn myself in," I say. Even though that's exactly what I was thinking of doing. When I open my eyes, Roya is looking at me like she can see right through to the knot in my stomach.

The rest of the girls start filing out of the bathroom past us, but Roya still hasn't moved. "Today, right?"

"Today?" I ask, trying not to stare at the curve of her collarbone.

"Yeah," she says. "Today. Me and you. Arm-in-arm?" She smiles at me, a small pleased-with-her-own-cleverness smile. "Yes, no . . . ?"

I had almost forgotten. "Yeah, today," I say, my heart pounding. Roya steps closer to me and her eyes flick to my mouth.

"It's a date," she says softly. Then she steps past me, and my heart is pounding, and she's gone.

All day I'm waiting for someone to bring up the arm. Waiting to hear a whisper in the halls, or to see a cop in the cafeteria. But other than an announcement in fourth period about the search party, no one is talking about it. Lunch is awkward and stilted, and we spend half of it in silence, staring at each other's untouched food. I pass by Josh's decorated locker and see that someone has ripped off the duct-taped teddy bear, leaving behind a swath of adhesive gunk. A sticky note that says "we miss u john" has been stuck to the middle of the gray stripe where the duct tape used to be. I rip it down and crumple it in my fist and drop it into my locker. When I clear my locker out for the summer, I'm sure I'll find it there, but right now I don't care. I just don't want to look at it.

When I get out of sixth period, I have a message from Roya waiting for me. **Parking lot fourth row in. Gotta boogie.**

I get into her car without letting the heat out properly. I start sweating immediately. Drastically, aggressively sweating. Torrential sweating. Roya's got the windows down and she starts the AC blasting the second the car is turned on, but it's still dire. She looks at me with an expression that says *I'm melting*, and I would laugh if I could breathe through the heat.

"Drive," I finally manage to croak. She nods and peels out of the parking lot at Paulie-speed. Her hair whips back from her face in the breeze, and the shimmer of sweat along the curve of her throat makes me lose the ability to breathe for about a minute. I stare out the window until I can get all of my thoughts into a line. "Where are we going?" I ask as she turns onto the highway.

"I want to show you something," she says. "Trust me?"

"Of course," I answer. She turns up the radio. At first I think that she's trying to show me something about the music, but then I realize that she just doesn't want me asking any more questions. So we sing along with the songs we know, and I stick an arm out the window and let the air rushing past the car lift my hand, and Roya drives.

She drives for an hour before I try to ask again. "Roya? Where are we—"

"Please," she says, her eyes still on the road. "We're almost there."

She parks by a stretch of road that looks exactly like the twenty miles that came before it and, I suspect, exactly like the twenty miles that come after it. Birch trees line either side of the asphalt, a long stretch of white that keeps going as far as I can see.

"Marcelina would love this," I say, resting my hand against the patchy white bark of the nearest tree. I don't feel anything but the scratch of wood under my palm, but I know that Marcelina would be immersed in the stories of the forest.

"Yeah," Roya says, but she sounds distracted and I'm not sure if she actually heard me. She's got a duffel slung over her shoulder, and she's staring into the trees in a far-off way I'm not used to. "Let's go?"

"Sure," I say, and I follow her into the trees. They're spaced far enough apart that it almost feels like a set piece in a movie, a fake forest, but then I turn to look behind me and realize that I can't see the road anymore. Without Roya, I know I'd never find my way back. That's the mark of a real forest: you can get lost before you realize that you should be trying to stay found.

I follow her through the trees, only occasionally having to step around the sparse undergrowth. Her hair is up in a high bun. The back of her shirt is dark with sweat. I watch the way her calves move with each step, the way the backs of her knees turn pink in the heat. We don't speak. She's not looking back at me. Whatever our destination is, she's entirely focused on it. Whatever our destination is, I'll follow her there.

The clearing comes upon us suddenly. Or maybe it seems that way to me. I'm not sure how long we've been walking, and I have no idea where the road is, but without warning, the trees fall away. I nearly run into Roya's back. She's standing with her arms by her sides, her eyes closed, her chin tipped back. She's breathing slowly, and every time she exhales: magic.

It's nothing I've ever seen her do before. Roya is frenetic energy, hunger, anger. But in this place, she's still and calm. Every time she exhales, a bare hush of a breeze stirs the leaves that are littered across the grass of the meadow. A loose tendril of hair plays across her forehead in the breeze, and a whisper of light suffuses her skin.

It's not that she's more beautiful than usual. She's always beautiful. But she's still, and I get to look at her without reservation, without worrying that she'll think it's weird of me to stare. I didn't realize how thirsty I was, but now I'm offered the opportunity to drink her in. And I take it.

When she opens her eyes, I don't look away. She looks

right at me, and I'm certain that she sees the longing on my face. I don't try to hide it. For the first time ever, I *don't try to hide it*. My hands are shaking. My heart is shaking.

She smiles.

She bites her lip.

"Sorry," she says. "I just . . . I like to take a minute when I first get here. To be present."

"No worries," I say, my voice rough. "Take all the time you need."

"I'm good," she says. And then she holds out her hand.

I look at it. She's wearing the gold bangle with the dark green stones. The lines of her palm are dark. The skin of her wrist trembles with the force of the pulse beneath the surface. She twitches her fingers, and I realize she's waiting for me. I reach out my hand and put it in hers.

Her fingers curl around mine, and she leads me toward the center of the clearing.

"I like to come here sometimes," she says. Her thumb is tracing the curve of my knuckle. I can't breathe. "When things get tough. It's where I first did magic, did you know that?"

"I thought the first time you did magic was at a family thing? The barbecue with the dropped cake . . . ?" I hear myself say the words as though from a distance.

"I always say that, but this is really the first place." I realize that she isn't looking at me. She stops in the middle of the clearing, and she doesn't look at me, and she traces the line of my thumb. "I got separated from my parents on a camping trip, and I wound up here. I could hear them looking for me, but I stayed quiet. I remember being scared that if they found me, they'd get mad and send me away."

"Oh." It's all I can think to say. Roya sinks to the grass and sits, still holding my hand. I sit across from her. Our knees are less than one inch apart, but there's no way for me to scoot forward without it being obvious that I just want her to touch me. I just want her to touch me.

"Yeah," she says. She's still not looking at me. "Anyway. I fell and skinned my knee on the way here, and it was bleeding like crazy, but by the time they found me, it was totally healed. No blood, no scar. Nothing. I remember trying to tell my mom about it, and she was sure that I had just gotten scared and imagined it, but I know it happened. That was the first time I did magic."

"How did you get lost?" I ask. My knees feel warm and I look down and realize that somehow, she has come closer. We are touching. Our knees are touching, and our hands are touching, and she's grabbing my other hand too. Holding it. And she finally looks at me. My breath catches when our eyes meet.

"I walked off," she says. "I was looking for my mom."

"Where was she?"

"No, you don't understand," she says, shaking her head and looking at me intently. "I was looking for my birth mom. I dreamed that she was in the woods, and I wandered off to find her. It was the middle of the night."

"How old were you?" I ask. The first time Roya did magic in front of me, we were eight and she still needed two night-lights. I can't imagine her in the woods by herself, in the dark. No moonlight would be enough to keep the shadows from looking like monsters.

"Four," she whispers. "I was so scared of the dark, but I wanted to find her. I wanted to find my birth mom. And I stayed here because I thought she was going to come get me." She squeezes both of my hands, and I squeeze hers back. She's looking back and forth between my eyes like there's something there, some answer to a question she hasn't asked yet. "I come here sometimes to think about stuff, or to be alone. I've never brought anyone here before."

I don't know what to say. I don't know why she's showing me. All I can say is "Thank you." I run the pad of my thumb across the palm of her hand, and she bites her lip. I'm stuck between absolute certainty that I'm imagining something between us and absolute certainty that I'm not imagining it at all.

"It's a magic place," she says. She lifts one of my hands to her mouth and presses her lips to my thumb, still staring directly into my eyes. My breath is loud in my ears. "Of course I wanted to show you," she whispers to the curve of my palm.

"Roya," I start to say, but I don't know what should come after.

Or, I do know what should come after, but I don't know how to say it. I've been biting back the words for so long now that I don't know how to push them past my lips.

But it doesn't matter.

It doesn't matter, because she's kissing me.

How can I explain what it's like?

It's like soft grass under your back on a hot day.

It's like the first ripe strawberry from the garden.

It's like watching someone fall asleep with their head on your shoulder, and knowing that you could brush the hair away from their eyes without waking them.

It's like coming home.

When Roya stops kissing me, she rests her forehead against mine and laughs.

"What?" I breathe.

"Look," she says, her mouth so close to mine that I can taste the letter *L* tumbling from her lips.

I look. I don't want to, because it means moving my head away from hers, but I look. "Oh," I say, and then "oh" again, because the first time wasn't quite enough.

The clearing is carpeted in flowers. All except for the place where we're sitting. Tiny purple flowers and huge, spreading yellow ones, and a fine tracery of white clover blossoms. The air is fragrant, and Roya is laughing and running a hand over the tops of the flowers closest to her. She flings herself backward and lands hard, but she keeps laughing as she sprawls her arms out on the flowers. Petals fly up around her like a snowdrift.

"That looked like it hurt," I say.

"It did," she says. "Try it."

I fling myself down next to her, and she's right, it hurts. And I'm glad I did it. I watch as flower petals spiral up in the air over our heads, and I listen to Roya laughing, and I can feel myself bleeding magic too. A swarm of butterflies circles overhead and settles in the branches of the birch trees, their yellow wings fluttering like autumn leaves.

"I've been wanting to do that for a long time," Roya says.

"Would you like to do it again?" I ask, then laugh at how slick I sound. I'm still laughing as her mouth finds mine, and then I'm not laughing anymore because she's not what I thought she would be. She's more. Her lips are soft, and her hands are both tangled in my hair, and she's straddling my hips and making a soft noise that means I'm more than she thought I would be too.

When we stop for air, her hair is loose around her shoulders, falling into my face. It's not dusk yet, but the light outside has taken on a long-shadow quality that means it will start getting dark before too long.

"Wow," I breathe.

"Yeah," she says. She touches her nose to the soft skin behind my ear and I pull up two fistfuls of flowers. "We should go soon."

"Yeah," I say. I don't sit up. She stays with me for the space of three slow breaths; then she stands up and extends a hand to me.

"Come on." She's smiling. Her lips are a little swollen. The word "bee-stung" springs into my mind, unbidden. "We have to take care of Josh before we go."

In the place where we were sitting before, there's a circle of grass. Roya digs her fingers into the soft soil and pulls up sod. She sinks her hands into the earth and turns it up as easily as she might pull fistfuls of cotton out of a torn-open teddy bear. I watch her, and she catches me watching her, and she grins at me. "Magic," she says, and I realize that she's not just pushing her hands into the dirt; she's pushing threads of magic, too, and the earth is moving for her.

"I wish I'd thought of that before I did all that damn digging," I mutter. She laughs at me.

"Can you grab the bag?"

"Sure." I pick up the duffel, which is half-hidden in a sudden profusion of bluebells. She takes it from me, and our fingers brush, and a flock of birds erupts from a nearby tree.

She doesn't say anything. She just unzips the duffel and overturns it, letting the arm inside fall into the hole. She shakes the bag, and a few bits of trash fall out—gum wrappers, pencil lead, eraser crumbs. She starts pushing soil back into the hole, over the arm. "What should we do with the bag?" she asks.

"I guess . . . leave it in the woods? Or maybe drop it in a dumpster somewhere?" I realize that we should all probably dispose of the bags as quickly as we can.

"I'll toss it on the highway," she says.

"That's littering."

She gives me a long look. "You're worried about littering? Really?" I shrug and she shakes her head. "Don't worry. I'll take care of it. Come here."

I sit beside her as she pats the last of the earth down over Josh's arm. She fishes in one pocket of her shorts with two fingers and withdraws something small and smooth. She drops it into my hand.

"An acorn?" I ask, turning it over between my thumb and forefinger.

"Yeah," she says. "To keep animals from getting at the arm." She plucks the acorn from my grasp and shoves it down into the soil.

"We can't make it grow, though," I say slowly. "That's a Marcelina thing."

"Alexis. We can do whatever we want," she says. She leans over and brushes her lips against my earlobe. "We're magic."

She grabs my hand and presses it down under hers, into the soil. She kisses me, and something new happens between us. Magic that feels like nothing I've ever done before. Something hot and vibrant. Something urgent and immediate. I feel the soil shift under my fingers, and then under my feet, and then we're both toppling backward. Roya pulls me up by my wrist, yanking me away from—

A tree.

An oak tree.

A small one, twisting up out of the ground. Five narrow, trembling branches reaching up like fingers. Leaves bud and unfurl as we watch, our hands clenched together tight. Gray bark hardens and cracks and splits and grows again. A gash opens in one side of the trunk; it oozes sap and then heals over within a few seconds.

"Holy shit," Roya says.

"Holy shit," I repeat, because there's nothing else that either of us can say. With a rustle and a shake of acorn-heavy branches, the oak stops growing. It's easily fifteen feet tall, with a huge, full canopy. It's beautiful.

It's ours.

"We did that," Roya breathes.

"Are you scared?" I ask.

"Of what?"

"Of what might happen next. Of what you might lose."

She shakes her head. "It'll happen how it happens, and you'll be with me for it, so why would I be scared?"

I don't say anything at all. I just grab her by the shoulders, push her back against the trunk of our new tree, and kiss her.

We make a pile of our clothes in the grass as the sun goes down.

Roya presses me down into the flowers as the crickets start to sing.

I gasp her name as the first few stars appear in the dusky sky.

I kiss her, and I kiss her, and I kiss her. And she kisses me back.

20.

THE DRIVE HOME FROM ROYA'S MEADOW IS soft-focus: she drives with one hand and gives me the other hand, and I kiss her palm, and we don't say a word to each other. The windows are down and the crickets are singing so loudly that we can hear them even over the sound of the road passing underneath us.

By daylight the next morning, though, I wonder if maybe we should have talked. Maybe I should have asked her if what happened in the meadow meant the same thing to her as it did to me. Even though all I want is to see her and the way she laughs and the way she smiles and the way she messes with her hair when she's thinking hard about something and the way she gasps when I kiss the hollow of her hip—even then, I don't want to see her because I'm afraid she won't meet my eyes. What if she's embarrassed around me? What if she says that it was just a joke, or a fling, or—worst of all—a mistake?

I check my phone for messages from her while I try to figure out what a girl is supposed to wear to a search party. The announcement said to wear comfortable shoes and included dire warnings about ticks and dehydration. I decide on jeans and a tank top: it's hot as hell, but I'm pretty sure that I heard once that long pants are good to wear when there are ticks around. I dig under my bed for my hiking boots, pushing aside the backpack with Josh's name on it.

My hand freezes.

I do a mental tally.

The head. The arms. The legs. The spine. The liver. The hands. The feet.

All those parts are gone. I had gotten so used to the feeling of knowing that we had more pieces to get rid of—so used to the guilt and uncertainty and pressure—that I hadn't realized we were done.

I tug the bag out from under my bed, and there's no heft to it at all, no weight. Before I even finish unzipping it, I know what I'll find. But I still have to see for myself.

I pull at the zipper tabs, and the loose piece of duct tape covering Josh's name falls to my bed. My palm covers the *J* in *Josh* as I pull the backpack open and look inside.

I was right. I try to exhale, but I can't seem to remember how. I was right. There's nothing in there. I was right, and I have no idea what will happen next.

The backpack is empty.

The heart is gone.

* * *

The search party is up on the overlook where Paulie kissed me. I catch a ride with Maryam, who passes me a mason jar of something she calls an iced marshmallow latte. It tastes like powdered sugar and toasted breadcrumbs. I tell her to give her dad a C-minus from me. She laughs, and then she tells me about all of his recent culinary adventures. His attempt at homemade cocoa puffs. His basil obsession. I realize, halfway to the overlook, that she's talking nonstop. It's not like her—she's big into listening and leaving room for conversation. I think she's doing it so I don't have to talk, and I'm unspeakably grateful.

When she pulls into one of the last open parking spaces at the overlook, I unbuckle my seat belt and turn to her. She waits for me with big, serious eyes. Her makeup is light, glowy, natural. She's here to work today, and she's here for me.

I finally get it. I trust her. I trust her with my secrets, and I trust her with my friendship, and I trust her with my gratitude. I don't need to apologize for being thankful for her. I don't owe her an apology—just gratitude.

"Hey, before we go out there. I just wanted to say thanks. I know that none of this is yours to deal with, and it means a lot that you've been here for me."

She rests her fingertip on my chin and stares into my eyes, just like she did on prom night. "Always," she says. "I'm always here for you. No matter what."

I nod. "I know," I answer. "Thank you."

* * *

There are a ton of people at the tree line, getting instructions. The cop from school is there. I try to move away from her, but she waves me over. My heart pounds as I approach her. She's watching me with those hawk-eyes. I try to keep my face still and calm, try to focus on the way that my breath moves through my lungs the way Iris always says. I try not to be scared.

And then I get to the cop, and her eyes pass right over me as she waves over the next girl. My breathing settles a little. *Maybe things will be okay*.

The cop assigns each of us to sections of a grid, telling us to stay arm's-length apart and keep our eyes on the ground. "Watch out for wildlife and tripping hazards," she says. "Don't touch anything you find. Just stop where you are and put your hand in the air, and someone will come find you." Her eyes settle on me again. "Just wait for someone to find you."

Or maybe things won't be okay.

A hundred feet away, Roya's mother is talking to another group of people, probably telling them the same thing. Roya is in that group, but it's like she feels me watching her. She turns and her eyes meet mine and she says something to her mother, who waves her off. She walks over to our group just as we're lining up and stands next to me. She's in her old beat-up uniform from when she was on the intramural basketball team in sophomore year. I guess she isn't worried about ticks. The shirt is a little too small and the shorts are a little tighter than they were then. I remember yesterday, when I was too busy checking Roya out to notice how tired and worried she was, and I reprimand myself. I look at the ground. *Don't be a jerk, Alexis.*

"Did you get assigned this part of the grid?" I ask.

"No," she says, and starts taking measured steps forward but not even pretending to look at the ground. "I just wanted to be over here. By you."

I sneak a glance at her. "Cool." I try to say it normally, but it comes out a whisper.

"How come you didn't come over and say hello?" she asks, stepping over a tree root.

"I don't know." I look at a tree fifty feet ahead of us. Am I supposed to go around it? Of course I'm supposed to go around it, that's a stupid thing to think, it's not like I could go *through* it. "I didn't think I was, um. I didn't know if you wanted me to."

"Why wouldn't I want you to?" Roya asks. Her voice verges on impatient. I sneak a glance at her, but I can't read her face at a sidelong angle like this, not while I'm trying to pretend I'm not looking.

I don't say anything. I let myself get absorbed in picking my way around a four-inch-tall thistle. How do I answer a question like "Why wouldn't I want you to?" The real answer is, "Because you secretly think you made a huge mistake yesterday," or "Because you don't like me the way you thought you did," or "Because I'm a bad lay." Or "Because I might have ruined our friendship by having sex with you and you don't know how to tell me that you don't want anything to do with me anymore." But all of those answers will sound like I'm looking for her to comfort me, or like I'm needy, or like I expect yesterday to have meant something more than what it probably did. So I don't say anything. Roya waits for me to answer her, but she's not very good at waiting. She does a big I'm-being-patient sigh and then immediately loses her patience.

"Hey, about last night . . . ?" She says it slowly and my heart sinks. "If you didn't, um. If you didn't want to have that mean anything, or if you didn't want it to be a thing . . ."

"No," I whisper before I can think better of it, even though I probably should say that it's fine and it's whatever and I don't care. "It meant something. It meant a lot." I focus on the terrain, looking for spiders or lizards or prickly plants that will snag my jeans. I try to feel the way the dry patches of grass crunch under my sneakers. I wish my heart would slow down. I wish she would stop looking at me.

"Well. It meant a lot to me, too." She reaches over and grabs my hand—*we're supposed to stay arm's-length apart*, I think, and even as I think it, she draws me a little closer to her. And then closer, and then she's walking right next to me like we're on a date instead of pretending to look for a dead boy in the woods. *It meant a lot to me, too.* What does that mean? It's the kind of thing you say to make someone feel better. It feels like a pat on the head. I shouldn't have said anything. Did I say something? I can't remember.

It's so hot outside, and so bright, and the air is so close and so thick. And Roya is so close.

She's right next to me. Mint smell and warmth. Something cool bumps my wrist, and I look down to see what it is—she's wearing the bangle again. She's been wearing it a lot lately. She stops walking, and I realize we've come to the tree that I noticed before, the one that will need to be gone around. But Roya doesn't let go of my hand. I can't make myself look at her face. My heart is pounding and the tree is in the way and she won't let go of my hand but she also hasn't said—

A finger under my chin, gentle pressure. She turns my head until I'm looking at her face. "What's going on?"

My eyes burn. "I'm really scared that you'll change your mind."

"Okay." That's all she says. She's looking at me, and she's so close. I wait for her to say something else—to tell me I'm being stupid, or that I shouldn't worry, or to ask what I think she'll change her mind about. But she doesn't. She waits.

So I keep going. "I don't want to start something if it doesn't mean the same thing to both of us. I—I know that you probably don't feel the same about me as I do about you and I just really don't want to make a mistake. And our friendship is more important to me than anything, so if you don't want to—"

She cocks her head. "Why do you think I don't feel the same?"

"Because you aren't in love with me," I say. I immediately regret it. "I mean, I don't mean like, I didn't—"

She kisses me. It's a light kiss, a stop-talking kiss, a

featherlight brush of her lips against mine. It works. I stop talking. I stop breathing. I stop thinking. I stop worrying. There's just her lips, right there, a thought away from mine. Her breath and mine, together.

"I don't know if I'm in love," Roya says. She pulls me closer, so close that her hair is brushing my shoulders. The big oak tree leans over us and I can't help but wonder if I'm meant to always be closest to Roya in leaf-filtered light. I can't help but wonder how much Marcelina already knows about us, because of what the trees have told her. "I don't know what that means. But I want to find out. And I want to find out with *you*."

"Since when?"

"Since always, dummy," she says, bumping my nose with hers. "Since forever. I don't know."

"But—"

"Look," she says, cutting me off. "I've been into you for a really long time. And I know that we've missed each other a lot. I know that we've both done the whole *there's no way she likes me back* thing for like a hundred years. But I'm done with that, okay? We hid body parts together. If we can figure that out, we can figure this out too. I want to figure it out." She brushes her nose across mine. "I want to figure it out *with you*."

She kisses me again, a longer kiss, a *believe me* kiss. And I try. I try to believe her.

"I should tell you something," I whisper against her lips. I don't want to tell her, but I know I have to. It would be dishonest not to, and if there's anything I don't want to do to

Roya, it's lie. "I was going to sleep with Josh because I wanted to make you jealous. I know it's stupid. It's the stupidest thing I've ever done. Well. Almost-done." She doesn't laugh. "But. I don't know. I thought that maybe if I slept with him, you'd get mad, and we'd have a big fight, and you'd yell at me for sleeping with some guy I barely know, and then I could say, 'Well, it's none of your business anyway, it's not like you're my girlfriend!'" She does laugh at that, barely, just a breath, and I'm flooded with relief. "And then you would say, 'Well, why not?!' and we'd kiss and all of this would happen."

"That's ridiculous," she says. And then she laughs again, another small, breathy laugh. A little incredulous. "And it's probably exactly what would have happened."

"I know." I shake my head, and because our foreheads are still pressed together, it makes her shake her head too. "I'm sorry. It was stupid and manipulative and it was the only way that I could think of to make you see me the way I see you."

"How do you see me?" she murmurs.

"Glowing," I murmur back, kissing her with each word. "Brilliant. Loud. Fast. Wild. Kind, when you think no one is looking." She laughs and her teeth bump my lip. "Magic."

"Then I see you exactly how you see me," she says. "Except add anxious and silly and kind, even when you think people *are* looking." She considers me for a moment, then adds, "And maybe a little scary."

I step back. "Scary?"

"A little," she says. "You did something to Josh that we

didn't know was possible. I know it wasn't on purpose, but. You know. He's dead. That's a little scary."

It hurts to hear, but I shouldn't expect anything less from Roya. She's honest, but not particularly gentle. She's not trying to make me feel bad. She's just telling me the truth. And it's true—I'm a little scary now. I've never been scary before, but I am. Just a little. I open my mouth to say something, I don't even know what. Something that will make it okay that I'm scary. But she stops me from saying anything. She stops me in the best way possible.

For a minute—just a minute—my whole world is a curtain of Roya's hair, and the smell of her vanilla-mint lip balm on my mouth, and the feeling of her fingers on the back of my neck. She kisses me the way she kissed me in the meadow: with everything she is, and everything I am, and something extra that's outside both of us. She kisses me so hard that the breath leaves my lungs and my toes curl inside my hiking boots.

She kisses me like there's no plan.

When she pulls away, there are sunflowers brushing against our hips. They've pushed up out of the soil in a circle around us, ringing us in bright yellow.

"I mean it," she says. "No matter what happens, remember that I mean it. Okay? I want this."

"I know." I don't know if I know, but I want to know, and maybe for now that can be enough.

21.

I SEE MOVEMENT OUT OF THE CORNER OF MY eye a scant few seconds before I hear Paulie crowing. "All riiiiiight!" When I look over, she's got both fists in the air, and her face is split into a wide grin. "Finally!"

"Break it up already," Iris calls from behind her. Next to them, Maryam and Marcelina cackle. Roya laughs into my mouth and gives me a tiny last kiss before she pulls away.

Not a last kiss, I remind myself. Just . . . the last for *now*.

"What are you doing here?" I ask when they get closer. "I thought you were with another group."

"We swapped with Angela and Gina and the Matts," Maryam says. "We figured it would be better if we were all together."

I bite my lip. "Actually, yeah. It's really nice to all be together for this." Roya squeezes my hand. "And since we're all together . . . there's something I should tell you guys."

We start walking, our paces slow and even. We're arm's-length apart, except for me and Roya. The two of us keep our fingers linked. Her palm is soft against mine. It's the only thing I want to pay attention to, the only thing I want to talk about: *me and Roya, Roya and me, look, we're a We, are you all seeing this?* But there's something else that needs to be said, and I need to say it while we're all alone together.

I squeeze Roya's hand the way she just squeezed mine, because that's something we get to do now.

And then I tell them all that Josh's heart has disappeared.

Paulie's eyes are on the uneven ground in front of her. "Could someone have taken it? Nico, maybe?"

"Why would they?" I ask. "The bag was in the same place I left it. No, I think . . . I think it just disappeared. When, uh. When Roya and I got rid of her last piece."

"What do we do now?" Marcelina whispers, and no one answers. We follow a trail of stirred soil deep into the woods, far from the ongoing searches. We pass through a thick section of twisting black oaks that look like something out of a scary story. I duck under a low-hanging branch and get trailing moss in my hair. I've never seen trailing moss before, except in documentaries about bayous and horror movies about haunted houses in the Deep South. Paulie ducks between two of the trees and disappears into shadow. I'm pulling moss out of my hair and looking at Paulie's retreating form, about to follow her, when a shadow detaches itself from the trunk of an oak just a few feet away from her.

"Paulie," I hiss.

"What?" she whispers back. I point to the shadow, and Paulie freezes.

It's the coyote.

Her ears are low, almost flat. She's staring at me, her yellow eyes wide with alarm. I try to send her calm and comfort and certainty that we won't do harm, that we've just stumbled across her path by accident. I try not to distract myself with prayers that she's not going to panic and hurt Paulie or me.

Because she might hurt us. She's an animal, a creature. She's not a dog and she's not a person and she has teeth that are made to tear into soft flesh like mine. And if she's scared of us, she'll do what she thinks she has to do in order to survive.

But then, impossibly, she takes a step toward me. It's slow, hesitant—her paw hovers a few inches above the ground before she lets it fall. Her eyes are locked on mine. Paulie is looking at me too, and I shake my head, hoping that she'll understand what I mean: don't do *anything*.

The coyote doesn't bite me. She approaches, impossibly slow, and pushes the top of her head into my palm.

Strange smell meat found yours come follow come now meat strange new come

Before I can answer—before I can really even begin to understand—the coyote turns and starts to walk slowly between the trees. She slinks with her tail low, glancing behind her.

It's not that I don't have a choice, but—what else am I going to do? Of course I follow her. As I pass Paulie, I have just enough time to whisper, "Follow me. Not too close."

Paulie's face is frozen with something between fear and

disbelief, but there's no time to explain. By the time I turn back to the coyote, the dappled shade of the trees has almost swallowed her up.

I follow ten feet back, my fingers still warm from where Roya was holding my hand before. I'm just close enough to see Paulie's movement. She turns to look at me occasionally, the line of her back taut. I can just hear Paulie, Maryam, Marcelina, and Iris following, another twenty feet between us. They don't talk. Good. Human voices might be too much right now, might make the coyote panic. *All of this is too much right now,* I think, and I have to bite back a hysterical laugh.

We go just far enough from the trail that I know we didn't stumble across the coyote by accident. It feels impossible, but—she came to find us. To find me.

She finally stops in front of a fallen tree, one that's overgrown with weeds and fungus. She looks behind me to the girls, her ears flat, her tail low.

She doesn't run, but she's close to it.

I put my hand out and manage to brush her head with my fingertips. *Friend friend friend friend packmate ally friend*—I'm saying everything I know how to say to calm her, but there are too many people here and they're all too close to her. She's got her lip lifted at me, showing a few teeth that don't look as sharp as I know they'd feel. There's blood caked on her muzzle.

She jerks her head from under my hand, and I flinch, but she isn't snapping at me. Instead, she lowers her nose to the overgrown weeds in front of the fallen tree.

It's hard to make out shapes in the uneven light that falls through the trees. I recognize the leg first.

"Oh my god." I say it out loud without thinking, lifting my hands to my mouth, and the sound of my voice is the last straw for the coyote. She takes off into the trees, loping lower than she would if she wasn't already trying to hide from us. She's fast—not as fast as she'd be out in the open, but still faster than my best sprint. She moves through the woods like a stiff breeze, and then she's gone.

My friends are still too far away to see what I'm seeing. I'm alone.

It's just me and the body.

It's just me and Josh.

22.

HE'S WHOLE.

He's here.

Josh is right here, in the woods in front of me, naked, sprawled out in the weeds. I fall to my knees and reach for him, press my hands to his chest, to his face. He's—oh god, he's warm.

"I think he's still alive!" I shout it at the top of my lungs, and I don't hear my friends come running because of the static in my ears, a high steady rush of panic. I don't hear them come running, but then they're there, and Roya is next to me again, pressing her fingers to the skin under Josh's jaw, and then to his wrist, and then to the inside of his thigh.

"No." She shakes her head. "There's no pulse, but—"

"But he's warm," Iris says, and she's across from us, touching Josh too. Everyone is touching him. Iris's hands start to flicker with uncontrolled light—she still hasn't figured out how to manage her magic without looking at it. "He's warm, maybe we can—"

"Don't," Maryam warns. "Don't try to heal him—remember what happened last time? And besides, you can't—"

"But we have to—" Marcelina starts, and before she can finish, Roya and Iris have locked eyes and shifted positions. Iris cups Josh's head, pushing his jaw forward and gripping the base of his skull. Roya laces her fingers together and presses the heels of her hands into Josh's sternum, presses hard and rhythmic, again and again, counting under her breath.

His arm flops around with each compression, and I look for the birthmark that I didn't notice when I was on top of him in his bedroom after prom. But then I realize I'm looking at the wrong arm.

The other one's missing, torn off at the shoulder. I remember the blood on the coyote's muzzle. Did she know she was helping us, or was she just taking her percentage?

I'm frozen. I'm useless. I'm not doing anything. They're trying to bring him back, doing CPR like—like they've practiced a hundred times, like they learned just in case, and I'm just sitting here thinking about a missing arm. I'm not doing anything. *I have to do something.*

After a minute, they switch places. Iris mutters, "Do we do breaths? I can't remember, they changed it," and Roya says, "Don't worry about it, just take over," and then Iris is doing compressions. As she presses down, something in Josh's chest makes a crackling noise.

"Hey," Roya says, looking me in the eyes. "Call my mom."

"But—" I hesitate, but she keeps her eyes locked on mine

as she holds Josh by the head, and I nod. "Right. Right, yeah." I take my phone out of my pocket and make the call.

As soon as Roya's mom picks up, I start talking. "We found him, we found Josh, we're doing CPR, he's here—"

"Where?" she interrupts.

"Where?" I repeat, realizing I have no fucking clue where we are. "Um, we're—it's a little off the path, it's—"

"Are you with people? Do they know where the trail is?" Her voice is calm, direct, and I want to lean into it. She knows what to do. Someone knows what to do.

"Yeah, hang on, let me—" I look to Marcelina, who's standing frozen, gripping Paulie's arm. "Do you know where the trail is from here?" She nods. "Yeah, okay, Marcelina knows where it is."

"Give her the phone," Roya's mom says, and I do. Marcelina doesn't take her eyes off Josh as they talk. I watch her because I don't know what else to do. I don't know what to do.

She hangs up and gives me back the phone. "She told me to go find the trail, and then call her and tell her, uh." She pauses, staring at Josh, until I snap my fingers at her. "Right. I'm supposed to call and tell her what marker we're at, and she'll come meet us."

"I'll go with you," Maryam says softly, and Paulie doesn't say anything, but together they all disappear into the trees, back the way we came.

"Fuck," Iris whispers. "I don't think this is working."

"One more round," Roya says.

"Can I help?" I ask, and Iris nods.

She grabs me and pulls me to where she's kneeling, behind Josh's head, and she shows me how to hold his head in place. His hair is so soft, the way it was when I buried his head in Marcelina's woods near that broken tree. "Just like that," she says. "Hold him still just like that. You're keeping his airway clear so he can breathe if—if that's something that can happen again."

His body jolts every time Roya shoves the heels of her hands into his chest. I stare into his face, a face I kissed. This boy who would be alive if it wasn't for me. I try to hold his head steady enough. If I just hold his head the right way, maybe he'll breathe.

Please let this work, I think. *Please let us save him. Please please please—*

There's crashing in the trees, and voices, and then everyone is everywhere. I hold Josh's head as Roya and Iris stand up, as hands grip my shoulders to try to pull me away. If I hold his head, he might breathe, and they don't understand, and they're trying to pull me away. I open my mouth to yell at them—but then there's a hand on my shoulder, and Paulie's sending a sharp spark of magic into me, enough to jolt me away from Josh. She puts her hands under my armpits and hauls me up and away from him.

"Let them help," she whispers in my ear, pulling me away from the body. "We've done what we can do."

I look up. Everyone is here—Paulie and Roya and Marcelina

and Maryam and Iris, and Roya's mom, and the gray-haired cop from the school, and a half dozen others, all crowding around and doing things to help. They're all helping, and I'm just . . . here. Useless.

I can't fix it.

Paulie leads me to where our friends stand, half-huddled in a circle, leaning on each other. They look exhausted. Roya is flushed and sweating, and her eyes have taken on the same don't-talk-to-me distance that they get after a swim meet. Iris is staring at the palms of her hands. Behind me, I can hear people loading Josh onto a stretcher. The sound of sirens is a rising howl in the distance.

"We did what we could," Maryam whispers, wrapping her arms tight around Marcelina. Paulie squeezes my shoulder. "You did everything you could."

She's right. I did everything I could.

It just wasn't enough.

23.

ROYA'S MOM PUTS OUR NAMES INTO A REPORT, then tells us that we can go home. She says she'll call us later, take our statements when our parents can be nearby for them. We leave together, even though she dismisses us separately.

We're quiet for the entire walk back to the parking lot. No one really knows what to say. We bump into each other. I tangle my fingers loosely with Roya's for a few paces, then drop them. It doesn't feel right. Nothing feels right.

When we get back to the cars, we stand together awkwardly, not wanting to say goodbye but not wanting to stay here either. After a little bit of uncomfortable shuffling, Maryam looks up at me, visibly reluctant to say whatever's on her mind.

"The arm," she says.

"Yeah?" I ask.

Paulie clears her throat. "Did you . . . Where did it go? The arm that was cut off?"

It takes me a moment to catch up to what she's asking. "I

didn't—no, I didn't rip his arm off," I say, trying to make it sound like a joke. Like something ridiculous.

Everyone looks at me.

"Do you really think I'd do that?" I ask.

"No," Marcelina says quickly. "Of course not. Not on purpose. It's just . . . maybe you did it by accident."

Roya takes my hand again. "It's okay," she murmurs.

I shake my head. "No, it wasn't me. I didn't do that. He was like that when I found him." It sounds like I'm lying, and I catch Iris looking out of the corner of her eye at Paulie. I don't know how to make them believe me, so instead of saying anything else, I hold out my pinky finger.

After a second, Marcelina links her pinky with mine. "Okay," she says.

"Right," Maryam agrees. She adds her pinky to ours. One by one, so do the rest of them. It's awkward—Roya has to bend her elbow at an angle that makes me cringe—but we all shake on it.

"No secrets," I say.

"No secrets," they repeat.

That awkward silence returns. Roya slips her arm around my waist and I lean into her. She's warm.

She's alive.

All of us are alive.

Iris clears her throat. "Can one of you drive me home? I, uh. I hurt myself while I was doing compressions on Josh." She holds up her hands. There are crescent-moon cuts there, fingernail wounds. The blood that's run across her palms and down her fingers is dry, but the wounds look deep and painful. "I held my hands wrong, I wasn't—I wasn't thinking. They tell you not to make fists, but . . ." She trails off helplessly. "I must have made fists."

A pull flickers deep in my belly.

I couldn't help with Josh. But I can help with this.

I take a deep breath, deep enough that white spots flare in my vision, and then I reach out and grab Iris's fingers. Everyone gathers in close to look at her hands, to see what I'm doing. I grip them hard, look her in the eye, and whisper, "Hold still."

And I give in to the pull.

No surprises this time. It's just like it was in my bedroom when I showed Pop my magic—tiny spirals of blood rise out of the crescents in Iris's palms, curling into themselves and freezing into vines. Snugly furled buds form at the tips of impossibly delicate stalks of blood, and they stay that way, curled up tight as a promise. By the time the vines drop into Iris's hands, her skin is healed.

"What the *fuck*?" Paulie gapes, her eyes moving between the vines and my face. "What did you—what the fuck? You can—what?!"

"Yeah." I feel awkward, trapped. Everyone is pressed together around me, and they're all looking at me, curious and excited. I don't know how to say *I guess I can do blood magic*. "I, um. Yeah. I can do that now."

"Is it healing magic?" Iris asks, her eyes lighting up. "Like Roya?"

"No, I think it's . . . I think this is its own thing. Its own kind of magic. The first time it happened was, uh. Prom night."

I hear Gina before I see her. "I fucking knew it. I knew you were magic." I turn and there she is, right behind me, tall enough to have seen between my shoulder and Paulie's. Everyone was so busy staring at Iris's palms, at the little flowers there, that we didn't see her.

How long has she been there?

Gina's eyes flick to Iris, and then to me. I realize, suddenly and without understanding why it took me so long, that I'm done fighting. It's too much, and I'm too tired, and Gina—Gina doesn't deserve this. She doesn't deserve to be so scared. She shouldn't have to carry something this big just so I'll feel safe.

She's looking at me, and I'm looking at her, and I give her a nod. *Go on*, I think. *Do what you have to do. Tell whoever you have to tell.*

But she doesn't say anything. She looks back at Paulie, her brows drawing together, and she shakes her head. Then she looks at Iris and shakes her head again. And then she makes a low humming noise, and her eyes start to fill with panic, and I understand what's happened.

Iris. The consequence.

Her, uh, mouth will seal over. That's what Iris had said.

But I can help with this. I know I can.

It feels like kissing Roya did: I can't tell you how I knew where her mouth would be even when my eyes were closed. I don't know how I knew that biting her lower lip would make her sigh like the fluttering of new spring leaves. I will never understand how I knew the shape of her hip under my palm before I ever touched her. But I did.

It's like that. It's the pull in my belly that's been there since the moment I saw the dried blood on Iris's hands. The pull that, if I'm honest with myself, has been there since the moment Iris cast that spell in Josh Harper's bedroom. The pull that I gave in to when I showed Pop my magic, and turned my blood into something beautiful and dark.

I don't know how I know how to give in to that pull. I don't know how I know that it's the right thing to do. But I do it anyway.

I flip Iris's hand over and squeeze it hard in mine, feel the beautiful little flowers of her blood turn back to liquid between our palms. Then I clap my palm over Gina's mouth, leaving a bloody handprint behind, and I reach for my magic, and I—

twist

—and her mouth falls open.

She gasps like she's coming up for air. She staggers and puts a hand on my shoulder, and as she does, I feel something shift in my bones.

I can do this.

"I hope you don't tell anyone what we can do," I tell Gina. "I hope you just . . . come talk to us about it. But if you do decide to tell someone about us, nothing bad will happen to you. It's up to you what you do."

Gina shakes her head, touches her lips. "I knew it," she whispers. "I knew it." She walks away fast, looking over her shoulder more than once on her way to her car. She's looking at me.

I can't tell what she's feeling. She looks curious, and excited, and afraid.

No matter what happens, I can't undo that fear. I can't ever make her forget the feeling of not being able to open her mouth. I can't make her believe that I won't hurt her, any more than I can bring Josh back to life.

But I can try to do things the right way. Even if it doesn't work out, Maryam is right—it's worth the attempt.

I take Roya's hand and we head to her car, which is parked in the shade of a big twisting oak. She leans against the back bumper and pulls me in close.

"You okay?" she whispers against my temple, her lips brushing my hairline.

"I'm trying to be," I answer, and it feels like the truth.

I'm trying. And I'm going to keep trying.

24.

I'M THE LAST ONE TO SHOW UP AT MARCELINA'S house. I know because they text me:

We're all here, where are you?

We're going to make s'mores, where are you?

Alexis get here already, before Roya explodes.

I'm late because I'm walking. I could have asked for a ride, but I'd rather walk. Tonight is the last night before the evenings will start to get really hot—I can smell the way the air is singed at the edges, and I know that tomorrow night, summer will be here. Not just because we graduated today, but because the heat is going to get thick and slow and heavy.

Right. I almost forgot. We graduated today.

It was fine. It lasted too long and none of the speeches were nearly as touching as they were supposed to be. Josh's parents talked about wishing they could have seen him walk across the stage, and there was a big pile of flowers on an empty chair that was supposed to represent him but really just looked small and cheap. Roya held my hand during the moment of silence. Everyone else bowed their heads, but I couldn't stop looking at the pile of drugstore carnations on that chair. It wasn't enough. I couldn't cry for a boy I didn't know and didn't miss, but I ached for the goodbye he should have gotten and didn't. For the life he should have had.

For the thing inside me that took it away from him.

And then it was over. I got a piece of paper that represented my diploma but that wasn't really my diploma because they mail those to your house. I shook my principal's hand. I stumbled as I stepped off the stage, but nobody started bleeding because of it. I threw my hat in the air and hugged my friends and cried because even though it was all a bit stale and a bit overdone, it was ours.

That's why we're having the sleepover at Marcelina's house—we're celebrating. The school year is over. Tomorrow afternoon, Paulie is going to get into her car and drive for hours and hours until she's in New York City, where she'll learn how to be who she wants to be. Tonight is the last night that we get to be students, the last night we get to be kids. We all know that there are people who will still think of us as kids for the rest of our lives, but really, this is the last of it. So we're having the last slumber party that we'll all be able to have together. We're going to stay up late and talk and eat and watch movies and probably wind up telling early-morning secrets because we're too tired to not share them.

And that will be the end of it.

So I'm walking. I'm running my fingers over leaves as I

pass, smelling the rosemary from Marcelina's neighbor's hedge stirring into the warm air. My feet hurt from standing forever at graduation, but that's okay. I'm walking through my neighborhood for the last time as the person I am now, and when I leave Marcelina's house to go home tomorrow morning, I'll be walking past this same hedge as someone else. As the person I'm supposed to start becoming.

I don't know if that person I'll become will have anything in common with the person I was a month ago. I don't know if I'm a whole new ship, now that all my sails and all my planks have been replaced. But I know that I'll keep sailing either way.

It's not fair that Josh died. It's not right, and I would give anything to bring him back. But I can't bring him back, and I owe it to him to be better than the version of me that killed him. So there are some things I definitely know about the person I'm going to become. I know I won't lie to myself as often as I used to, now that I understand how those lies I tell myself hurt other people whether I mean them to or not. I know I'll try to let my friends love me as much as I love them, no matter how hard that is.

I know I won't pretend to be any less powerful than I really am. Because now I know for sure: the worst part of me isn't the strongest part of me.

And the strongest part of me is so, so much stronger than I ever realized.

* * *

I can hear them as I walk across the grass to Marcelina's front door. I can hear Paulie loudly telling some story or other, and I can hear Maryam interrupting her to add parts. I can't hear Roya, but I know she's sitting there hugging a pillow and grinning at both of them and waiting for the moment that she can drop some joke that will make the entire thing brighter for everyone. I can't hear Iris, but I know that she's sipping on something—probably Uncle Trev's super-sour lemonade, maybe with some of Roya's mom's stolen vodka mixed in—and enjoying being quiet for a minute or two. She does that more now, after whatever broke inside her at the edge of the woods that day we tried to bring Josh back.

We all do things a little differently now. None of us have gotten back the things we lost. I suppose it's only fair—Josh didn't get back what he lost either.

I pause with my hand on the doorknob and breathe in the not-quite-summer air and try to figure out how I can hang on to this moment, the moment before, the music-swelling importance of it.

But then the doorknob turns under my hand and the door falls open and Gina says, "Finally!"

Oh yeah. Gina's here.

She didn't tell anyone about us. But she did ask us questions. She wanted to know how, and for how long, and who could do what. And then, once we'd been honest with her about everything we could do, she showed us what *she* could do. She opened up her hands and held two little flames steady in her palms, and she cried and we cried because we'd found each other. Because she didn't have to be alone anymore, and because we had a new member of our weird little magic family.

And then Iris cried even more, because Gina pulled out a notebook of her own research and asked if we knew anything about how this all worked.

She's been helping Iris study us, trying to understand the roots and rules of our magic. They've gotten really close, and they balance each other. She's helped Iris to accept that sometimes, it's okay to not have all the answers. Sometimes, not having the answers means hurting people, and that part is terrible. But a lot of the time, not having the answers means letting things be what they are.

Because whatever this thing is, it's beautiful. And whatever it is, it's ours.

The sleepover is everything we all hoped it would be. It's perfect. We throw things at each other and make a mess and at midnight Roya says she wants some cookies, so we make cookies out of whatever we can find in the kitchen. Gina and Paulie draw closer and closer to each other over the course of the night, until finally, they disappear into the backyard, arms around each other. When the door shuts behind them,

Maryam and I share a smile, and nobody says anything because it's insane that it's taken three whole weeks for Gina and Paulie to hook up.

Around four, I'm snuggled up with Handsome and Fritz. Handsome is breathing deep and heavy, and Fritz's paws are twitching with some kind of dog-dream. I lay a hand on his wide flat head and try to figure out what he's dreaming about, but all I can get is a sense of wind making his ears flap. Listening in on his dream isn't as good as having my own, but I sink into it all the same, trying to remember what it's like.

Maryam has fallen asleep on the couch with a bowl of popcorn in her lap. She's been planning nonstop, putting together mood boards for the apartment she and Roya and I will share, mapping the neighborhood we'll be living in. She's really excited about the mosque a few blocks away from our school—she keeps talking about finally finding an imam, someone she can talk to about faith and magic, so she can decide which rules she wants to keep living by and what she believes in. Iris's head rests on her shoulder. Paulie and Gina are in Marcelina's room, and none of us have checked on them, but I'm pretty sure that they're asleep together. Marcelina is softly stroking the leaves of a deep purple basil plant she grew.

Roya is watching me.

I ease my way out from under Handsome and Fritz and head for the front door. The dogs, exhausted by the amount of attention they've gotten, don't stir. Roya follows me—I can hear her soft footfalls on the thick, ancient carpet of Marcelina's hallway. I don't look back. Not because I'm scared that she won't be there, but because I know that she will be.

"What's up?" she whispers as we step outside. Her hands finds my hips and she presses her lips to my temple as she finishes the *p* in "up."

"I have to do something," I whisper back.

"Do you want company?" She draws lines on my shoulders with her fingertips, and the way the moonlight reflects off her cheekbones is transcendent, and I want to say yes. *Yes, Roya, yes, I always want company, your company, you, yes, you, us, yes.*

But.

"I have to do this alone," I murmur into her hair. "I'm sorry. But I'll be back soon and then maybe we can watch the sunrise?"

"Perfect." She gives me a squeeze and pulls away and then changes her mind and kisses me. She kisses me like it's the first day of summer. She kisses me like a patch of blue sky breaking through a gray morning. She kisses me like she's saying yes.

I could kiss her forever.

I would kiss her forever.

But I have to do this alone.

"I love you," I whisper, and she whispers it back, and then she kisses me again and then she's gone. The door closes with the softest of clicks and I'm alone outside.

Alone doesn't feel the same now as it used to feel. Before prom—before Josh—alone felt scary. It felt like maybe if I wasn't careful, alone would be permanent. But as I walk across Marcelina's lawn and into the trees, alone feels temporary. It feels like a gift that the morning is sharing with me: a moment with myself and the waking-up forest and the taste of heat already on the air.

I walk without direction. I know that when the time comes to find my way back, I'll be able to. I can ask a bird or a colony of beetles the way home. And more than that, I can feel it. I can feel the pull of the sleeping magic girls in that house. I can feel Roya waiting to kiss me and fall asleep together. I can feel the path I'm cutting through the forest, the broken leaves and bothered mice.

It doesn't take long for me to reach the lightning-struck tree. I step around the place where I buried Josh's head—the earth is still a little rounded there, and I give it a wide berth. I walk around the tree in a circle, looking up at the branches. The long black scar is still there. I wonder if it'll ever fade. And a lot of the leaves are still brown. But at the very tips of some of the branches, in the graying light of the predawn sky, I can just make out a few buds of bright green. New leaves.

I lay a palm on the trunk and press until the bark hurts the tender parts of my skin. I close my eyes and I try. I know that I'm not Marcelina, and I can't tell this tree anything or hear anything back from it, but I try to tell it that I'm happy it's doing better. I hope it knows. I hope it understands.

This is what I needed to see. I needed to see the place where I dug a hole for a boy's head. I needed to see the tree that his bones fed.

I'm startled by a noise—a whistle of wind, a heavy wingbeat. I look up to see a hawk dropping from the branches of the lightning-struck tree. Her wings don't flutter, she's not a fluttering kind of bird, but she's not diving for prey, either. She lands on a gnarled tree root and cocks her head at me.

She looks so different from the hawks that fell out of the sky the day we failed to bring Josh back to life with our magic. She's just like them, the same species, probably the same size. But with all that life in her—she looks bigger.

"Hey," I whisper. She doesn't respond, because hawks don't talk, but she watches me with one yellow eye. I can't make out her markings, but I can see that eye, and I can see that she's staring right at me. I sink to the ground slowly—not slowly enough, as she still ruffles her wings at me, but slow as I can go. As I sit, the hawk hops down off the tree branch. It's light enough out that I can just barely make out the spots on her wings. She steps toward me, walking with broad, bold steps. She's not afraid of me.

I'm afraid of her. More afraid than I thought I would be. Her beak is huge and hooked and dangerous, and her talons sink into the soft soil as she approaches me. She's a predator. She's made to destroy soft things.

She's perfect.

My heart is beating hard and fast, and some part of my

brain is screaming at me to *run run run* from this thing that is born to be danger.

But then, some part of me is born to danger too.

I lift my wrist until it's parallel to the ground. She looks. Hesitates. Takes another step forward.

And then, with a flutter and a terrifying lurch, she's on my arm.

She's heavier than I expected her to be. She smells like meat and feathers and something that I can't put my finger on but that makes the *run run run* part of my brain scream. Her talons dig into my skin. I feel blood running down the length of my arm, curling into tight spirals in the air around me. I don't look away from the hawk, but there's something feathery about the red rising next to my shoulders.

She studies my face, the one pupil I can see contracting. She shakes her feathers once, squeezes my arm in a heart-clenching grip of her talons.

And then *she's* gone, and my arm is burning, and it's over. I'm alone. I stand up, my legs trembling with fear and relief and fatigue.

I turn back the way I came and head for the house. Roya's waiting for me, and I've got a sunrise to watch with her. I wind my way between the trees, feeling unbearably light, the flesh of my arm knitting itself back together. I trail spirals of crystallized blood that will melt away as the dew evaporates at dawn.

I breathe in the first day of summer.

I breathe out magic.

Acknowledgments

THIS IS A BOOK ABOUT THE FRIENDS AND FAMILY that hold us together. It's about uncertainty. It's about learning to accept love and support. It's about how scary that can be, and how hard a skill it is to learn. It's a book about doing hard things unalone.

To DongWon Song, my agent and friend, who has seen me through the good times and the grieving times;

To Liesa Abrams, my brilliant editor and champion of this project;

To Ryan and Christina, who let me be strange;

To Mom and Dad and Katie and Scott and Rachel and Mathew and Becca and Amy;

To Mark Oshiro, who helped me to find the person I needed to be in order to write this book;

To all my early readers, including Sarah, Sharon, Ashley, Melanie, Charis, Hilary, and Mark;

To Kaye, for helping me get it right and for telling me where I got it wrong, with kindness and patience;

To Mallory O'Meara and Elisabeth Fillmore, both of whom have given me real talk and shown me real kindness;

To all my communities—PQ, MF, the coven, the squad, the group text, the group chat—I know I will never have to hide a body alone as long as I have all of you;

To Team DongWon (all of you are magic);

To Tinkerbell, who is not allowed on the bed and who is an outlaw;

To everyone who saw me through the writing of this book and all the other ones, who congratulated and consoled me, who held my hand during bad news and hugged me after good news, who made me eat and sleep and hydrate and go outside, who showed me around new cities and kept me from getting lost;

To everyone who believed in me and to everyone who didn't;

To you, for reading this book:

Thank you.

About the Author

Hugo Award winner Sarah Gailey is an internationally published writer of fiction and nonfiction. Their nonfiction has been published by *Mashable* and the *Boston Globe*, and they are a regular contributor for Tor.com and the B&N Sci-Fi and Fantasy Blog. Their fiction credits include *Fireside Fiction*, Tor.com, and the *Atlantic*. Their novels have been published by Simon & Schuster and Tor Books, and their novellas have been published by Tor.com. You can find more about their work at sarahgailey.com. You can also find them on social media @gaileyfrey.